Daniel Isn't Talking

Marti Leimbach is the author of several novels, including the international bestseller, *Dying Young*, which was made into a major motion picture starring Julia Roberts. Born in Washington DC, she moved to England in 1992 where she lives with her husband and two children. She teaches at Oxford University's Creative Writing Program.

Also by Marti Leimbach

Dying Young
Sun Dial Street
Love and Houses
Falling Backwards

MARTI LEIMBACH

Daniel Isn't Talking
A NOVEL

FOURTH ESTATE • *London*

First published in Great Britain in 2006 by
Fourth Estate
An imprint of HarperCollins*Publishers*
77–85 Fulham Palace Road
London W6 8JB
www.4thestate.co.uk

A catalogue record for this book is
available from the British Library

ISBN-13 978-0-00-721700-7
ISBN-10 0-00-721700-5

Typeset in Sabon by Palimpsest Book Production Limited,
Polmont, Stirlingshire

Printed in Great Britain by Clays Ltd, St Ives plc

1

My husband saw me at a party and decided he wanted to marry me. That is what he says. I was doing an impression of myself on the back of a motorcycle with my university sweetheart, a young man who loved T. S. Eliot and Harley-Davidsons, and who told me to hang on to him as we swept down Storrow Drive in Boston, the winter wind cutting through our clothes like glass. If I allow myself, I can still remember exactly the warm smell of his leather jacket, how I clung to him, and how in my fear and discomfort I cursed all the way to the ballet.

We sat on the plush red seat cushions and kissed before Baryshnikov came onstage, the whole of his powerful frame a knot of kinetic energy that leapt as though the stage were a springboard. I always insisted on sitting up front so I could appreciate the strength of the dancers, the tautness of their muscles, the sweat on their skin. My lover of motorcycles and poetry once licked my eyeball so quick I hadn't time to blink, and told me he dreamt of crossing a desert with me, of living on nothing but bee pupae and dates. In warm weather he trod across the university

1

campus in bare feet and a four-week beard, singing loudly in German, which was his area of study, to find me in the chaste, narrow bed allocated to undergraduates. There, while the church bells chimed outside my window, he took his time crossing my body with his tongue.

'I'm Stephen,' said my husband, a stranger to me then. Dark jeans, expensive jacket, an upper lip that is full like a girl's, against a startlingly handsome face. 'Are you plugged into something?'

My legs were straddling empty air, my back vibrating with an imagined Harley engine, my arms wrapped around the nothingness in front of me. I was laughing. I wasn't sure at first that Stephen was even speaking to me. I was surrounded by young women – he could have been addressing one of them. But the crowd I was entertaining with this impression seemed to shrink back with Stephen's approach. Apparently, they all knew him, knew the type of man he was and to back off with his arrival. I didn't know anything. My lover, now dead, was killed in a highway collision on his way to work one morning. I couldn't even drive a motorcycle, knowing only to hang on to the boy in front of me, whose head was shielded by a shining black helmet. His precious head.

'Pretending to be on a motorcycle,' I said. Suddenly, the whole idea seemed stupid.

'Do you like motorcycles?' asked Stephen.

'I used to.'

'Would you like a drink?' he asked, nodding toward the bar. 'A glass of wine, perhaps?'

I said no, I don't drink. This wasn't actually true, but I had no idea I was speaking to my future husband. He was just some guy. None of my answers were supposed to matter.

2

He smiled, shook his head. He wasn't easily dissuaded. 'Let me guess, you *used* to drink,' he said.

He was the first man that night who looked right at me instead of slightly over my shoulder, who didn't make me feel he was comparing me to a whole list of others. And the first man who had offered me a drink, I might add. 'I'll have a glass of white wine,' I told him.

He nodded. And then, without a shimmer of uncertainty, he reached out and touched my hair with his fingertips as I searched the floor with my eyes.

'Canadian?' he asked.

'American.'

'What brings you to England?'

A combination of circumstances, that was the truth. But it was far too much to explain. 'I don't really know,' I said.

He laughed. 'Yes you do.' He was so confident, his eyes steady on me as though he'd known me all his life. 'You didn't just get lost.'

'Yes, that's exactly it. I got lost.'

He put his hands in his pockets, pushed his face a few inches closer to my own, then away again, smiling. He behaved as though we'd just concluded some tacit agreement and I found myself unwilling to challenge him. 'I'll get your wine,' he said, and disappeared into the crowd.

'Give me a time frame for this,' says the shrink. He has a clipboard and a mechanical pencil, a reading lamp that shows his skin, dark and smooth, like an oiled saddle.

'Six years ago. Spring. On windy days the flowering trees sent blossom through the air like confetti.'

*   *   *

3

Now we are to talk about my mother.

'She died,' I tell the shrink. He waits, unmoving. This is not enough.

So I explain that it was cancer and that I wasn't there. When later I saw the time indicated on the death certificate, I realised that I had been at an ice rink, looping circles in rented skates in a small town near Boston. What does that say about me? About my character? The truth is I couldn't have watched it happen. I mean, the actual moment of death – no. She'd lost both breasts, had a tube stuck into the hollow which would have been her cleavage, shed her hair and her eyebrows. Even her skin peeled in strips. I'd been through all that with her, but this final part was different. There was no helping her.

The worst part, she once told me – this was before things got too bad, before she was entirely bedridden – the worst part, other than the fact that she was dying, was the humiliation of having to go around in maternity clothes. Her belly, its organs swollen with cancer, gave the impression that she'd reached the third trimester of pregnancy. Shopping with her amid the fertile exuberance of expectant mothers had been for her a macabre, debasing affair. We did it. Somehow.

'I should be buying these things for you,' she said, holding her credit card in the checkout line. I was twenty-two and looked more or less like all the other women in the shop trying to figure out how big a bra to buy now that they'd outgrown all their others. Except I wasn't pregnant, though secretly I would have liked to be.

'I could only give birth to an alien,' I said. 'We'd have to buy Babygros with room for three legs.'

'You will have the most beautiful babies,' said my mother. 'You are the most beautiful girl.'

I remember there was a jingle that kept playing in the shop, a nursery rhyme tapped out on a toy piano. I smiled at my mother. 'Yeah, but cut me and I bleed green,' I said.

Just before I left for the airport she said, 'Let me see you again one last time. Who else can make me laugh?'

I promised her that. I promised her in the same manner with which I made her meals she could not eat, took her to the bathroom in the middle of the night, called the ambulance, sat with her as she lay in bed, exhausted, the telephone on one side of her and photographs of her children (now grown) on the other. I promised I'd be back in no time at all, but the afternoon she died I was gliding along a frozen rink in my woolly socks, my mittens.

The fact is I had no intention of being there when she died. I could not face it. I am a woman of great energy, compulsively active, given to fits of laughter, to sudden anger, to passionate and impossible love affairs. But the truth is I am a coward. Or was a coward.

I call my shrink, Shrink. Not to his face, of course. I also call him Jacob. He seems as fascinated by me being American as I am by him being black, a Londoner, and having almost no visible hair on his body at all except this one thing, his greying moustache, which he is often seen poking at with a slim forefinger. He has the delicate hands of a surgeon, but everything else about him is stocky, compact. His leather chair is faded where his head rests, and there are cracks around the edge of the cushion where his legs bend.

'So that's it, that's all you want to say about your mother?' he says. He sighs, crosses his legs. His laconic air is in direct contrast to my own pulsating, nervous energy. He says, 'She died and you weren't there. OK, how about before that? What about when you were growing up?'

My shrink is a man who wants to reveal me, and yet I know nothing about him. I am sure this is the right and proper way for a patient and therapist to operate, but it feels cold to me. I cannot think of anyone in my life now who wants to see inside me for what is good and right, only those who want to find what is wrong. And that's so easy – everything is wrong. I tell Jacob, 'My mother was at work. I don't remember. It doesn't matter.'

'Run that by me again?' he says.

'What about how I feel right *now*?'

It is as though I've eaten a vat of speed; my mind races along trailing incoherencies and half-finished thoughts. There's a continual restlessness in all four of my limbs; I am hungry almost all the time, except when I eat. Two bites and I feel sick. All this has come upon me gradually over the past months. That confident, breezy woman who Stephen saw at a party all those years ago is not me any more. I am her shadow.

'Jacob,' I sigh. 'Be a pal and medicate me.'

He says, 'Melanie, you're going to need to relax about all that or else we won't get anywhere at all.'

But I can't relax, which is why I am here. I used to read books by the score but now I am unable to concentrate. I go to the library, trying to find a book that might help me, but even the self-help books seem indecipherable. I'm lucky if I can remember a phone number. So instead I wander. I visit all-night cafés on the Edgware Road where teenagers suck sweet tobacco from hookahs; I go traipsing round the New Covent Garden Market, picking lonely flower stems from the shiny cement floor. I'll be at a train station at midnight with no ticket. I might be writing a list on a notepad held in my palm. Or staring at the blank walls of the station or wherever I am, which is anywhere you can linger instead of sleep. During the day, my hands sometimes tremble with fatigue. I squint at sunlight, splash cold water on my face, review the notes I have written to myself reminding me what to do. I set the alarm on my ugly electronic watch, a watch I found in a public toilet at Paddington, in case I fall asleep by accident. I have children to look after, to sing to, play with. I regard them as one might the Queen's largest jewels. They receive my best – my only – real efforts.

'I'm just after some help,' I tell Jacob. 'I am worried all the time.'

'I'm trying to help you,' he says. He smiles and his teeth are like piano keys, his lips like a sweet fruit, tender and large. His children are grown now. That is all I know about him. 'Tell me what troubles you,' Jacob says. I am meant to pour myself into him as though he is an empty jug. This I cannot do.

At home I frantically organise clothes and toys, collect the sticks from ice lollies, the interesting wrappers from packets. Egg cartons turn into caterpillars; jam jars become pencil holders, decorated in collage or made garish in glass paint. Setting out the paints and crayons and shallow dishes of craft glue, I prepare for when Emily wakes, my little girl who loves animals and art. Daniel will not draw, will only break the crayons in half, rip the paper. I tell myself he is young yet. A voice inside me says, Wait and you'll see! But the voice isn't real and the boy won't even scribble on paper. This is part of the trouble.

'My son,' I tell Jacob. He nods. I am meant to continue.

Every morning I take the children to the park, hanging on to them as though someone might snatch them from

7

me, drug them and spirit them away from me for ever. This is a great fear of mine. One of my fears. The only reason I haven't been to the doctor for Prozac is that I am convinced that the doctor would alert social services who might then come and take the children away. This is a completely ridiculous idea and I know it – but that's why I'm at the shrink's. Although I have to admit I'm not getting anywhere here.

I say now to my shrink, to Jacob, 'Medicate me or I will fire you.'

'What's that mean?' Jacob says. 'Fire?'

I shake my head. I feel like a seed husk spent beside a loamy soil, like an emptied wineskin, drying in the sun. 'It means I stop paying you,' I sigh.

He smiles, nods. But he does not, at this point anyway, prescribe.

Emily has a mop of blonde curls billowing around her face, smiling eyes, aquamarine. Her baby teeth, spread wide in her mouth, remind me of a jack-o'-lantern, and when she laughs it is as though there are bubbles inside her, a sea of contentment. She carries Mickey Mouse by his neck, and wears a length of cord pinned to her trousers so that she, too, has a tail. Kneeling on a chair beside the dining table, she instructs me on the various ways one can paint Dumbo's relatives, who wear decorated blankets which require much precision. Unlike most children, who only paint on paper, Emily enjoys painting three-dimensional objects and so, for this reason, we own nine grey rubber elephants, some with trunks up and some with trunks down, that she has decorated many times. She has yet to find an elephant she thinks is a suitable Dumbo, and so we just have the nine so far.

Daniel has one toy he likes and hundreds he ignores. The one toy he likes is a wooden Brio model of Thomas the Tank Engine. It has a face like a clock, framed in black, with a chimney that serves almost as a kind of hat. The train must go with him everywhere and must either be in his hand or in his mouth. Never in Emily's hand and never washed in the sink, as I am now doing. No amount of reassurance from me, no promise that this will take only one minute, *less* than a minute, does anything to soothe Daniel, who pounds at my thighs with his small hands, screams like a monkey, opening his mouth so wide I can see down his throat.

'Daniel, please don't cry.' I give him back the train but it is too late. He's so upset now that he cannot stop. His eyes are screwed shut, his chin tucked as though trying to ward off a blow to the face. I am on my knees in front of him, putting my arms around his shoulders, but this causes him to wrench away, falling with a thud on to the carpet just as Stephen walks through the door from work.

'I could hear him from the street,' Stephen says. He's holding his post in one hand, his mobile phone in the other. Standing at the door, his tie knotted crisply, his jacket folded over one arm, he looks as though he has entered the house from another world, one that is ordered and logical, one that is calm. He steps around Daniel and goes to the back door, waving to Emily who is making towers of blocks on our small patio. She runs to him and I hear the clap of her arms around his waist, her happy chatter as she tells him she made a tower as tall as herself. Stephen brings her over to where I am with Daniel, holding her on his hip.

'Why is Daniel crying?' Emily asks.

'Because I washed his train.' I try to smile, to make a funny face. 'He'll be OK,' I tell her.

'Daniel, SHHHHH!' she says to him, but he pays no attention.

'Do you think he's allergic to something?' Stephen asks.

'I think . . .' I don't want to tell Stephen what I think. I only had that train for half a minute. It seems to me Daniel cries more and more with each passing day for all sorts of bizarre and inexplicable reasons. And I have no idea why.

'*What* do you think?' Stephen asks. His voice sounds sharp, but it might just be because he is trying to be heard over the noise.

'That it isn't normal.'

Stephen puts Emily down, telling her to get her Mickey Mouse. 'I want a word with that mouse,' he says mock seriously, which sends Emily into fits of giggles. Then he squats next to me on the floor, putting his arms out for Daniel, who ignores him. 'It's the terrible twos,' he says in a manner that tells me this is not a suggestion but a declaration of fact.

'He's almost three.'

Stephen sighs. He is so used to my worries about Daniel that they must feel a burden to him now. I can tell this is the case, but I can't make myself react any differently. He gets up and goes back to the post, sifting through envelopes. After a moment or two he says, 'Young children cry. Isn't that what you always tell me?'

But not like this. I spend every day with young children. I see them at toddler groups. I see them at playgrounds. None of them are like Daniel. 'That's not why,' I say.

Stephen opens his mouth to say something, then smiles and shakes his head. It's a gesture that is meant to be *what* exactly? Sarcastic?

10

'I am not making this up, Stephen!' I try to stroke Daniel's back but he pulls away from me. 'Daniel, honey.' He will not let me touch him, hold him, and yet he is crying as though something awful is hurting him, as though a bee has just stung him or some other, acute and private pain has taken him over. I have to resist the urge to pull off all his clothes and look at every inch of his body to ensure that nothing is wrong – that there is no swelling or redness or bee sting, for that matter. The only thing that stops me is that I know I will find nothing. You see, I've done all this on other occasions, and I've never found a thing.

'Just leave him,' says Stephen. He studies a bill, turns it over, and I can tell from looking at him that he is tallying the numbers. 'He'll be fine,' he says absently.

'I can't leave him. He's not fine.'

Stephen rubs his hand over his mouth, draws a breath. 'What is at Toys "Я" Us that can possibly cost two hundred pounds?' he says, holding up the bill.

'Toys,' I say. I look at Daniel. 'This is all wrong.'

'He's crying. It's what kids do – you always tell me that.'

But *this* is not what kids do. Daniel is pushing his head against my calf, and now dragging his forehead along the floor.

'I think we should buy shares in Toys "Я" Us,' Stephen says, picking a new bill from the pile, slitting the envelope with his car key.

'Stephen –' I feel myself panicking a little. I know I ought to have some explanation and some sort of . . . what would you call it? . . . *remedy* for what is happening here, but I do not. Daniel seems to be using his head like a floor mop. What would other mothers do? They all seem so capable, so commanding; but it seems to me that all they ever argue about with their children is why the broccoli is left on the plate, or why the child can't find his shoes. Nothing like this. Daniel is hysterical and I'm feeling not too far behind him. And now, to my horror, he is not only dragging his head across the floor but pushing it down into the carpet, as though trying to hurt himself on purpose, which only makes him cry more. 'Stephen, *look* at this!'

But just then Emily appears at the bottom of the stairs, holding up her Mickey Mouse and smiling.

Stephen says, 'Daniel has a headache, that's all.'

But I notice he's looking at Emily when he says this. It's as though he cannot bring himself to see what I see. In front of me, Daniel is pushing his head into the corner of the room and pressing it there with every ounce of strength that he has.

2

If Stephen is away – on business, for example – I sleep
with Emily on one side of me and Daniel on the other.
Like this I can attend to the movements of either of them,
can feel the heat of their skin, the stirrings of their dreams.
It is the only time I can really sleep, huddled between
them, kicked by them, occasionally woken by Daniel who
cannot sleep through the night yet. I never complain about
the broken night's sleep. When I wake for those few
minutes, the darkness seems a comfort. I feel my heart is
a timepiece set in motion by my children's breathing, and
that the bed is our refuge, a place where nobody can touch
us. As long as we stay here together, warm beneath the
duvet, the darkness is velvet. Thomas the Tank Engine can
stay clutched in Daniel's hand. Dumbo's family, in their
gaudy circus blankets, can watch us from the nightstand.

Because I have been particularly high-strung of late –
what Stephen calls unstable and, if I am honest with
myself, what I also would call unstable – I slept last night
with the children like so, one to my left and one to my
right. It's the only way I could recover after Daniel's

tantrum. I needed him close to me – quiet, peaceful, loving. I needed to feel connected to him. I don't think Stephen understands this – I don't think *anyone* understands – and so I've woken this morning feeling slightly ashamed of myself, as though my behaviour makes me feeble and pathetic. Stephen has spent the night in Emily's bed, which is a proper single bed, quite comfortable, but not where he wants to be. Getting ready for work he is crabby, remote, gathering my attention now as I stretch into this new day, limp in one of his old rugby shirts, not quite able to face the morning.

'I don't have a babysitter for tonight, Stephen, I'm really sorry.'

'Did you *call* a babysitter?' he asks, dressing in front of me. He is crisp as a new banknote, his hair springs up from where he's combed it wet from the shower. He pushes his leg through the elastic of his boxer shorts, gathers his suit trousers at the waist, loops the belt. Bowing his back like a sprinter at the starting block, he turns the laces of his shoes.

'Of course I did. I called several.' This isn't true but I have no other excuse. He wants us to go to some sort of business dinner party thing tonight and there is no way – no way whatsoever – that I'm going with him. 'I'm sorry,' I say. And I *am* sorry, too, but not because I don't want to go out tonight. The truth is I feel self-conscious. I don't want people to see how fretful I am, how troubled. I used to love to go out, but now it is as though I've lost all capacity to speak to other people at such things as dinner parties. They always seem so well adjusted and normal to me, making me feel even weirder. 'I'm not myself lately,' I tell Stephen.

Stephen sighs. 'What I want to know is what this guy is doing for sixty-five pounds an hour.'

'Who? Jacob? He listens. I talk to him,' I say. 'Don't blame Jacob because I don't want to go out tonight. It's not his fault.'

'See, I knew it. You don't *want* to go.'

Oh damn, I've blown it. 'I *do*,' I say, trying to smile. Stephen gives me a long look, then shakes his head. He works his fingers down his stiff, immaculate shirt, weaving the buttons through their holes. 'You can talk to *me* for a lot less than sixty-five pounds an hour,' he says.

'I'm getting him to prescribe something. Maybe Valium. Maybe Prozac. I haven't decided. They keep coming up with new drugs, it's getting harder and harder to choose among them all.' I try laughing, but it doesn't work. I'm so exhausted it sounds like a grunt.

Stephen goes to the closet and extracts a tie, flipping the silk through his fingers until it forms a perfect knot. Then he goes down the short flight of stairs to where his coat hangs on the banister. I can hear him now, pushing his hands in and out of the pockets, disrupting his keys which give off tiny, musical notes as he tosses them in the satin lining of his coat. He comes back upstairs with a small brown vial.

'I told a friend of mine at work what you're like these days and he gave me these,' he says, lobbing the vial on to the bedclothes. 'Antidepressants or something. Now, are you coming out with me tonight or not?'

'Not,' I say, but I stash the pills in my nightstand.

The pills are long and thin and white. Just one sends my head into a fuzz and makes it so the radio song I heard five hours ago is still crystal clear across every thought, raining down into my ears. Like this I cannot play My Little Pony correctly because I cannot make up the stories

Emily needs in order to use the ponies' new kitchen and their new glittery tiaras. I keep saying, 'They are making a pie to take to the party.' And she keeps saying, 'But *then* what?'

'Then they make the pie?'

Emily's big eyes turn to me, heavy under her furrowed little brow. 'Mummmmy!' she says impatiently.

'OK, it's not a pie. Give me a moment. It's a . . . uh . . . it's a cake?'

I wander off to look for Daniel, but discover I cannot find him. In my ears is a terrible girl band and I cannot make them shut up. Not only do I *hear* them singing, but I also *see* them dancing. It's like a sound and light show inside my head. Poking my fingers into my ears makes no difference, nor does covering my eyes with my hands and spinning, which is exactly what Daniel does when he is distressed. I call for Daniel but, of course, he doesn't answer. He never answers. I am hoping that he will reappear, drawn by my voice, but he does not. I look in my bedroom, in all the closets and cupboards. It feels as though the house has swallowed him. He is Houdini, disappearing before my eyes. Downstairs, I search behind chairs and curtains. With every second that passes my panic rises. I cannot find him. I am searching for open windows, for some part of his body lying on the floor, dead from choking or poison or a sudden, inexplicable collapse. My mind is a kaleidoscope of unspeakable images: small, still limbs; eyes like marble, like glass. He is dying, my baby, and I cannot find him no matter how fast I run through the house or how loud I yell his name.

'Daniel! DANIEL!' I still can't find him, but now it's Emily who has my attention. She wears an expression as though she's been scolded, sticks out her lower lip, preparing for tears. I scoop her up, balance her on my hip and keep searching. After many minutes I find Daniel inside the shower, rolling his Thomas the Tank Engine along the ledge of the pan. His face does not register surprise when I fling open the shower door. Parking Emily on the sink ledge, I reach into the shower for Daniel. When I pick him up he does not look at me, but stretches toward the train, his hands clasping and unclasping.

'You said you'd talk to me, *so talk to me!*' I tell Stephen. I've sat both children in front of the television to watch *Teletubbies*, an inane programme that I am sure is not good for them, but Emily likes the way the custard machine flings pink glop, not to mention all those oversized French rabbits. Daniel, on my lap, sits with a fixed expression, staring at the television, often leaning forward so that his face is way too close to the screen. Emily, taking my advice to sit further back, occupies the armchair along with a dozen or more plastic ponies from her collection. Between episodes she sings the *Teletubbies* theme tune while her ponies dance in her hands.

'I don't understand the problem,' says Stephen, speaking to me from his office. 'You looked for him, you found him. He was in the shower but there was no water running, so no danger of drowning –'

Among my many fears is that our children will drown in the tiny, ornamental pond in our garden. Before I consented to move into this house I insisted workmen arrive and cover it with three layers of metal wire. They did as I asked, but kept sneaking glances at each other. When I made cups of tea for them they said, 'This is just tea, right? Nothing in it?' Similarly, I had the lid for the septic tank in our summer cottage buried under half a dozen paving stones. I was told by the septic tank emptying service that this was not folly on my part. It would take thirty seconds for a child to die in a septic tank, the lid opening easily with one finger. He, the man from the septic tank service, drank his tea without any questions at all. 'Please,' I beg Stephen. 'Come home now. Turn off the computer, get up from your chair, put on your coat.'

My socks don't match and there's a split in my jeans, along the seam of the crotch. I haven't washed my hair in two days and my eyeglasses are so gunged up that the world through them seems to have grown a skin. Meanwhile, Daniel needs a new nappy, but I'll have to change it in here because if I take him away from *Teletubbies* now he may not get back into it, which will mean I have to chase him around the house to keep him from endlessly flushing the toilet, which he will only play with like a toy but will not consider sitting on. Then I will have to stop him climbing up the curtains, or stacking the books like a ladder so that he can reach the glass-encased clock on the fireplace mantel. He will not play with me, although every day I try. I get out books in bright colours, push matchbox-sized cars up and down garage ramps, hide from him then appear like a vaudeville clown, leaping before his eyes. He turns from me. His pre-occupations are a barrier between us, a sheet of glass through which I cannot reach him.

'I *know* how to come home,' says Stephen.

'What did you say?' My head is a sound machine; the singing girls still won't go away. Daniel is leaning forward, straining in my lap. If I allowed him, he'd have his nose against the screen. 'I don't like these pills you gave me,' I tell Stephen. 'I don't like what's going on here at all.'

* * *

18

I make him speak to me while he's standing on the platform at Paddington, while sitting on the train. Even though I cannot hear him and the phone cuts out continually, requiring frantic redialling, I ask him, beg him, *plead* with him not to go away. As he walks down the road, turning the corner leading to our street, he must speak to me. Good things, I say, please tell me good things.

By the time he reaches our house he is fed up, his face vaguely disapproving as he enters the house. Emily, rushing to his arms, asks if something special is going to happen today. Is this a holiday? Is that why you are here in the daytime, Daddy? Daniel has given up on cartoons and is now staring at the pattern on the carpet, tracing it with his finger.

'I'll play ponies with you,' says Stephen to his daughter. 'But then I have a very important call.'

'My ponies are having a nap,' says Emily. Her eyes move to the sofa cushion where a whole cavalry of plastic ponies sleep beneath a dish towel. 'And they have a very important call, too. So you will *have* to play with me.'

Stephen moves across the room to Daniel, who is quietly sitting on the carpet. 'He seems fine to me,' he says.

'He disappeared,' I say. I am cutting the crusts off a sandwich for Emily. Daniel won't eat sandwiches. He will eat cookies and crackers and milk and cereal. But no meat and no fruit and no vegetables. I give him vitamins each day and I make cakes with carrots in them or with grated zucchini. 'I called for him for ages but nothing happened. It was as though he didn't hear me.'

'Daniel, were you hiding?' Stephen teases. Daniel looks up, meets his father's gaze, but does not smile back at him. 'He was playing a game, Melanie, why don't you just calm down?'

19

'A *game*?' I say, and toss the knife into the sink so hard it makes a dent.

But Stephen isn't worried about Daniel. He's worried about Emily because she is four years old and not yet in school.
'She's going to be behind,' he insists now.
'Behind what?'
'Behind the others.'
Everyone else we know sent their children to daycare, then to nursery as soon as they could get them out of nappies. But Emily shows no interest in school. When I walk her past the busy playgrounds, full of rushing children and squeals of laughter, the barking shouts of the footballers, the rhythmic chants of the girls with their jump ropes, she gives me a look as though to warn me off even the suggestion she be imprisoned in such a place. Rooms filled with primary colours, desks stocked with jars of coloured pencils, will not attract my daughter. Emily prefers instead to fax to her father's office pictures she makes of Pingu, the penguin from the Swiss cartoon. She weighs bananas at Tesco's, mashes bread for the ducks at Regent's Park, visits pet shops where she names each and every animal, even the crickets, which are only there as food.

Stephen does not approve of this no-school business. The government has recently issued some kind of report indicating that children who go to pre-school perform better throughout their primary years. The day of the announcement, Stephen brought home the newspaper and flung it on to the kitchen table, which was being used as a Play-Doh factory, covering up all our good monsters with the *Independent*.

'Hey, don't wreck our stuff,' I said.

'Your stuff,' he laughed.

'Well, Emily's stuff, I mean.'

'Have a look at this,' he said, pointing at the article.

The googly eyes came off one of the monsters and I stuck them back on. I glanced at the headline on the newspaper and nodded, then found another monster to adjust.

'Read,' Stephen said, and went upstairs to change.

Later, when Emily and Daniel were asleep, he told me he'd made appointments with three different schools and that we were going to visit these schools, ask the appropriate questions and get Emily's name down on at least one of the registers.

'She will perform better if we start now,' he emphasised.

'You make her sound like a trained seal,' I said. 'Anyway, what do school kids *learn* that make them "perform" better? Certainly they do not know how to use fax machines or make a chair out of papier mâché.'

That was one of our rainy-day projects, the chair. Emily and I made it out of a broken broom handle and chicken wire left over after that rather dangerous – I thought – pond in our garden was covered. We layered the chair with runny glue and newsprint, then painted it pink and yellow. It's lopsided; it smells a little; it might be a health hazard. But I feel it indicates our daughter's creative genius, so, even though it attracts a persistent insect I cannot find in my British flora and fauna book, it stays.

'They learn to read and write,' answered Stephen.

'Not at four.'

'They play with other children.'

'Emily plays with other children.'

I didn't tell him that the previous afternoon at the park

she kicked a boy in the head because he was rushing her as she climbed the ladder for the slide. Apparently, she stood on his hand, too, which may or may not have been deliberate. The kicked child's nanny was nowhere to be found and I had to carry him around the playground as he cried, searching for the nanny, which meant I left Daniel in the swing seat on his own. When I returned I found an older child swinging Daniel too hard, as he screamed hysterically. That would have been worth a pill or two, but I wasn't taking them then.

Now Stephen holds my head in his hands, massaging my temples, squeezing together the lobes on either side of my skull, tracing my hairline with his fingernails.

'Tell me what hurts you so much,' he says to me.

'Those fucking drugs you gave me,' I say. 'God, how does anyone in your office work on those?'

I can hear his laugh above me. 'I'm sorry. That was stupid of me.'

'I'm so worried,' I say. 'Worried about the children.'

'You just need some help. More than that useless cleaner.'

'Veena. She's not useless. She's my friend.' Veena is a philosophy Ph.D. candidate. She is terrifically smart, and good company, but is in fact terrible at cleaning a house.

'Well, the last time I saw her she scrubbed the skirting boards until you could eat off them but left the kitchen sink full of dishes.'

'Yeah, well,' I said. 'Veena doesn't like dust.'

To be honest, Veena is a little weird about dust. She runs a damp cloth along the tops of doors and the back of chests of drawers. She has a special duster she uses for radiators, one she made herself and which she says she should get a patent for. 'Such a lot of terrible dust you have,' she says. If she manages to get beyond polishing the picture frames, she might actually run a vacuum cleaner. 'You are having need of tile floors and shutters, not all these thick carpets and flouncy fabrics gathering dust,' she has told me. When I protested to her that in every Indian restaurant I've ever been to there are nothing *but* flouncy curtains with complicated pelmets, she made a face and told me London dust is very nasty stuff, plus nobody bothers to wash such things in this country.

'Why not a nanny?' asks Stephen now. He is using his most gentle voice, his most loving hands.

'No. The only thing I like is being with my children.'

'Then why are you so miserable?' he sighs. 'It's ridiculous.'

But it is not ridiculous. I have read how animals react hysterically, sometimes even violently, in the event of imperfect offspring. One night, while watching television, I saw the awful spectacle of a wildebeest born with the tendons in its legs too short. The legs would not straighten and the newborn calf buckled under the clumsy disobedience of his faltering limbs. Five minutes was all it took for a cheetah to find its opportunity. The wildebeest cow circled her crippled calf, bucking and snorting and running her great head low at the lurking cheetah, who seemed almost to gloat at this unexpected opportunity of damaged young. She ran at the cheetah, but the cheetah only dodged and realigned itself closer to the struggling calf. The mother then tried distracting the cheetah, enticing it to chase her. Trotting gently before it, inches from its nose, the wildebeest offered in lieu of her offspring the sinewy meat of her own buckskin hock.

'Turn it off,' I told Stephen. He was sitting in his favourite

23

chair, his feet resting on Emily's playtable, his dinner on his lap.

'What? Right now? Let's just see what happens to the calf!'

I took the remote control and pressed the button as though it were a bullet to the cheetah's heart. 'I know what happens,' I said.

3

Stephen's surname is Marsh. His Uncle Raymond has a family tree that shows the history of the Marsh family right back to a sprawling black-and-white farmhouse in Kent where I was once brought on a sunny August afternoon in order to observe the origins of this great family to which I am wed. The house was a low-ceilinged maze of musty rooms added on over centuries, charming but archaic, a difficult house that needed constant repairs to its thatched roof and, because of planning restrictions, lacked a garage or a paved road to its entrance, which was through a field of cows. The house was impressive, even if it did require a monstrous amount of attention just to remain habitable, and turned my thoughts immediately to such things as lead poisoning and water-borne diseases. What was I supposed to learn from it? I didn't understand. 'Ah, you wouldn't,' observed Stephen's father, Bernard, 'as you come from a country of immigrants.'

Now the family seat, so to speak, is a post-war brick house in Amersham. It has two bedrooms and a large,

anonymous living room with a textured ceiling and lots
of ugly brass lamps on the walls; but they can cope with
this house, while the other was too much for them now
that they are in their later years. Because Bernard is forever
spilling tea on the floor, they've laid a dark, patterned,
low-pile industrial carpet from one end of the house to
the other. I am a fan of their new-found practicality, having been subjected to endless numbers of competitively
designed terraced houses and roomy flats throughout
London. They are owned by Stephen's colleagues, all of
whom have recently had to sell their two-seat sports cars
in favour of five-seat Volvos, now that they've become
parents. As beautiful as I find the fireplaces and polished
floors, the thick plaster undulating gently up to vaulted
ceilings with all their fine moulded glory, I cannot help
being preoccupied with thoughts of inadequacy, as I am
indeed a daughter of immigrants. My father, now dead,
was the illegitimate son of a Jewish violin maker.

'Interesting carpet,' I whisper to my sister-in-law,
Catherine. 'It reminds me of something. Airport lounge?
Pub?'

'I can't help but think Mother has been the victim of
some sort of textile crime,' says Cath, studying the gold-
and-maroon pattern on the floor. 'And they've got the
garage stuffed with remnants in case Dad spills.'

Cath is unmarried at thirty-four, which gives both her
parents great cause for concern. She's a doctor, a GP, tall
and magnificently built, with thick hips and a powerful
tennis arm. Having been made to play cricket with her
brothers on beaches, to kick footballs into nets on school
holidays, and play tennis on unkempt lawns at the old
house for most of her childhood, she has an athlete's presence. She is my one ally in this family and I adore her.

'Would you like somewhere to deposit that lad of yours?' she asks now, nodding at Daniel, who sleeps in my arms. Like his mother, he has odd sleeping patterns that seem to defy the ordinary government of day and night. He will have about five hours from midnight and then a few hours in the afternoon, but only if someone holds him during the nap. Otherwise, he wakes and cries, arching his back and screwing his eyes shut as he howls. No amount of rocking or lullabies or cooing in his ear will make any difference at all. The only place he will sleep other than in my arms, is in the car. I should be a taxi driver, for all the senseless miles I clock in the early hours.

Cath says, 'I'll take him. Or perhaps we should give David something to do.' Stephen's brother, David, has been parked in front of the cricket the whole of the day, leaving his seat only to visit the buffet lunch, the majority of which was supplied by his wife, who remains mostly in the spare bedroom with a migraine. Their three boys, outside on the small frozen lawn, have been kicking a football for hours against the side of the house. Once in a while Tricia comes out of the spare bedroom, screams at them to stop, then goes back into the bedroom. Meanwhile, David wrings his hands at the Test match, which appears to be taking place somewhere hot. The players are all in wide-brimmed white hats, their noses covered in zinc oxide.

'I'll hold on to him,' I say. If I hand him over surely Cath will notice how much heavier he has gotten, how much bigger. It isn't that I don't want Daniel to grow – nothing of the sort – only that I don't wish to draw attention to how immature Daniel can seem, such a big boy and yet still sleeping in his mother's arms.

The lunch consists of several Marks & Spencer's quiches, a plate of sausages for the children, a green salad and several bowls of variously dressed cold dishes. I brought Cornish game hens in a complicated sauce, which was a mistake. As usual I tried too hard and my effort makes me look as though I've turned up to a child's birthday party in a Chanel suit. I don't know why the game hens, arranged on a platter of roast potatoes and watercress, are just so wrong for this family lunch, but they are. I understand why Emily doesn't like them, however. She thinks they look like the corpses of Easter chicks.

'No soggy vol-au-vents from you, then,' says Cath, eyeing up the platter. 'Very impressive.'

'I would think they are overpriced, being mostly bone,' says Stephen's mother, Daphne. She looks hard at the game hens, pursing her lips with a mixture of triumph and disdain as though to say she is not fooled by appearances, nor impressed by oddities such as these half-sized birds.

'I was told to bring quiche,' shrugs Tricia, dropping two dissolvable aspirins into a glass of water, then stirring the bubbles with her finger.

'These *are* quiche,' I say cheerfully, pointing at the game hens.

But the game hens grow cold, remaining for the most part on their nest of watercress. And my profiteroles are also a disgrace, being passed over for the blackberry crumble with Bird's Custard and a summer pudding, still slightly frozen from the box. Why do people with so much money fill themselves with such garbage? Is it some English eccentricity I will never understand?

Stephen leans toward me, whispering, 'You know, if you ate more, you might grow breasts again.'

'Stephen, don't be vulgar,' says Daphne. Like a schoolboy standing at a closed door with an inverted cup, she misses nothing.

'I'm sorry, dear,' says Stephen's father, sitting in his chair. He has not moved for many hours, and is engrossed in the cricket. 'Were you talking to me?'

'No, Dad, Stephen was just being himself,' says Cath, rolling her eyes.

But at least Stephen defends my game hens. He finishes off two, declaring them 'charming' to anyone who cares to hear. I fumble with my plate, trying not to disturb Daniel, who sleeps all through lunch. Lying across me on the couch, he looks more like a puppet for a ventriloquist than a boy. In the end I find it is too much trouble to eat, and anyway, I'm not hungry.

'Sit with me,' I ask Stephen.

'I am sitting with you,' he says, from the other side of the room.

Daphne steps through the house with a regal air. She wears a floor-length woollen skirt, a crisp high-necked blouse. I am too casual in chinos and a jumper. But then, last time there'd been such a gathering, I showed up in a silk skirt and heels, only to discover they expected me to go on a 'family walk' through half the Chilterns. I should have known I had it wrong this morning when we were dressing. Stephen polished his shoes before we got in the car.

'Why don't you put that child down?' says Daphne now, looking with mild disapproval at her sleeping grandson.

'He's attached to me,' I whisper, at which she gasps.

'You have a very odd sense of humour,' she says, moving away.

Her next complaint is how fat her elder son has become.

29

'You need to make time for the gym, dear,' she tells David, perched momentarily beside him on the armchair, like a visiting bird.

David doesn't look away from the TV screen. He's the only one who seems to like the profiteroles and has no intention of being distracted from them, or from his cricket. 'Too much on at work,' he says dismissively. Then he points his fork at the profiteroles. 'Did you make these things?' he asks me.

I shake my head no.

'Bloody good,' he says. Like most men of his type, David is under the impression that women cook to gain compliments from men. When we don't cook, but instead buy food, the compliment is forfeited, unrequired. I have been instructed by my mother-in-law on more than one occasion always to admit to baking a dish from scratch, regardless. 'Up to and until they see the bar code, it is yours,' she told me. I am not seeking to impress but rather to deceive. If I can present a reasonable lunch, then the rest of my life is similarly ordered. That is my statement, an If/Then statement. The logic of ordinary housewives. A complete lie.

'They don't look like something you'd make,' says Daphne, glancing from David's bowl to me. 'Though I suppose *someone* had to make them. What I want to know is how they get the cream into that incy-wincy, tiny little hole?'

'With a gun,' I say. Something about my tone startles everyone in the room. Stephen, David, and Daphne look at me all at once now, blinking. Raymond, who is in a corner with a book on the history of London, stares at me over his bifocals. Stephen's father rustles from his chair as though woken from a dream. 'A pastry gun,' I add, trying to smile.

In fact, I bought the profiteroles that morning at a pastry shop while cruising with Daniel, who would not go back to sleep no matter how much I drove. The pastry shop is run by a group of young Italian men who I gather are somehow related. At 5 a.m. they are in the shop, preparing for the day. The shop has dark shutters, newly painted white brickwork, spotlights that shine out to the pavement. I could hear voices inside, smell the dough, the sugar. Stumbling inside, I surprised them all. They tried to tell me they were closed; then suddenly a short man in baggy black trousers and what might have been a pyjama top charged out from the kitchen at a pace. He was older than the others, their father, perhaps. His hands were wet, his beard unshaven. He was balding in a pattern that made him look as though he had a huge forehead. He saw Daniel, with his blond hair and his favourite train, and stopped at once, wiping his palms on a towel tucked into his belt.

'Yeah, OK,' he said, waving us inside. Maybe he thought we were homeless or the sad outcasts of domestic violence. He opened the door, glancing down the road one way then the other, then shut it again. The others shrugged, going back to work. I sat on a stool and watched them roll out pastry, unload boxes, whip up cream. I couldn't understand much of what they said to each other in Italian, but I understood they were figuring out if I was American. While Daniel picked dough from the floor, I bought box after box of pastries they gave me for next to nothing. I answered questions like, 'Why Americans drink so much bad coffee?' and 'Why Americans like so much to have wars?' Their own coffee made my head spin. I was more interested in breathing its steam than in drinking it. How long could I stay there? I wanted to stay for ever. But

31

Emily would be awake soon. It was time to go. 'I'm sorry I disturbed you,' I apologised from the doorway. The sky was streaked with pink and orange, the traffic increasing by the minute now at 6 a.m. 'Come back, Miss America,' one of them called. The older one saw me leaving. He came from the kitchen barking orders at his sons. His face was hot, his shoulders enormous for so small a man. I noticed his fingernails coated in flour, a wedding ring that dug into his flesh. I smiled at him. 'Come back another time, *signorina*,' he said.

For the occasion of this family lunch, Stephen's uncle Raymond has brought the Marsh family tree, which is the size of a school map and requires careful folding. Raymond is a lonesome character with a vast lap and many chins. He moves by use of a cane, which was his father's and which he wishes to bestow upon Stephen or David when the time comes, which, at eighty-four, is not far off. Beside him, on the edges of a floral settee, is Daphne, who smiles into the family tree, this great canvas of alien names. As always, she seems impressed by the intricate detail of children produced by assorted, untraced females added on to the Marsh lineage by means of tiny crosses from Raymond's fountain pen. She's been to the beauty parlour to have her hair set in curls. Between glimpses of the enormous family tree, she admires Emily's hair, which you cannot get a comb through, but is nonetheless completely natural, flocked in ringlets that drape down her neck.

'Where has all your lovely hair gone?' she asks me now. When Stephen met me I had wavy blonde hair halfway down my back. I'd published some essays in a literary review and I don't know if it was the hair or my budding journalism career that got me invited to that party in

London where we met. 'I've heard about you,' he said, walking with me along the Strand. This was certainly not the case, but I didn't mind. 'I've heard about you, too,' I told him. He was far too sure of himself with a woman. It unnerved me. 'Well, about people *like* you,' I added, then listened to him laugh. I was wearing my hair loose, cascading around my shoulders like a shawl. He told me later how he longed to put his hands in my hair, his tongue in my mouth.

Now my hair is just ordinary, straight, shoulder-length, half the thickness it used to be. I've done some articles on a freelance basis since having the children and may, one day, return to work. But that's not what is on my mind these days.

Daphne says, 'I mean, what *did* happen to your hair?'

'I don't know,' I say truthfully.

'Did it fall out?' she continues.

I don't answer this. I'm not even sure it's a question.

Daphne says, 'Do you think it is because of . . .?' She makes a little motion with her hand.

'Stress?' I say. She shrugs. Time to draw this to a close. 'Could be hormones,' I tell her. 'You know, sex hormones.'

'Oh, yes,' she says, pursing her lips as though we have just spoken of something about which she greatly disapproves. 'They are such nuisances.' She turns now to Raymond, clearing her throat. 'I see you've spelt Took correctly. So few people can, and yet it is very much an English surname, you know.'

Took is her maiden name. She spies it in the lower edge of the map. Indicating with a bony, arthritic finger that does not point exactly where she intends, she smiles.

I am there, too. My name on the Marsh family tree: Melanie Lavin. An addition to the name Stephen James

Edward Marsh. But I notice that I am only pencilled in. Why am I only pencilled in?

Leaving Daniel on Stephen's lap, I make my way to the loo, passing Cath, who is looking at books on the ornate, glass-fronted shelves in the hallway.

'Somewhere here is *something* I want to read,' she says, studying the titles. 'Statistically speaking, that is.'

'I'm only pencilled onto the family tree,' I tell her. 'Though I notice the children are in ink. Are they expecting an annulment, do you think?'

Cath laughs. 'I don't know how anyone stays married to my wretched brothers. If I were Tricia I'd have more than a migraine, I can tell you. I'd have a settlement by now. You're better off with Stephen. At least he speaks.'

'It's not even *dark* pencil. It's as though they got some feather-light lead and just scratched in the suggestion of my name.'

From behind us comes Daphne's voice. 'I heard that!' she says, tottering through the narrow hall with Raymond trailing behind. 'And the reason for pencil is that you were written in at the time of your engagement. Very simple explanation. You make such a fuss without understanding the *why* of things.'

'The *why* of things, Mother?' says Cath, coming to my defence as she always does. At the wedding she slipped me a Valium and told me her prescription pad was available to me at any time. Perhaps I ought to use the opportunity of this family lunch to mooch some Prozac, those small wonder pills. But I've grown suddenly shy of any sort of drug, having been traumatised by the mystery pills Stephen gave me. 'What on earth are you talking about?' says Cath. 'They've been married five years.'

'Yes, but if you remember, they had a very brief

engagement and there had been that long-standing girl-friend, Penelope, and it caused us to wonder if Stephen might just change his mind.'

'Oh, for Godsakes, Mother,' Cath snorts.

Daphne draws her chin back, lifts her finger as though testing the wind. 'You don't know how many times he changed his mind before, dear. Your brother can be dead set for one thing, then suddenly turn. So rather than ruin Uncle Raymond's lovely tree we pencilled in Melanie's name.'

'How ridiculous,' says Cath.

'It doesn't matter,' I say.

'We'll put your name in ink right away,' says Raymond. He takes a handkerchief from his trouser pocket, wiping his brow in a flustered manner. 'I do apologise.'

'I thought you didn't go in for family trees and tradition,' says Daphne, sizing me up with her cloudy grey eyes. 'But I suppose people change.'

Bernard, having heard the argument, arrives in his slow, faltering gait, with something he feels needs to be said. 'Stephen was with Penelope for many years. She was practically one of the family,' he tells me with authority. He suffers from a lung condition so that his speaking voice is filled with wheezy sighs, but he means business. 'Not that you aren't one of the family,' he adds quickly. 'Don't be silly.'

'Daddy, sit down,' urges Cath.

'Are you happy now?' Daphne asks me.

Meanwhile, Stephen and David watch the cricket. Emily draws heads for the game hens, cuts them out and sticks them into the opposite cavity to where the head goes, announcing to anyone who cares to hear that we will wake her brother if we keep arguing like this, and that he will scream.

*   *   *

In the car, on the way back to London, I say, 'Once more, just so I remember, how long were you with Penelope?'

'Six years,' says Stephen. 'God, I hope we aren't going to go into all that again.'

He takes a long breath, one of his warning signs that we could have a big argument if I carry on.

'That's one more year than we've been married,' I say. 'Not that I'm counting.'

He says nothing.

'You were supposed to smile,' I tell him. But he doesn't smile. And I know why, too. It isn't that the joke is old – though of course it is. It's a variation of a Jewish mother joke that my father told my mother and my mother told me. But I can't pull off the humour any more. Along with everything else, I am losing my lightness, my wit, the thing that always got me through. Inside me I feel as though I am losing a battle in a war that hasn't even been declared. As for Penelope, I know that Stephen still talks to her, that they are friends. Occasionally she sends us postcards from the faraway places she studies, reporting the concerts she has heard done on instruments made from stones and reeds. But this has always been the case, and no reason for concern.

In a traffic jam on the M40, just outside of London, Daniel wakes up. He wails, angry at the confinement of his car seat.

'Oh great,' says Stephen.

'He can't help it,' I say. 'He hates car seats.'

Stephen doesn't say anything, not to me, not to Daniel. I tell myself this is only because Daniel is crying so loudly and because Stephen is tired, that's all. How can he be expected to talk over this noise?

'All right, I'll do something,' I say. I can't bear it

when Daniel screams like this either; there's no point in pretending it's only Stephen who is riled. Daniel is knocking his fists into the sides of his car seat. Emily and I name his tantrums the way that meteorologists name hurricanes. Tantrum Annabel, Tantrum Betty, Tantrum Caroline. If I don't want Tantrum Louise, I have to move fast. So I slip out of my seat belt and go to sit with him in the back.

'Can I have the front seat now?' asks Emily.

'Of course you can!' Stephen says, patting the empty seat beside him. Emily climbs into the front seat, a smile on her face. 'Hello, Pretty,' Stephen greets her. Crouched in the back now with only Daniel, I roll Thomas the Tank Engine around the edges of the car door, on to Daniel's legs and up to his chin. He screams, bangs his head against the back of the car seat, kicks his feet violently and spills so many tears that he makes his shirt wet. Finally, I unlock the seat belt. While Stephen and Emily discuss what exactly a grandparent is and how Stephen is Granny's little boy from a long time ago, I quietly lift my shirt and let Daniel find whatever milk might be left in my breasts. He is nearly weaned, but not quite. I have tried – believe me, I have – but among my weaknesses are children's tears.

'Oh, come on, Mel,' says Stephen. He's watching me through the rear-view mirror. 'You *aren't* breastfeeding him, are you?'

'I can't get him to settle.' In a manner as though I am striking a bargain, I say, 'Please, let's just get home.'

'Are you going to be breastfeeding him when he's fourteen?'

Cath would say, 'Oh, shut up, Stephen, you sod. The chap is only a baby, let him be.' Penelope, whom I have met from time to time, would laugh at him, whisper in his ear that he is only jealous. 'You'll just have to wait for yours,' she'd say, tossing back the fringe of dark hair that decorates her forehead. But I don't say anything. Daniel has stopped crying, which is what matters to me. And Emily is laughing at the thought of Granny being young and Stephen being a little boy. And that is the only other thing that matters to me.

4

Stephen dated me at the same time his girlfriend, Penelope, was having an affair with her university professor. I would have learned a great deal about Penelope if Stephen had taken me to his flat, a large floor-through at the top of a Victorian conversion in Belsize Park, as all of her clothes were strewn across the floor's oak-wood planks, along with various bizarre musical instruments – most of which looked like elaborate sticks or pots. Balingbings and bamboo xylophones, African gourd drums and Romanian pan pipes shared space with a grand piano from 1926, which aged gracefully on one side of the room. Penelope is an ethnomusicologist, which means she studies music such as Manchurian shamanic drumming, Brazilian death metal, Scots pipe music and even some Continental street busking. I wish I could report that she is a dry-thinking, doughy girl who dresses in woollen trousers and enjoys open fires, but Penelope is the sort of person who, though quite capable of pulling off a day at Ascot in a big hat, prefers miniskirts and boots up to her thighs, cuts the necks out of her sweatshirts and wears them hanging about her shoulders, sleeps in the nude amid satin sheets and takes pride in the fact that she can accomplish most sexual acts even underwater. Well, this is what I've managed to wheedle out of Stephen anyway – and yes, I wish I'd never asked. Penelope's parents, as it happened, were believers in the theory that humans evolved from fish, and spent every family holiday risking their children's lives in scuba gear and wetsuits. Thus, the child had learned at least how to hold her breath.

She is not a beauty, Penelope. She has a hook nose and stringy hair, eyes that seem overly wide apart in her face, like those of a cow. But she has something about her that far outclasses the likes of Stephen, who it must be said is a man who understands his limitations and so, perhaps unwisely, surrounds himself with extraordinary people to lighten his spirits and to give him something to think about other than whatever happens to be on television that week. Even *I* can see Penelope's appeal, her showy sexuality, her beautifully articulated vowels. When she met me once by accident on the street, she did not say, 'Oh, *you*,' with haughty disregard, but instead asked me to say a number of words for her: zebra, aluminum, advertisement, Alabama. The sound of these words seemed to fill her with a moment of exhilaration, such that the nostrils of her bony nose quivered, hearing the long 'a' of Alabama, the protracted 'oo' of aluminum. Like Henry Higgins, she could place an accent without trouble, and she declared correctly that I was mid-Atlantic, but with some time further south, possibly Virginia. To Stephen she said, 'Hi, pet,' and then moved on.

But Stephen did not mention Penelope, or give hint to the fact she'd bought that flat with him, nor that his relationship with her was crumbling with the arrival at the University of London of a member of the elite among French ethnomusicologists, Dr Jacques-Pierre Devereaux, world-renowned expert on Asian idiophonic sound, who had whisked Penelope away to do field work in Thailand. He took me chastely to Hampstead Heath, where we sat on the lawn by the lake, watching a fireworks display.

'What would be your eight desert island discs?' he asked me. I had no idea what he meant, having not at that time ever heard the Radio 4 show in which celebrities are asked what they'd listen to if stuck on a desert island. I didn't understand that this question was loaded with the invitation to display a sharpness of mind and deep cultural understanding of classical music.

'*Peter and the Wolf?*' I said. I could not think of a second. Stephen was stretched out on a tartan rug, his chin resting in his hands. Fireworks filled the night air with booming sounds, with bright colours reflecting now against his skin. His face took on an almost tribal aspect. When I declared I had no second choice, he pushed his gaze in the direction of the lake, wearing an expression as if he was suddenly, irretrievably bored. I am not a stupid woman. This gesture alone should have been indication enough to me that Stephen expected a woman to entertain him in that Edwardian manner of being pleasantly witty in conversation, knowledgeable about history, proficient at the piano or perhaps even the harp. In other words, that he would be no great friend of mine whatever he thought of my legs. But I shrugged, blew the grey wisps of a spent dandelion in his direction, and announced that I preferred the music of seashells and mermaids, of bellowing whales and chattering dolphins. Wouldn't the desert island be a symphony enough for me, providing as it did all of these sounds, not to mention the ceaseless clap of waves against rocks, the delicately lapping surf?

He seemed pleased with that answer. Clasping my naked ankle, he pulled me gently beside him on the rug, kissed me and called me darling.

I can only imagine what Penelope would have answered to such a question.

'So, is this what is bothering you?' asks Jacob now. His eyes are large and round in the dim light of his study. His leather chair creaks as he shifts his weight, leaning toward me. 'This woman? Penelope?'

I shake my head. I don't even know why I've wasted his time with this information. Wasted my time.

'Then can we talk about what is really going on?' Jacob asks.

'I don't know what is really going on,' I say.

When I want him, I must go to him, find him, take him by the hand. In the sunlight, he lies on his back, his legs kicking the glass doors in a steady rhythm, his small fingers shoved down his nappy. He will not speak or look at me while I sound out words for him. It appears a deliberate effort, this turning away, for he seems to search for everything but my face, my eyes that seek him out, my lips that produce the words I am so desperate for him to try. 'Mummy,' I say, hoping he will imitate. Beside me is Emily, her mouth pursed reproachfully at her brother, who is pulling away from me now, having decided that if he cannot be left alone to kick the door he would rather be in another room. 'Say Mummy, Daniel!' Emily urges. But he will not speak to us or stay with us. He wiggles free and begins to climb. A spot of sunlight has divided into a rainbow across one side of the wall, and he is scrambling up the back of the sofa now to lay his tongue against its colours.

'I've made an appointment for Daniel to see a consultant about his hearing,' I tell Stephen. 'So you're going to have to move the school thing.'

He is sitting at the table eating his lunch as he studies the *Financial Times*. He flaps the paper to uncrease it, glances at me, then returns to the headlines. He says, 'This is a top girls' school and it has exactly two places available for the autumn.'

I decide that if he isn't going to look at me, then I am not going to answer, at least not out loud. Instead, I shrug. I send my eyebrows up and tilt my head this way and that, as though considering what Stephen is saying. None of this can he see because he is too busy reading the *Financial Times*. But then he lays the paper on the table, folds his arms across his chest, and sighs. 'Melanie, I am listening,' he says reasonably. 'I think we should both be there. Why aren't you eating anything?'

In front of me is a cheese omelette, peas and grilled tomato, all of it grown cold. 'I am eating,' I say. 'I'm *about* to eat.'

He says, 'Emily should be there. They'll want to meet her.'

At the other end of the table is Emily in a plastic smock with a big flower printed across the front. She is painting a blue cap on to a plastic monkey the size of her hand and seems wholly disinterested in our conversation. 'She's four years old,' I say. 'What are they going to do, give her a *test*?'

I'd meant to be sarcastic, but Stephen looks at me

squarely and says, 'Yes.' Then he takes my fork and stabs at the omelette. Adding on a few peas, he holds the fork to my mouth. Then he smiles, a gorgeous warm smile, and it seems to me that I haven't seen him smile at me in so long I stare at him, mesmerised. He looks so sweet all of a sudden that I wish we could just stay like this. He says, 'You are going to eat. Emily is going to go to school. Things are going to be normal around here.'

I open my mouth for the omelette, chew slowly, still watching Stephen, who I realise now is just trying to manage our family the same way he manages his office. If I let him, perhaps he will succeed.

'What about Daniel?'

'What about him?' he says.

'The appointment with the consultant.'

'How many consultants do you need?' Stephen cuts some more of my omelette, hands me the fork, then nods to indicate that I should eat. 'Didn't you already take Daniel to a consultant? I certainly have a bill for a consultant.'

'He wasn't so good, that doctor. This next one is the very best.' I chew slowly, then put my fork down, standing now to clear the plates. 'I don't want Emily tested,' I say.

He is annoyed, but all he says is, 'Move the appointment.'

'I'm really worried about Daniel.'

'About his hearing?' asks Stephen. 'You think there's something wrong with his hearing?'

I consider this. 'No, unfortunately, I doubt it's his hearing,' I say.

Stephen looks at me as though I've just said something very sinister, disloyal; immediately I am shamed. Then he says, 'There's nothing wrong with Daniel, full stop. He's a boy. Boys are slower than girls. As for Emily, she won't even know she's being tested.' He points his chin toward Emily. 'Emily, do you care about being tested?' he asks her.

Emily glances up from her monkey. She has a splash of paint across her cheek and some in her hair, too. 'Yes,' she says.

'Oh, come on,' Stephen says. 'You don't even know what "tested" means.'

'Mummy thinks it's bad,' she says.

Stephen rolls his eyes at me. 'Oh great.'

I say, 'It's as though she's applying for a job.'

'That's ridiculous. Everybody tests kids these days,' Stephen says. 'It's all part of the programme.'

Daniel has given up on the rainbow and wanders now into the kitchen where we are talking. I go to hug him but he refuses my body, rolling his shoulders to evade my grasp. Tiptoeing across the kitchen floor, he arrives at the refrigerator, expertly tackling the child lock, to remove two pints of milk. Emily adds a blue jacket to the monkey, who I suppose she wants to look like the circus ringmaster for Dumbo. He'd be more authentic if he didn't have his fangs bared.

'Then what's going to happen when they test *him*?' I say, meaning Daniel, who is now pouring the milk straight on to the floor, without even looking up to see if anybody is noticing.

When finally Stephen and I slept together, it was not in his flat but in Cath's, which she'd left empty while on holiday in France. I didn't quite understand why we were there (he'd said that he had to stop by to water the plants) or whose flat it was, and I must report that I felt a bit like a hooker. Things I couldn't help noticing: how we made love on the floor, not the bed; how he washed out the coffee mugs we used and put them away so it seemed nobody had ever been there. When he told me he loved me I didn't believe him. I judged him to be the sort of half-nice fellow who thinks he has to love a girl to sleep with her, and I didn't answer back. You might think that would be the end of things, as I was meant to return to America anyway – I was only in Britain for a year, completing a kind of ersatz degree at Oxford on an exchange basis. Not a proper degree, you understand, just something they fling at Americans so they can get their own students over to the States for free. I'd said on the application that I had a sincere interest in British literature, which wasn't entirely untrue. But having completed my undergraduate degree and having no idea what else to do with myself now that I was supposed to be out in the world doing *something*, I thought Oxford sounded nice. Pleasant. Cultured. I had the image of streets laced with coffee houses and obscure specialty shops, crowded with bicycles and peoples of every nation, of dazzling young men in greatcoats and wire-rimmed spectacles, of tweedy professors searching second-hand bookshops in their slippered feet. And it was exactly like that. A great place to hide from the world, so long as you didn't trip over the drunks or fall headlong through the windows of one or other topless dance bar.

'Stay with me,' Stephen urged. 'I adore you.'

I didn't know how torn up he was over Penelope's sudden exit from his life; I was still floating in the aftermath of my mother's death, then my motorcyclist's death. In the wake of such events, his seemed an appealing proposition. The truth was I didn't want to go back home.

It felt easier to live freshly in England. So for many months I lived in London among Penelope's musical instruments, her bizarre tapes of chanting monks and crashing metal and homemade pan-pipes from distant lands. One only had to flip a switch to hear drums that seemed to whip up the blood inside you, mouth harps that extolled the loneliness of mountains. I never intended to fall in love with Stephen, just to bide some time and think of what I should do next. It was a strange, uncontrolled period in my life. For the first time ever I had no place I was meant to be, nobody to whom I owed an account for my time or an explanation for my whereabouts. For hours each day I lay on the couch listening to tiny violins played by equally tiny men who hailed from Chiapas, Mexico. I read all of Martin Luther King's writings, and discovered that I would be quite capable of believing in God if anyone ever cared to mention Him any more. Toward the end of the summer, just about the time I thought I'd better return to America – for surely there is a reason to live in one's own country? – I discovered as though by accident that I'd fallen in love with Stephen.

We were in his muddy blue Volkswagen driving out to South Wales. There was a particular beach we liked that made only a pathetic nod toward tourism and was more or less vacant most of the year. I looked at his profile as he sang along with a Van Morrison song, his hand on my knee, and I realised I loved him dearly, the way you do a great friend or a member of your family. He had a knack for making me feel good, bringing me tea in bed and reading me jokes from a book just like my brother used to do when we were kids. He was an expert camper and knew, for example, how to pitch a tent in the wind and cook an entire breakfast using only a tiny gas cylinder. One day we saw a rosewood vanity box in the market on Portobello Road. He brought it home and made it into a record player, that old-fashioned relic of a machine, with speakers so small we could tuck them on the window sill behind the bed. Even now, when we make love, he moves over me silently and thoroughly and selflessly, kissing me afterward, his hands in my hair.

'And that is *how* often each week?' asks my shrink, his notepad on his thigh, his mechanical pencil hovering above.

'That isn't the problem either,' I tell him.

He sighs, shakes his head. Slaps his pen on the clipboard.

But this session, session number two zillion, we hit on it.

'What am I scared of?' I say, whimpering. One hour, sixty-five pounds, thirty minutes of London traffic each way, a splitting headache, no workable drugs, and all I've done is cry. 'What am I *scared* of?'

He nods. Says nothing. Fixes his lips into a serious expression. Another time, not now, I might wonder what Jacob thinks about during the session when all that happens is a lot of crying. But I'm not thinking about Jacob.

'There's something wrong with my baby,' I say, sputtering through the sentence, all snot and tears, my ears ringing, a stabbing pain in my throat.

'What is wrong with him?' asks Jacob slowly.

I feel my child is slipping away from me. It is as though he's lost, or hovering distantly along the horizon, even when he is right up close, even when he is in my arms. I don't know why I feel this way, or what to do to hold on to him. Somewhere in the world, right now, a new baby has been born and everyone is celebrating that he is just so perfect. All around me spring is bursting forth. There's flowers and birdsong and mothers with babies. All of this depresses me, and I cannot stand to admit it.

'I don't *know* what's wrong with him,' I say. Daniel uses my hands like tools, opening my fingers and putting them on to his train so I will roll it. He spins on the wooden floor until he falls down, laughing, paces the edges of the garden so that there is a balding path, will eat nothing at all except biscuits and milk, has one stupid toy.

'He's got *one* toy!' I say. 'It's like he's hypnotised by it.'

'What's the toy?' asks Jacob. This is typical and what I love about Jacob. He doesn't say, 'Then buy him another toy.' He knows I'd have already bought him half the shop.

'A train.'

Jacob considers this. 'I used to have trains. My son had trains. I can remember the track took up the whole dining-room table and we built a station out of shoeboxes.'

'Exactly!' I say. 'But Daniel doesn't build the track or care about the station. It's just this one stupid train!'

'Have you taken him to a neurologist?'

That word – neurologist. I hate that word and all it signifies. It seems to me that once you are talking about neurology you are talking about sealed fate.

'He's going in two weeks to a paediatrician,' I say. 'The ENT consultant who gave him the hearing test said he was normal.'

'What *exactly* did the consultant say?' asks Jacob carefully.

So I tell him. 'They put him in a soundproof room and had him build a tower out of coloured bricks. They wiggled things that made noise and flashed lights. They took some kind of photograph of the inside of Daniel's ear. Then they said he was normal, take him home.'

Jacob nods, rubs his finger over the hair on his lip,

pokes his pale tongue into the corner of his mouth and says, 'So then what?'

'I took him home.' I took Daniel home and he stood on the table, trying to reach the light bulb, screaming because he could not. Then he laid the videos out across the living-room carpet with all their edges in perfect alignment. Then I tried to get him to look at me by stealing his train and holding it at the end of my nose. I took him to the park and let him sift sand through his fingers, which is all he would do. No playing tag, no feeding ducks. He used to love to feed the ducks. I went home and thought about how he used to chase them, laughing, how he used to throw balled-up pieces of old bread into the water and watch the ducks skim the surface with their bills. I got out photographs of him at that same duck pond, his face alight, his hands raised to throw more bread. I cried all night so that Stephen had to sleep on the living-room couch. In the morning I threatened to kill myself, which is how I ended up in Jacob's office now, and why I am afraid to leave.

5

Do everything you can in life to avoid ever visiting a developmental paediatrician, particularly one in the NHS. It is not that they are wholly incompetent, nor that they will state flatly everything wrong with your baby, although either one of these may be the case. It is first that you must arrive at a car park lined with tall, rusting chain-link fences set into the untidy grounds by means of cement posts. You then put yourself through a gate that has a tricky lock placed high on a wall so that none of the children can escape, and pass through a series of anonymous hallways with cheerless chipping paint, linoleum floors that smell of disinfectant, posters about various sorts of conditions – dyslexia, Down's syndrome, schizophrenia – until you enter playrooms full of badly damaged children. These children do not often smile, cannot easily speak, play not with each other but with objects that are not toys. And if you are there for the same reason as I am, today, you see in every one of these children the shadow of a person you love more than you can describe, and who is just three years old and has only this to look forward to in his life.

Daniel has begun to collect disc-shaped objects, which at first I thought was a good thing because it meant less attention to Thomas the Tank Engine. He has taken to balls and balloons and coins and draught pieces. Milk bottle tops and metal washers and clockfaces, the lids of mayonnaise jars and shining CDs. He holds as many of these objects as possible along with his Thomas as we walk through the nursery at the Frilman Centre, where we are to visit Dr Margaret Dodd about what is being called a 'developmental delay'. Daniel keeps dropping a coin or a lid or a marble, which means we have to stop, retrieve the object, give it back to him and toddle along again, until he next drops something else. At this excruciatingly slow pace we make our way through the car park and the cement garden that leads on to the main building. By the time we reach the nursery, I have to pick him up in order that his revered objects do not get pilfered by the other children, who seem similarly disposed to carrying around useless items, or at least behaving very oddly toward their toys. One girl has a plastic Barbie she keeps hammering against a table, then flinging through the air, then hammering on to the table again. A boy with remarkably quick movements carries an armload of cars in a manner disturbingly similar to how Daniel is carrying his own assortment of cherished garbage.

Dr Dodd has Daniel's notes in front of her. She is a woman hard to describe. Her face seems entirely without form, as though her features have receded with her advancing years, so that you find yourself regarding her in terms of what she is not. Not tall, not voluptuous, not thin, not short, not extremely old but definitely not young, and not terribly interested in Daniel. While she interviews

Stephen and myself, another woman attempts to entertain
Daniel with a table of toys that he is to name and make
do things. Dr Dodd wears a white coat and a name tag.
The name tag is the most definite thing about her. She
speaks in the perfunctory manner of a dental hygienist
and jots all our answers on to a form that she has clipped
to a board on her knee.

*When did he first sit up? Crawl? Walk? When did he
first speak? When you say he has a few words, does he
use them together or just as single words? Exactly how
many words does he have? Does he have trouble with
changes in routine? Does he ever engage in 'pretend' play?
What does he eat? How often does he sleep? Does he
seem particularly worried by loud noises? Does he spin?
Does he perseverate, do the same thing over and over
again?*

The pitiful answers to these questions are that he was
perfectly normal until sometime around nineteen months
when we noticed he didn't talk. We could remember
him saying 'ball' which he applied to anything round,
including clementines and buttons. He then began to use
the word 'help' but dropped the word 'ball'. Then he
didn't say anything at all. He is ingenious at undoing
locks, switching on televisions and unfastening car seats,
but not so clever at playing with toys. We can't get him
past the lights-and-sounds plastic baby toys he had as a
nine-month-old, and no, he doesn't sleep at night. Or
really, much at all. As for loud sounds, I am unable to
use a public restroom because if somebody presses the
hand dryer he goes screaming in terror. All loud sounds,
from barking dogs to doorbells, send his hands flying to
his ears, where they remain as he runs blindly away from
the noise.

Because Stephen has an appointment later in the day, he is wearing a Jermyn Street suit, a thick silk tie. His shirt alone costs more than I would spend on a coat, and he has shaved carefully so that his face is perfect. As Dr Dodd continues with her questions and I put forward my sad replies, I watch as Stephen loses himself in the violence of what is happening here. His back slumps. His knees fan out, his big hands hanging between them. His tie coils on his right thigh. He is staring at the colourless linoleum tiles as the woman behind us tries uselessly once more to get Daniel to say the word 'car' and to keep him anywhere near the table of toys she has set out for him. Daniel keeps wheeling away from her as she grabs his arms, then he drops like a stone when she attempts to get him to stand at the toy table. All this is happening slightly out of our vision, but we hear it along with the battery of questions. While the commotion of Daniel's attempt to escape from the woman continues, I am forced to report on the mental health of my family, that my father killed himself in the basement when I was four years old, that my mother went through a depression around the time of her cancer diagnosis. The only time Stephen looks up, in fact, is when the doctor asks if I am receiving any psychiatric help at present, to which I reply, firmly, that I am not.

'Well, you might reconsider that,' she says. 'Your son is very likely autistic. Frankly, you may need help coming to terms with this. Let me see what the speech and language report is.'

I cannot bear to look at Stephen. All the times he has been annoyed with me for being so focused on our children, for providing every opportunity for their pleasure and comfort at the expense of his and my own, for busily singing nursery rhymes instead of going with him to films, building dollhouses out of cartons instead of arranging dinner parties, for failing to accompany him to his firm's Christmas party, but instead sitting on the floor having picnics with Emily's stuffed toys and playing peekaboo with Daniel. Then suddenly I have a thought that makes me feel sick to my stomach: *when did Daniel stop playing peekaboo?*

'Stephen,' I say urgently. 'When did Daniel stop playing peekaboo?'

He shakes his head, doesn't answer. He's looking at Dr Dodd. She's saying something but I cannot seem to focus. All I can think about is how so many of the mothers practised 'controlled crying' and found suitable nannies, while I gave myself wholly to every whim of my children. This method of child-rearing is a mistake according to those who think we should tame toddlers and thwart manipulating pre-schoolers, but I took pleasure in the sanguine, parasitic and entirely innocent fashion with which my children enveloped me. And yet, I am right now riddled with guilt because I cannot remember when Daniel stopped playing peekaboo. I feel, yes, that I've ruined him, this precious gift, my baby that within seconds of being born made me laugh out loud with the delight of seeing his squashed face, his dark eyes. Physically, he is a most perfect child. He has cupid lips and a shy half-smile, skin the colour of a ripe peach. He is lovely beyond imagination and I have failed him. I don't know how I could have let this happen. Or how I can look up from the floor or ever raise my head or call him my own again, having let him down so badly. *Baby, baby, please don't be sick*, I hear my own voice in my head. *Little boy, come back to me.*

'He has frequent ear infections,' says Stephen. Apparently, we are being asked questions again and I've missed my cue to speak. I feel my mouth is full of elastic bands – I cannot seem to make it work properly. I rely on Stephen, who seems all at once to be solid and defined while I float up to the ceiling, watching us all as though from a great distance. Tell them about his fevers, Stephen, I think. Tell them how often he is unwell. 'And he gets high temperatures and swollen glands around the neck,' adds Stephen. And his stomach, tell them, please darling. Tell the doctor how many nappies we get through each day, then about the constipation. Four days and nothing, sometimes five. 'He's got problems with his bowels,' says Stephen.

Dr Dodd adds these facts to the file. Then she has a quick word with her colleague, who has finished her evaluation of Daniel's speech and language. He is being returned to me, my boy, and is clasping his disc-shaped objects, his Thomas and his mother all at once. I clutch him to me – too hard – and he squirms away, then settles with his back on my chest, using me as a chair. The report on his speech is that he has almost none. Functionally, he is less than six months old. I hold him and all his collection carefully in my arms, my head pounding, my heart fluttering inside my chest, every breath a heavy weight inside me.

'Well, thank you very much,' I hear Stephen saying, then his hand on my arm lifting. I leave the chair, walk the corridor, wait for the many locks and codes to be sorted so we can get back to the car. I am unsteady as though I've been drinking. The walls come at me all at once; I'm not ready for the kerb. Thank God it is Stephen driving because I would not be able to. My nerves are threadbare like antique cloth. My hands are cold and yet I am sweating. As we travel home it is as though we are driving through a strange land; the shops and signs and banks of houses feel as though they are designed for people other than ourselves, as though we don't belong. When we stop at a light it feels too sudden. The cars beside us and in front of us appear too close. On the motorway I would swear we are speeding out of control, close to crashing, yet when I check the dashboard it reports that the car is well within the speed limit. Stephen drives carefully, both hands on the steering wheel, his eyes forward and alert. I am unable to sit still. I squirm and feel my breath coming unevenly. My leg is shaking. I pull my knee up to my chin and hold it. I keep checking Daniel, who is in the back seat staring out the window, moving his train's wheels over his lower lip.

We have a favourite nursery rhyme CD and usually I put it on, singing the songs along with Emily. Without her here the silence is palpable, dire. I realise all at once that it has been Emily's exuberance, in part, that has shielded me from the knowledge of Daniel's condition. She always talks enough for two; her interests keep me busy answering questions, telling stories. It was easy to imagine that Daniel was part of all that, but now I see that he might not have been, that I have missed the obvious. He does not seem anxious for the CD to play; he does not seem to notice his father and me in the car. He's always been like this – of course he has – a diagnosis, a label such as autism, does not change the child. And yet I feel that a change has taken place. I cannot help feeling as though I started the journey this morning with my beloved little boy and am returning with a slightly alien, uneducable time bomb.

Dr Dodd explained to us that Daniel will improve in

some ways, but in others he will deteriorate and become noticeably more 'autistic', whatever that means. We were urged to understand that autism is genetic and that a history of depression on both sides of the family (Stephen's father, Bernard, is also given to depression) is proof that this is evident in Daniel's case. Indeed, the consultant seemed very satisfied when she heard my father had killed himself. The suicide absolutely decided it for her – Daniel's predicament was clearly the result of unfortunate genetic coding. The fact that there was no history of autism itself was irrelevant to her, and the idea that my son might have some immediate treatable medical issues was never even acknowledged. If I could have willed my mouth to speak, I would have emphasised that he was terrifically unwell within weeks of receiving his MMR vaccination and that the photographs of him from that day forward plainly show him in marked decline.

It wouldn't have mattered, of course. She has a whole slew of reports about the safety of the MMR, and anyway, didn't my father put a gun in his mouth and shoot while his children slept upstairs?

Yes, I might have replied, if I had dared to reply, if I could have gotten words out, if I wasn't entirely in shock. But my father could laugh and joke, put us on his shoulders and dance. He had a wit that could lay someone out if they tangled with him and a smile that swept a room. He was not dysfunctional, not unable to read emotions, and certainly not autistic. He was forty-eight with an inoperable tumour that made him feel his head was going to explode. Though I don't pretend to know the details of what happened in that basement, I can assure you it wasn't exactly his life he was aiming for with that gun.

*   *   *

At home I find Emily with Veena, sitting in front of the fireplace enacting the scene from *Dumbo* in which the ringmaster, the fierce monkey with the blue-painted coat and hat, forces the poor elephant to jump from a great height into a pail of oatmeal. We made Dumbo from Febo clay and baked him in an oven, paying special attention to his large ears so that they did not crumble. He has enormous eyes and an innocent expression. It isn't just those ears which set him apart from the others, which are the sort of plastic animal you buy at Early Learning Centre and are very correctly moulded, though far less beguiling until Emily painted circus blankets on them all.

'Where is your husband?' Veena asks. Remarkably, after the announcement of Daniel's diagnosis, Stephen dropped us back at the house and went on to work. I have a meeting, he said. Try not to worry, he said. Take a pill if you have to, and let Veena look after the children.

In this numbed, surreal post-diagnosis state, I could think of no objection. Except to the pills. I fed the toilet with them, then filled the vial with aspirin.

Veena says, 'I believe British imperialism to be a kind of genetic coding. Your daughter requests that I take her to India so she can ride an elephant like a royal person.' She shakes her head, smiles. She smells of orange tea and has her hair braided down her back in a single, weighty rope.

'It's the Dumbo influence,' I tell her, 'not the British.'

'Same thing,' she says, tucking a lock of loose hair behind her ear.

'No, Dum*bo*,' I say. 'The elephant.'

'Dumbo the elephant? What are you talking about? The child says she needs a palace.'

We give the children lunch and Veena sets about sucking the dust from the drapes with the long hose of the vacuum cleaner. The whole of our downstairs is just one big room, so I follow her with her Hoover, keeping an eye on Daniel to see that he eats the food and doesn't just roll it between his fingers. Over the noise I try to explain to Veena that Daniel is autistic, and that he is going to get worse unless we do something, but we don't know what to do. Even as I say this it doesn't seem real to me. It's like being in one of those movies where they've discovered the world is going to end in ten days unless a solution is found. But there is no solution.

'What a silly you are,' she says, aiming the hose. 'Your boy is fine. It is only that he is a male and destined to grow up to be a male.'

'No, no, *nooo*,' I say. 'As bad as that sounds to you – you, in particular, Veena – *this* is actually very much worse.' I have a need to push the information at her, to press it into her and force her to take hold of it. It's a feeling that will not go away and that, I believe, will visit me often and with everyone, guaranteeing the end of many of my friendships. Whispering so that Emily and Daniel don't hear, I say, 'He's autistic. That's what they've said. He will not grow up like a normal child. It is the worst thing that can possibly happen!'

She shakes her head. 'Where I come from,' she says, 'they burn women.'

'Vee*na*,' I say, begging with my voice.

'Eat something before you die,' she tells me.

But I cannot eat. I cannot sip the tea or even the water that Veena sets before me. It is a condition of my existence now that the simple, keep-alive activities of eating and drinking and sleeping are beyond me. I sit with my cheek against the wood of our dining table, my hands hanging down, my eyes half open, staring.

Veena watches me for a moment, then shuts off the Hoover and comes to me, taking my hand. What I notice right away is how dry and small her hand is in mine. And how her eyes are so deep a brown I have to search for the pupils. And how sad she looks. I realise now that this is my fault; that I have made her sad by telling her what has happened. She looks across the room at Daniel, at Emily, and I register at once that she is thinking how it is worse for them. With a single confirmed diagnosis their whole lives are different. And then I see something else in her face. An awareness. A resolve. She lets go of my fingers and sits up straight, then says to me steadily, 'I am a philosophy student and an Indian woman. This makes me a very dark person in many ways. Each day I see around me a world falling about like a stumbling drunk. They hold prisoners of Muslims and say they are not racists. They let the white skinheads terrorise the blacks and say they are not racists. I have come to this country as an escape from my own, worse country, where people are still considered untouchables and where it is known that boys are kidnapped and castrated and made to live as eunuchs. I am sorry, dear Melanie, but you are a white woman living in a white paradise. This is not the worst thing that can happen.'

'Untouchables?' I say.

'Gandhi tried to rename them Children of God, but they call themselves the *Dalit*, which means depressed.'

'Veena, I'm depressed.'

She nods. She has heavy glasses that slide down her boxy little nose. She breathes in deeply, then lets the breath go all at once. 'I understand,' she says. 'But right now he lives, and so do you.'

Strangely, Veena's words are a comfort to me.

6

Our house is tiny, fourteen feet wide, two levels. It used to be the garage to a very grand house next door. It has a small garden stocked with ornamental roses and tons of lavender. In the summer the bumblebees, big as mothballs, hum outside the window. I love that the plaster is smooth and cool even in August. That in the winter, when you wake up, the air smells like frost and it smells like coal. To me, our house seems palatial, a miracle in the middle of this dense city. When we first moved here, shortly after Daniel was born, I used to lie in bed with the two children and look outside the windows, where the float glass is different in each of the panes so that the tree branches don't appear to align correctly, watching as the sun fired the sky with colour. Stephen got dressed for work and we spoke in hushed tones so as not to wake the children. I liked to watch him get dressed. He's tall, with enormous presence. Barrel-chested, big wrists, broad hands, thick neck. I looked at our perfect babies, sleeping one on either side of me, and my handsome husband and I thought nobody has ever been so lucky as me. No one has ever been so content with what she has.

But I didn't know what I had. You see, Daniel seemed completely normal. You might think that a baby with autism gives you some warning so you won't love him quite as much as you do your normal child. Maybe he doesn't cling to you or hold his arms round your neck, or laugh when you give him piggyback rides or reach for the swing seat. But he did all those things. I was Daniel's trampoline and his hammock; he made my hip bone his seat and opened my heart with his laughter. There are hundreds of pictures of Daniel sliding down a slide at the playground, stomping puddles with his new wellies, riding his toy train, putting on the eyeglasses for Mr Potato Head and dancing. The change is gradual; the symptoms devious in the way they come and go. You don't love him any less because he doesn't speak to you. Or when he cannot seem to get the hang of the new garage and all the shiny new cars you buy him, or has no interest in the games you try to play. When he won't let you touch his head, let alone wash his hair, or when he cries almost all day and you have no idea why. You don't love him any less – you just think you are failing.

Stephen will not talk to me at all about him. He goes to work early, comes home late, retreats into his laptop and is unavailable for comment.

'This, what you are doing here, is not helpful,' I tell him. I am lying face down on the couch while he sits at the other end, poking his keyboard, answering emails.

After a very long while he says, 'If you knew there was something wrong, why didn't you get help?'

'So it's *my* fault?'

'I asked why you didn't get a doctor. Sooner. Obviously, you *knew*.'

And now I wish he'd go back to not speaking to me. Email somebody in Hong Kong or *whateverthefuck* he does.

When I wake in the morning there are a few seconds' reprieve before a sense of doom and anguish alerts me again to my son and my predicament. It would appear that he is to fail to attain any of the normal milestones of childhood growth, will likely become more remote and wilful, possibly even dangerous to himself and to others. To Emily? Yes, possibly. I have been told that for the sake of the siblings one must sometimes find alternative accommodation for the autistic one – but not to worry, that would be many years from now. Not to worry? Not to *worry*? As for right now, I am to accept as fact that he will need special education in a school designed for children who cannot learn like other children. There is apparently nothing I can do but gently escort him through his childhood until one or another institution or, if we are lucky, sheltered community assumes his care as an adult. The unfortunate truth of autism is that it cannot be cured, or even effectively mitigated, and that the condition is a genetic mistake for which we will for ever pay the consequences.

'Stephen, please, don't go to work today. Stay here with us. Please,' I beg him now. What day is it? Tuesday, I think. All my concerns tumble around my mind like clothes in a dryer. I toss one up, then another, the next, and so on. I tell him this. I tell him that the day seems inordinately long and that I cannot see how to navigate it, that I am lost.

Stephen understands, pats my arm, nods his head. But he does not stay.

Stephen's uncle Raymond, that dear man, rings to tell me not to regret giving Daniel the MMR. His voice is loud in the receiver; he speaks as one who has endured early efforts at telephonic communication, who has shouted into tortoiseshell receivers fixed on wall phones, gone through operators in order to place calls. Now he tells me that in his time he has seen children die of measles; they died in droves when he was a boy. Temperatures of a hundred and six, their brains burned inside their skulls. I mustn't regret a thing.

'Please come and see us,' I say to him. Raymond lives on the other side of London. He owns the same house in which he grew up and that he shared with his mother until her death some thirty years ago. He has taken me round the upstairs to show me the scars in the ceiling where a bomb came through the roof during the war. He has stood me by the window and pointed to the areas, now dense with houses, where once there was nothing but craters and buildings in ruins. He's seen things he will not tell me about, the experiences of being a soldier. 'I would not wish my memories upon you,' he once said, then asked me if I could find a use for the cake pan his mother used to bake birthday cakes for him and his brother when they were children. Whether, too, I might like some of his mother's damask linen.

'I will come,' he says now. 'But meanwhile, you mustn't blame yourself.'

'I don't,' I tell him, a lie. I am fast becoming a good liar, which I discover is a means of camouflage for the protection of others, those who have not been conscripted into this battle with autism, those who have normal children, for example. Or those like Raymond, whom I feel I am discovering now as one discovers an ancient and magical place. I would like to curl up on his mother's window seat, admire the large oak tree he planted as a boy, talk to him about the way London has changed in his lifetime, consult the past, disregard the future. Where is that cake pan? I will bake a Victorian sponge, slather it with cream, talk about decoding machines and doodle-bugs, battles fought on foreign beaches, places I have visited only in history books, anywhere far away.

'These things happen,' says Raymond. 'Nobody knows why.'

Speculation abounds, however. I thought only hippies didn't vaccinate their children. And I remember the day I held Daniel's chubby thigh as the nurse readied the syringe.

The headmaster of the prep school thinks Emily is a delight and is very happy to offer her a place in pre-prep starting the autumn term. He is ultra-blond with a long, effete forehead and a thin, sculpted nose. His face has a dapper, ruddy complexion as though he spends most of his free time sailing, which I guess he does. He sits at a large oak desk surrounded by prints of famous sailing ships, the sort you might find hoisted on a dry dock and visited by tourists. All along a bookshelf are bottles containing models of such ships. I regard them as one might a taxidermy collection, which the headmaster notices.

'My hobby,' he says, rather grandly. Cartwell is his name. He has a big brass plate on his desk engraved in swirling, girlish letters so that everyone knows.

'You do these *yourself*?' I am amazed he will admit to such a thing. There's something distinctly creepy about this man. My mind drifts to thoughts of strange potions in backrooms or remains under floorboards.

Cartwell nods, making a little movement with his hand as though he doesn't want to boast too much about it. We are invited to sit down in two captain's chairs at the side of his enormous desk. Turning to Emily's file, he says, 'She's an unusually articulate girl, isn't she?' He reels off her test results as though reading a sales report. I notice his peculiar habit of continually rearranging the objects on his desk as he speaks. In the last few minutes, for example, he has moved a paperweight from the lower left corner to the upper right corner, lined up his pencils, wiped the surface of his blotting paper with the back of his hand, stacked a group of Post-it notes and ordered a number of business cards. All I can think, as he outlines for us the results of the diagnostic tests they gave Emily, is how these habits seem somewhat obsessive and unnatural. Also, that I am quite sure he buffs his fingernails.

I say, 'Have you looked at Emily's drawings?'

Amid many test reports on Cartwell's desk are dozens of Emily's cartoons: Mickey Mouse, Donald Duck, Pluto, plus several pictures of Dumbo flying through the air. I brought the drawings to show the school because I believe they illustrate something of Emily's personality, her interests, what makes her who she is. I think she's a genius, but Mr Cartwell only frowns at the images. 'Yes, er, they are very nice,' he says as though staring at a pungent mound of disastrous ethnic cuisine he has no intention of ever tasting. 'Would you like them back?' he asks now, handing them over.

I am about to launch into a discussion about how

important art is to Emily when Stephen takes his shoe and puts it on top of my boot in a secret communication that means Don't Say Anything. Stephen does not often try to control me in conversation, although he does have an uncanny way of subduing my opinions. But this gesture at this particular time is a mistake on his part. I am not in the mood for it. There's something about the way Cartwell keeps assuring us that Emily won't be held back by children with 'problems' because the school carefully screens such children out that has me on edge. Plus all the rearranging of knick-knacks on his desk. I keep thinking that Cartwell himself clearly has problems. His face is grim, serious, as though explaining a procedure for qualifying neurosurgeons rather than talking about children. He keeps clearing his throat in rapid grunts that sound like someone imitating gunfire. Stephen's foot on mine presses in an annoying manner and it feels to me to be exactly the sort of obstacle that requires swatting away. So while Cartwell goes on about his wonderful school and the screening procedure that makes it so, I take my umbrella, the old-fashioned sort with a long, pointed steel end, and knock it firmly into Stephen's Achilles tendon.

Stephen's face barely registers the assault on his ankle. In a different mood I could not only admire but actually be mildly attracted to him for being able to endure so much physical pain without allowing it to show on his face. The problem – for him – is that he cares very much how we come across. He can't actually move away, nor can he tell me to stop attacking him with the umbrella – unless he wants to look really weird.

'You have nothing to worry about with Emily – she

will fly through,' says Cartwell, as the drama of the umbrella continues under the table.

Stephen glances briefly at me as though to say, I Mean Business. This annoys me so much that I remind him of the umbrella by tapping his shoe with its steel point. 'Even at the pre-prep level we do not accept children with any special needs or behavioural problems,' says Cartwell as Stephen kicks with some force to fend off a blow to his ankle.

The sound of this causes Cartwell to pause.

'Did you hear something?' he asks.

'Like what?' I say. 'Like a man kicking an umbrella?'

Now Stephen is even more irritated. He knocks my boot with the edge of his shoe while Cartwell continues his speech about the quality of his school's pupils. I land the umbrella once more against Stephen who, with amazing self-control, gives no sign whatsoever that he has just had a rather serious knock on his ankle bone. I watch him nod, agreeing with the sage counsel of Cartwell, who explains that children with problems are to be avoided, of course. That is what we are buying. One of the things we are buying.

'You've indicated you have another child,' says Cartwell now. 'Daniel is his name? How old is Daniel?'

'He's three,' says Stephen.

'Marvellous,' says Cartwell. 'He'll be ready to join his sister here shortly, then.'

I'm about to explain that Daniel is exactly the sort of child who is apparently wholly unwelcome by his school when Stephen, risking serious injury, puts his foot back on mine again. I turn my head to him, catch his eye, and then get him so hard across the shin that he has a sudden intake of breath.

'I'm sure I heard something,' says Cartwell. 'Did you hear anything?'

'I thought so too,' I say. 'Almost like the sound of bone cracking.'

Cartwell begins an unsteady laugh, then looks uneasy. Then he arranges Emily's file so that the edges of the test results line up perfectly, glances back and forth at Stephen and myself.

'Perhaps we had better let you go,' says Stephen, rising.

All the way out of the school Cartwell and Stephen compare notes about their own prep-school days, chuckling about the way things have changed. I see that the deal has been clinched. I trail behind them as we are led out of the school building. Inside, I feel myself shrieking objections to everything associated with this pompous and, it must be said, really very strange headmaster. I'm thinking, how can we send our daughter to a school in which the headteacher puts boats in bottles? And makes promises that he will shield children from having to have contact with any child like my own son? But I can see I will lose this one. Stephen shows only a slight limp and he's determined – oh yes – that Emily will go to this school.

The autistic teenage son of a man in Buckinghamshire bit through his father's thumb. I read it in the newspaper on the way back from the interview with Cartwell. They had to find the thumb and sew it back on. Meanwhile, the boy ran out of the house.

So who found the boy?

In America a young autistic man went into the bank and yelled, 'Stick 'em up!', his finger pointing like a gun. He was shot during his arrest, because he wouldn't put down his weapon.

In court, the parents have been told that it is nobody's fault. Nobody is to blame. Their son was shot for having a finger gun and the parents have been told 'these things happen'.

Stephen's voice on the message tape says, 'Look, Mel, I'm sorry . . .'

But when I pick up the phone he says, 'I just didn't want you to blow it for Emily –'

'Not sorry then,' I say, and hang up.

Later he calls and says, 'But *you* hit *me!*'

'Still not sorry,' I say, and down the phone goes.

But that night I am tearful, upset, not wanting a fight. I sit on the doorstep with Daniel, who has a thing about the iron railing in front of our house. He scans it with his eye, drops down as though doing a deep knee bend and then pops back up all at once like a jack-in-the-box. You might not think that's so bad, except he's been doing it for an hour now. Judging by the enthusiasm he still shows for the pattern of parallel lines that make up the railing, he'll be at it for another hour if I let him. I've been sitting here thinking that maybe Emily needs some doors open to her. That if the pre-prep is a place that will do that for her, then maybe that's a good thing. Maybe she should go. This thought disturbs me, depresses me. But so does the thought of Emily stuck in a house with nobody but her mother and her autistic brother.

Down the road I see Stephen. He's talking on his mobile, balancing his case, walking in long, determined strides. When he sees me on the step he stops, stares at me.

'What are you doing sitting there?' he says.

'I'm sorry about the umbrella attack,' I tell him.

He shakes his head.

I tell him, 'I'm sorry about everything.'

Almost midnight and I still cannot sleep. The alarm clock glows. The refrigerator hums; the muddied sound of distant cars rumbles in the air. I am alert to everything, to the gentle rising of Daniel's chest, the warmth of his breath upon my cheek. I watch him sleep and I have only one wish for him. A wish that should never need be: that he was normal. Just normal. Just an average child. Not a superstar, not a genius, just a kid.

I watch the sweep of the clock's second hand, hear the distant chime of bells. Even though he cannot hear me, I find myself speaking to him. 'Here comes tomorrow,' I say.

My shrink has brand new trainers, bright yellow, like two giant bananas tied to his feet. His dark tracksuit is in contrast to the trainers, which are distracting and odd. He has come to our house because I called him just before he went to the gym and I could not speak, not even to tell him my name. I just held the phone to my ear and listened to him say 'hello, hello' over and over again, and could not bring myself to interrupt his day, his scheduled appointments, his tidy life. The way he figured out it was me was by comparing the number on his caller ID screen with his patient list. Then he put down the phone, got into his car and drove to my house.

Now he sits on the couch and looks at me as I rock on the floor. Veena has taken the children to the park and I feel guilty I am not with them.

'I can't even do *that*!' I sob.

'Right now, this minute, at 3 p.m. on this Wednesday,' says Jacob, 'no, you cannot.'

'Why am I so useless?'

'You are not useless. You are in shock. Frankly, I am in shock. I had no idea what was wrong with your son. Melanie, please, I have to say this. I am so sorry.'

What I want him to say is that he disagrees with the diagnosis. He saw Daniel on his way out the door with Veena, walking on his toes, looking at the wall, being strung along by Veena, whose hand held his wrist. But Jacob doesn't say he disagrees with the diagnosis. Nothing like it.

'Tell me why you are not disagreeing with the diagnosis,' I say. He says nothing. I wait for him to speak and he doesn't. 'Tell me!' I say, but all he does is shake his head.

Then I say, 'Then explain what you thought was wrong with me before you found out what was really happening. With Daniel, I mean.' It is not too late to join the children at the playground. Except I still can't seem to get off the floor.

'Anxiety disorder. I suspected perhaps marriage problems,' says Jacob.

'Oh my God, my marriage!' This sends me into a new episode of unretractable tears. We wait through that, both he and I. I have a sore muscle just below my ribs from all the crying, and I've broken some blood vessels just beneath the surface of skin on my cheek. I saw them in my reflection when I went to pee: a blotchy patch of tiny red dots. Who knew you could cry that hard?

'What *is* wrong with me then?' I ask Jacob. 'Now that we've gotten the initial impressions out of the way.'

'You are grieving,' he says. 'You are experiencing a very serious loss.'

'But Daniel's not dead,' I say, remembering Veena's words.

'The boy you thought he might be is lost, however,' says Jacob.

'You call yourself a *shrink*!' I say, sobbing out of control now. I pick up Duplo bricks and a coffee mug, hurling them across the room. The mug ricochets off the fireplace surround and I'm so mad at it for breaking that I throw a book, a tub of crayons and, finally, my eyeglasses. Luckily, the eyeglasses don't break, so I stop throwing things. I sit still and don't breathe. This is on purpose. I sit with my head on my knees and I don't let in a single breath. I am drowning, I think. But Jacob won't let me drown.

'Melanie,' he begins.

Later, still sitting on the floor, my head inches from Jacob's silly banana shoes, I whisper, 'Jacob, what happens if Daniel dies?' I say that several times in a row, and without a pause between the questions. Even to me, I sound weird.

'He won't die. He's going to live, and so are you.'

'But I want to die. But I can't die. Because if I die who will help him? Jacob, please listen to me. Please, don't go away or look at your watch –'

'I didn't look at my watch –'

'Just in case you were going to look at it, don't look. At the watch, I mean. Jacob, I have to describe this to you. You know how when you have a baby, a little child, you think how if you die that the child will be broken-hearted? I mean, this is a tiny soul who cannot stand to be away from you for more than an hour and who, if he should fall, needs you to hold him and *only* you?'

Jacob nods, although I doubt he ever thought about such a thing as dying when his children were young. Anyway, his children are grown up now. And I have a feeling that nobody other than me imagines such events. It is because I have watched such great, unthinkable things. My mother died in pieces – it seemed to me they were always carving more from her body. My lover, my best friend, hit the asphalt of a Massachusetts highway at sixty miles an hour one morning because someone in a four-by-four didn't bother to look.

I say, 'OK, so you know if you die it's going to tear him up. So you cling to every shred of health you have and you take careful pains to ensure that you get through each day. If only on a subconscious level, you think you better not take any risks. Life insurance won't be enough. Savings accounts won't be enough. He needs *you* because *you* know how to tuck him into bed and which stories he likes and how long to hold open the book and where to take him on a Saturday morning. You love him and he loves you. No, it's more than that. He's part of you, like your arm or your face. He lays claim to you and counts you as his, as he might his own foot. But if you *should* die, you know that some day he will grow up anyway. He'll grow up and he'll drive a car and make love to his wife and have friends he laughs with, collect books or go to football games or whatever. You know that he won't stay that hurt, desperate, devoured child who is told his mum won't come back. Now, Jacob, let me tell you what happens to Daniel, to my baby. My baby who does not grow up because he's autistic. You see, when I die, he is not grown up yet, is he? He is not driving a car or turning over in bed to hold his wife or being a man in a world full of men. He is still that tiny child who cannot understand why his mother isn't here any more. What happened to her? Who took her away? This is not a *possibility* that he will be that broken-hearted boy, but an inevitable *fact*. Because I cannot live for ever.'

That's all I can get through. That's it. For an hour or more Jacob stays with me, however.

7

The first I ever heard of Bruno Bettelheim was in a sociology class at university. We were given his paper on how victims of Nazi concentration camps would sometimes come to emulate their captors, so that within the camps existed a kind of secondary Nazi force, Jews controlling Jews. Bettelheim spent some time describing how bits of the Nazi uniform were coveted by many prisoners, and how some were said even to march among their fellow prisoners hurling abuse and anti-Semitic remarks.

'I don't think I believe this,' said Marcus. He was sitting on the edge of my bed wearing a pair of boxer shorts and waiting for the aloe vera gel to cool the sunburn he got riding his motorcycle with his shirt off. He kept making faces as he read, which may have been because his shoulders hurt so much or may have been because he thought Bettelheim was greatly exaggerating what he claimed to have witnessed in concentration camps. He kept shaking his head. 'It just isn't true,' he said.

I didn't think much about Marcus's comment and probably would not even remember him saying it except that

since Daniel's diagnosis I have become feverishly interested in anything to do with autism. Bettelheim, it turns
out, not only embroidered stories about the Jews in
concentration camps, but was the famous inventor of the
idea that childhood autism was caused by poor mothering.
It is this second fabrication that grabs my attention.

So I find out a few things. I find out that by 1939
Bettelheim was in America creating a whole new life for
himself as an expert on autistic children. That would be
OK, except there was no reason to believe he knew
anything about autistic children. He said he met Freud
(which was unlikely), that he received training as a
psychoanalyst (which was untrue), that he published two
books before coming to America (no one has ever seen
these books) and that he was part of an organisation in
Europe that studied the emotional problems of children
and adolescents (for which there is no evidence). The
only training Bettelheim had was a Ph.D. in philosophical aesthetics, which has to do with questions like,
What is art?

And yet he somehow convinced everyone he was an
authority on autistic children. He set up a school outside
Chicago that claimed to give specialised treatment for
them. He compared the mothers of autistic kids to
devouring witches, infanticidal kings and SS guards in
concentration camps. He was taken seriously and came
to hold tremendous influence on the course of treatment
for autistic children all over the world. Nobody dared
argue with him. Had Daniel been born at a different time
it would have been understood that it was me who
destroyed his psyche, that I had dehumanised him and
that in his despair he became autistic. Bettelheim, who
invented nearly all his credentials, would say that on a

subconscious level I wanted Daniel dead – and he would be believed. That the world should take notice of and even acclaim this charlatan who made his living by damning the mothers of unwell children, pressuring parents to relinquish their children to him on a residential basis, and then tricking everyone into thinking he could restore them through psychoanalysis, is a humanitarian crime. And yet, this is what happened. If we don't hold in our minds just how easily we were duped by Bettelheim and his ilk, it could happen again.

This is what I tell the doctors at this supposed centre of excellence for autistic children, when they ask me if I would like Daniel to enrol in their programme. This programme, it turns out, is based on the wrongly derived, scandalous notion that autism is a problem that requires psychoanalysis. They want to spend time guessing at what went wrong during a 'critical moment' of Daniel's psychological and emotional development.

'ALL moments of a child's life are critical,' I tell them. 'Your stupid institution here is following the wrong road, one that was paved by an insane and morally criminal man.'

'Excuse me, Mrs Marsh, I don't think you quite understand,' says a sandy-haired shrink – God, she's younger than I am. Into her hair she has braided a decorated cord of colours. She puts down her notes and gives me a beautiful smile. Must have just gotten the braces off.

'Understand? I think I have given you a fairly thorough account, Miss,' I tell her. Doesn't she have homework to complete? An exam to study for? Some stubborn acne to medicate? I think, *why* is my son so low on the list of priorities that he gets treatment from her, who is probably not even a beginner shrink, but a student, and who is wearing *lip gloss*? Not that I want this 'treatment', which isn't 'treatment', which is only bullshit, in any case. Do they also believe the world is flat?

The junior shrink looks at her colleague, the real shrink. You can tell he is a real shrink because he is older with a hollow chest and soft, white hands as though he's never done a bit of work in his life. The real shrink says, 'Mrs Marsh, we don't actually think it's your fault about your son.' He has a face like a shovel and a receding hairline revealing scalp moles and what might be a cancer up there. I'm more apt to believe what he says, if only because of the scalp moles. I would tell him so but he might take it the wrong way.

'That's lovely that you don't blame me. So why psycho-analyse him? Let me ask you this, would you psychoanalyse him if he had something wrong with his heart or lungs or kidneys?' I offer a few additional comments about Bettelheim, their great genius who would claim that I had a secret wish my baby would die. As for charging the National Health Service a hundred pounds an hour to speculate uselessly on what might have caused a develop-mental crisis in Daniel, I say, 'I think the taxpayers should know what you are doing here. Certainly, you're not *helping*. Why don't we use the money to find someone who can teach Daniel to *talk*? Surely, even *you* can see that being mute has disadvantages.'

'We *do* help them to talk,' says the real shrink. 'We help them to say the difficult things about the way they *feel*.'

'Is that right?' I say. 'The difficult things? Well, right now, little Daniel here who is coming up for three, cannot say Mama. In fact, he can't recognise his own name in conversation as far as I can tell. I think you might find yourself hard pressed to get him to express complex phobias.'

'Mrs Marsh,' he says, 'we are qualified –'

'Qualified by *whom*? For *what*? That's my point. There are all these supposed experts around, but they don't seem to be able to do anything to help the person who needs help, which is Daniel. What's it mean to be an expert if you can't make anything better? I mean, what are you getting paid *for*?'

The doctors look at each other. Salt and Pepper, these two, standing beside each other like two dolls in their white coats.

'I think we're done here,' I announce now, taking Daniel's hand.

But I can't always be so tough. I fall apart in the silliest places – playgrounds, supermarkets. I think the supermarket is the worst. The only way to get Daniel through what is (for most people) an ordinary shopping trip is to give him a heap of sweets to keep him still in the trolley seat. If he doesn't have the sweets he screams, undoes the flimsy seat belt, and tries to throw himself out apparently without any thought about the physical damage he'd suffer by doing so. He would succeed at throwing himself out, too, except I use my own belt, buckled snugly around his middle, to keep him in place. So when he tries to hurl himself over the rail he can't get very far, although he does scream and look completely weird if not the victim of some kind of parental abuse. Comments from me to the other shoppers ('This is just to keep him from falling') only serve to make me look like a freak and exactly the sort of person who would make any child miserable enough to want to drop from a height onto his own head.

There is an alternative, of course. I can chase him through the aisles as he speeds like a dervish, his hands reaching for whatever he might wish to investigate, to open, to eat, to smell. It means I won't actually accomplish any shopping, or at least not much, and I will probably find myself with a fair bill to pay for items hurled from shelves as Daniel makes room for his feet so that he can climb up to the really good stuff.

What I want is a third option, though I know this is just too ambitious, which is to let him have a *little* treat while seated in the trolley. *One* ice lolly, for example, or a *few* biscuits.

I cannot see this working.

Right now he is leaning toward the rows of chocolate biscuits, seeking with his nose the way a dog might, finding just the ones he wants and then pressing his face right against the packet, his eyes open, staring into the ballooned lettering, his lungs filling themselves with the smell of McVitie's chocolate digestives. He seems to get immense pleasure from this, a sensual delight greater than I can understand. Even Emily watches him, her expression one of fascination. I suppose, like me, she seeks to discover what delight Daniel finds from this activity of sniffing and staring. And now he takes the packet into his arms and holds it in much the same way a child holds a teddy bear. Then he grabs another packet and tucks it under the opposite arm, his hands turned inward and across his chest, his elbows fanning out as though they are wings.

I pick him up and place him into the trolley seat. He gives me no help whatsoever with this procedure. He won't bend his knees or look down to where he needs to place his legs. All his concentration is focused on the biscuit packets. I push his thighs gently through the seat. Emily helps guide him in by pulling on his shoe until it comes off in her hands. Then she drops the shoe like it's a live toad so that I have to retrieve it from the floor.

And now comes my next choice. Do I let him have the whole packet of biscuits – and yes, I mean the entire packet as he is gnawing his way through one of them already – or do I bargain, try to get him to have just one or two of the biscuits?

Today, I am going to bargain.

I take an identical pack to the ones he is holding, thumb the red tab on the wrapper, lifting it gently, until part of a chocolate cookie is exposed. Because I am becoming attuned to the things that make Daniel unusual, set him apart, I notice the aroma of the cookies as he might, a mixture of flour and butter, sugar and chocolate. I inhale deeply and I have this strange feeling as though I've sucked all the flavour from the air leaving Daniel nothing for himself. But he doesn't appear unhappy about it. Every ounce of concentration is focused on the shiny surface of chocolate that coats the cookie, the crumbs that linger on the wrapper. 'Say cookie,' I tell him.

Emily throws her hand over her face. 'They're called *biscuits*, Mummy,' she says.

'OK, fine.' Right, of course. They are called biscuits. How can I expect him to say 'cookie'? How silly of me. I look at Daniel again. He is reaching for the biscuit, staring at my hand as though it is the grabber in one of those machines at amusement parks that pulls a random toy from a stack of others by means of a mechanical arm. He does not look at my face or appear to be estimating whether he can persuade me to relinquish the biscuit.

'Biscuit,' I say. But he seems to pay no attention what-soever to my words. I just want him to try, to make an

attempt, to give some sign that he wants to talk to me.
But Daniel does nothing, says nothing. He reaches for the
cookie and then kicks out because he cannot have it.

'Biscuit,' I whisper. Oh, why can't he just try to say it?
He strains against the seat belt in the trolley seat, leans
over the bar. I take a step back and now he's furious,
kicking his legs, pushing the handle of the trolley with
both hands while rocking his body back and forth. He's
crying so loudly that people are looking, which makes me
a little panicky. I move the trolley along with one hand,
holding the biscuit packet away with the other. One of
the many bits of advice I read in parenting books when I
was pregnant was that when a child is having a tantrum
the best thing you can do is remove him from the scene.
If you are outside, go indoors. If you are indoors, go
outside. I can't remember the logic of why this works,
though it certainly seemed to work for Emily when she
used to tantrum. She was always so interested in the world
that moving her to a new spot within it commanded her
attention. But Daniel doesn't care that we've moved past
biscuits and cakes, past sweets and crisps, and are now
skirting the back of the store and turning toward the
frozen-food section. His cheeks are red; his hair suddenly
sweaty. There's a heat coming from him that is almost as
noticeable as the tremendous noise he makes, his eyes
tearing, his fists pounding the trolley in a way that really
must hurt. It pains me. By the time we reach the frozen
vegetables, I am nearly crying myself.

'This is Tantrum Sindy,' says Emily.

'Sindy?' I try to smile. 'Where did you learn that name?'

'Sindy dolls. I want one,' she says.

'Of course,' I say absently. My mind is racing. I keep
trying to placate Daniel. And I keep asking myself why I

try so hard. Isn't it enough that I get around the shop without staring at all the other boys Daniel's age, sitting in their seats or skipping along beside their mothers? Without watching them as they talk – pointing at the things they'd like to eat, asking questions about whether they can go to see the toys – envying them, sometimes dangerously close to crying out right there in public my own desperate desire to hear Daniel speak? Whenever Daniel produces even the most incomprehensible sound, I drink it in like someone who has crossed miles of desert with no water. I am desperate to hear him. I know what he'll sound like – if he ever decides to talk at all. He'll sound like all the other little boys I know. He'll have the same squeaky, high-pitched voice that I hear all around me. And yet I am desperate for this voice. I am pleading with him now to please stop crying.

'Have the biscuits,' I say finally, stabbing through the packet with my thumbnail, spilling out dozens of disc shapes into his lap. He's so delighted. Discs he can eat. He takes them in his hands without looking at me, stacks them neatly and licks the surface of each in turn as though instilling his own mark.

'What about me?' whines Emily.

Emily! Of course! I grab a biscuit from where it rests on Daniel's thigh, which is covered in crumbs now, and she makes a face like she might cry.

'He licked it!' she moans. So I grab another, and then the first one drops, breaking into pieces at my feet. Emily stares in horror, then looks up to Daniel to see if he's noticed, to see if he'll start to scream again. But he doesn't scream – thank God – and Emily accepts the next biscuit I give her, though I think it may have been licked, too. Out of the corner of my eye I see other customers watching us. They may have been watching the whole time or maybe just this last bit, where I indulge what they imagine to be a spoilt child with all the biscuits he can hold. I stare back at them. I think, *Damn you, you have no idea.* Gradually, they turn away as I try to sweep up the broken biscuit with a tissue, stuffing it now into my coat pocket. Oh, this is pathetic. I just want to go home, but I cannot, because of course I have to pay for all this shopping, which means somehow I have to get through the queue. I can only hope I have enough biscuits to do so.

And that is when a woman in a bright green coat walks up to me with a smile. She has a halo of greying hair, soft eyes behind thick plastic frames. She wears stylish earrings and lipstick but no other make-up. I am used to people making comments about my kids – or rather about Daniel – and I prepare myself for what she might say. I just wish I was in a better frame of mind to hear it. That I had some witty or insulting remark I could make back. But my throat is full of pepper and my eyes feel like they are boiling. I just want to run. If she'd get out of the way now I might do just that. But instead she stops before me and looks at Daniel, then me.

'He's lovely,' she says.

There's a beat of silence between us. Her eyes lock with mine. I shake my head back and forth, feeling a pressure in my skull as though a dam is breaking.

'He's *not* lovely!' I splutter. I am crying now, crying in front of this stranger, in front of the whole shop. People are looking, then turning away. 'He's not lovely at all!'

'Mummy!' says Emily, holding me around the thigh, her face tilted toward mine, puzzled. 'You're not crying,' she says, and it is a statement not a question, as though she is calling it into being.

'He reminds me of my boy,' says the woman. She has a whispery voice, expressive eyes. She seems so desperate to tell me something. I have to listen, though really I'd rather she just left, too, like the other shoppers who have the good sense to abandon this aisle. She says, 'You know, at McDonald's he used to go around all the tables and take one bite – just one – out of every burger he could get his hands on. People just . . . well. I thought they'd kill us!' She laughs now, steps closer to me. 'And once he was having such a tantrum in the car that the police pulled us over because they thought he must be being abducted.'

I rub my eyes on my collar, look up at the ceiling, at the signs that tell you the contents of aisles, at the long strips of overbright lights. My head is throbbing like a wound. I look at Daniel, who is getting increasingly upset because he cannot hold all the biscuits he insists on holding. Some are crumbling; some are falling to the floor.

The lady says, 'He wouldn't go into a public lavatory. The hand dryers just threw him.'

I nod, look down. I know what she is telling me.

'I had to take my husband with me whenever we went into a public place, especially one with food!' she says. 'I think you are very brave.'

She won't use the word because she's too nice. And she's afraid of hurting me. So I say it instead. 'Your son is autistic?' I ask, knowing the answer already.

She nods.

'Can he talk?' This feels to me the only thing that matters. That one day I will hear Daniel speak. I cannot tell you what it would do for me, just to have his words in my ears, the sound of his voice. If I could hear it, it would be music.

'Talk? Oh, sweetheart,' she says, looking a little sad for me, looking the way my mother used to when she wished she could cheer me up over some issue that upset me, but that she knew would come out all right. 'Of *course* he can talk. And so will your little boy. He will talk.'

My knees can barely hold me. Daniel is screaming again because too many of his disc-shaped biscuits have fallen now. He's angry, throwing some down, picking others from his lap and trying to stack them. Emily is pulling at me, wanting me to pick her up. Can I hold her without falling over? I can barely keep myself from shaking. 'How do you know?' I say, rather harshly. I don't want it to sound harsh, but it does. 'How do you *know* he will talk?'

This woman . . . oh, God, I hope she doesn't walk away . . . she says, 'Because your son is not as bad as you think. He's really not so bad. I've seen a lot of them – not that I'm an expert, just a mother. Your boy will talk. And one day you'll be able to take him in here and he won't make a scene. All sorts of things will change for the better – you'll see.'

I nod, but I'm not sure I believe any of what she is saying. She writes her phone number on a bit of notepaper and I fold it carefully into the front pocket of my jeans. That's where I keep every important thing that I don't want to lose no matter what. My car keys are there, for example, my credit cards. And now her number. And her name, too. She is Iris, like the flower.

8

My father-in-law, Bernard, only cares about his own son, Daniel's father, my husband, Stephen. Stephen is a man perfectly capable of talking, dressing himself, working, laughing at a joke, driving, attending parties, flirting, dancing. These are just a few of the things Stephen can do which Daniel cannot and may never do – but Bernard is worried about Stephen.

'You *do* know your father is a git,' I tell Stephen. He's just returned from a day at his parents' house trying to reassure Bernard that all is well, even though all is not well. All is more or less in the toilet.

'What do you want me to do about it?' he says unpleasantly. Then he plugs himself into his MP3 player and is away.

Bernard believes, but does not say, that Daniel's autism is in part a judgment from God. During the brief time Stephen and I lived together unmarried he used to lament that we were 'living in sin'. One afternoon, at the age of seventy-six, Bernard drove to London to have lunch with Stephen in a restaurant near Stephen's office. There, in the middle of a room full of business lunches, he took Stephen's hands in his own and asked, almost tearfully, if living together meant we are were having 'relations'. This was the bit he could not bear to imagine, that his thirty-year-old son was having sex with a woman to whom he was not wed. When Stephen admitted that yes, he was having sex with me, his father slumped on the table with the weight of this awful news.

'What kind of perfect life has this man led that the thought of his grown son having sex is such a tragedy?' I hollered, hearing Stephen's account of the lunch. 'In America, parents are *relieved* when their thirty-year-old son is having sex with a woman!'

Anger. Outrage. Resentment. Stephen didn't feel any of what I felt. He had in his mind the sad, tearful face of his elderly father, how he'd driven through the London traffic, how he'd taken his hand across the table.

'It's your fault,' I told him, 'for hiding five years of rampant, crazy sex – as in underwater-type crazy sex – with *whatsername*.'

'Penelope,' said Stephen.

'I know her name! Why didn't you tell him about *her*?'

'What? Tell my father I was having sex with Penelope?'

'Well, yes. When you came up for air, I mean.'

This time Bernard is worried about Stephen because he thinks that Daniel will ruin Stephen's life. He keeps saying, 'To have a child like that is an awful thing.' Being a relative newcomer to the world of parents of disabled children, I don't yet have the exact parlance to describe how this remark offends me, but it does. Plus this issue of a judgment from God, which is not visited directly upon us but skirts along the edges of every conversation and report from Stephen's family. Bernard is suffering with matters involving Christianity, morality, sins of the fathers, all that. And is very worried about Stephen . . . oh yes, and Daniel, too, although they keep saying Daniel will never 'know' so he'll be happy. As though Daniel is not quite fully human or something. Meanwhile, I am supposed to be 'supportive' of Stephen's parents.

David calls and wants something – I don't give him the opportunity to explain – but it has to do with 'the family', meaning himself, Stephen, Cath, Daphne and Bernard.

'Look,' I say, 'I do understand and it isn't that I don't care about your dad,' although frankly, I do not, 'only that your dad isn't my first priority right now.'

David says nothing in reply, but then he might have been watching the football anyway. I certainly can hear it in the background. And I think he is a little in shock. Stephen's parents have always been everybody's first priority. I have no idea why.

'Try to get Stephen to visit his dad,' urges Tricia, wresting the phone from her husband, who apparently has been mesmerised by a pivotal moment in the game. 'He's going into another of his depressions.'

So now the preoccupation for Stephen's family is this: what will happen to Bernard if he gets depressed again. He is too old to take much more of this. He has a weak heart, a problem with circulation, with his lungs, with sleep, with getting through the day.

'Well, me too,' I say to Tricia.

'Yes, but you're young,' she says.

'And what about Daniel? Doesn't anyone care about him?'

'They all do. They are grieving.'

But I don't quite see it that way. Daphne, who is caught up with small issues like how to get her hair just right or keep her ugly carpet from staining, regards more obvious, larger problems in life with considerably less concern. She calls, looking for Stephen, and then tries to find something to say to me, whom she regards as a kind of unfortunate fact of Stephen's life, the way the mothers of teenage sons regard such intrusions as pop music and big muddy trainers that lie ponging in the hallway. She tells me now she knows the diagnosis is bleak, but isn't it 'marvellous' that nowadays they have such lovely homes for children like Daniel. And they can do such wonderful things.

'*What* wonderful things? He's already got a home,' I say. It is a favourable condition for her that she reports this to me by telephone. If I'd been in her presence and actually watched her say such a thing to me with her bright smile and stinging eyes, I cannot tell what might have happened.

'Well, I know he does, of course he does . . .' says Daphne. But it is no good, I see where she sits on the subject of Daniel. Tricia says they are grieving people, but I don't see grieving people. What I see is an old man more concerned about his own son than he is about mine. Well, OK, I won't blame him for that, but *grieving*? And what about Daphne, who thinks Daniel should be in a home, if such things still exist? She's imagining a stout white building with pleasant gardens and a name like 'Little Springs Centre' or 'Magnolia House'. In her mind she is travelling by car down the smooth, soundless drive shaded by oak trees, surrounded by discreet tall fences. 'Isn't it *marvellous* how beautiful it all is!' she is saying, as though the residents in this opulent prison are luckier than the rest of us.

'Your mother rang,' I whisper to Stephen. We are all sitting on the floor watching *Sesame Street* and eating pizza.

Emily giggles at the Cookie Monster and watches the letter Q do a ballad about how great it is to be the letter Q. Daniel seems to like the letter Q as well. He's looking at the television anyway. I say to Stephen, 'She wants to put Daniel in a home.'

'Don't be ridiculous. She never said that,' he says.

'I heard her.'

'She's just worried about how we'll cope –'

'How *you* will cope.'

'She didn't mean anything by it,' he says.

'So she told you, too, right? She said the same thing to you?'

'I'm not talking about this,' Stephen says. And he means it.

But things get better because Daniel likes Elmo. He looks at Elmo and laughs. He bounces up and down, his fingers in his mouth, his eyes shining. I take his hand and make it so that he is pointing and then hold it, pointing, at the screen until he is almost doing it on his own.

'That is what is missing,' says Stephen, rising to his knees, and staring open-mouthed at Daniel. 'What you are doing there. *That*.'

Daniel's chubby hand is just about able to point at Elmo, and his face is bright. He looks like any other child and so, for the time being, we are all laughing. Emily loves the pizza, making long strings of the cheese. Stephen is delighted with his boy. Right now, this second, I'd say we are the happiest we've been in a long time. Because Daniel is pointing. Or trying to.

We've been asked by Emily's new school to enrol her in a pre-school before she arrives in the autumn at their pre-prep. This is to 'prepare' her. So, if I understand correctly, we are meant to prepare her for the school that is meant to prepare her for the school that prepares her for the school from which she will eventually go to university. It seems a bit much to me, but when I protested to Stephen that I felt this was overkill for a child not yet five years old, he looked at me impatiently and said, 'Don't stand in her way.'

'*Don't stand in her way?*' I said. I followed him out of the house, still in my pyjamas, my hair flying every direction. 'In her *way?*'

But Stephen isn't the sort of man who will engage in an argument on a city street. 'I'll see you tonight,' he said in a perfectly even tone, as though there was nothing wrong at all.

So now, at everyone's request except Emily's, I get her ready in the mornings for eight thirty. I strap Daniel in the pushchair, take Emily by the hand, and we walk half a mile to the pre-school, where Emily gets to use glue and glitter to make us cards, sing songs during circle time, and argue about who gets what toy at playtime.

'What do you like best about it?' I ask enthusiastically.

'Going home,' she says.

'That's a good one. You have good jokes,' I say.

'I am not joking,' Emily says.

I say, 'OK, but there must be *something* else you like.'

She thinks about this. 'During milk time you get a biscuit.'

'Not bad,' I say. 'I don't get any such thing during milk time. Your school sounds great!'

'The biscuits are yucky,' she complains. 'And I only ever get *one.*'

She doesn't want to go. I don't want her to go. But the pre-prep says this is good for her and so she goes.

'I miss Daniel,' she says, dropping her school bag on the pavement, bending over the pushchair, her lips pursed, kissing the top of his head.

'You do? You miss him?' We are standing outside the pre-school gates surrounded by mothers and nannies and dozens of tiny, beautifully clad children holding their sugar paper stiffened by wooden sticks and pasted-on seeds. The theme for this week is spring and they've done a study of the germination of beans. 'Oh, Emily, he misses you, too!' I say, fairly singing my exclamations. 'He loves you! He loves you so much! He needs you! We all need you so much!'

The mothers and nannies around me have noticed this moment I am having with my daughter, who loves her baby brother, who misses him and lays claim to his affection with a kiss on the head. They are not impressed by my mushy response. Eyes roll. Some of the nannies look as though they might gag.

Around five in the morning or so, when Daniel can't sleep, I take Emily from her bed and tuck her in next to Stephen. If she should wake, I want her to feel at once the comfort of him next to her. Then I put a sweatshirt over Daniel's pyjamas, find his thickest socks, his canvas shoes, and go directly to the Italian pastry shop and sit on their shining stools. Round and round I go with Daniel in my lap. He laughs, holding his hands out, squinting his eyes. Round and round until I am so dizzy I might fall off.

The guys there remind me of wild cats, so young and sleek, looking exactly alike with their dark hair, their dark eyes. They are lean and full of themselves, treating the kitchen like a kind of gym, hurling pans to each other, pivoting on their heels with trays of hot bread. They sing in English to the radio, stomp around in workmen's boots, their aprons tied loosely, batted by their thighs. They throw bits of uncooked pastry at me to get my attention. Their father or uncle or whatever he is – Max is his name – wipes the sweat from his face with his meaty hands, barking orders to them in Italian to please not throw food at the lady. But they make me laugh, trying to pretend it was all an accident, that the dough just flew from their hands, landing down my blouse. One of them – he couldn't be more than sixteen – gets down on one knee and proposes to me, his apron wadded in his hands as though he is holding a bouquet.

'I'm already married,' I tell him.

'But are you *loved*?' he says.

'This one is especially stupid,' says Max, swatting his son on the head.

A dark January night, rain thumping the window pane. There's been some sort of problem with the boiler and the whole house is steaming hot. On one side of the bed, in a messy heap, is every book I could find on autism, on language in children, on play therapy, on child development. Many of them are from Iris, my lady from the supermarket, who told me that she didn't really recommend the older books. So much has changed, she told me. The books occupy the whole of one side of the bed. On the other side there's myself and Stephen.

'Don't make me pregnant, please,' I whisper to him. His head is above me, I speak into his chest. 'Not that you are planning to . . . I didn't mean that . . . only just be careful.'

He stops, and there is an awful silence between us. Then he rolls off me and stares up at the ceiling.

'Is there no place we can go now, *nothing* we can do?'
he says, his voice getting louder with each word.

'Please, don't be angry –' I begin, but it is too late.

'I'm not *angry*!' he shouts. And now the whole room
seems to echo, and I brace myself for whatever he's going
to say next, which is that we cannot even make love
without me thinking of children – existing or potential –
and being worried about them in one way or the other. I
am troubled, too, that he will link all this anxiety back
to Daniel, to autism, to the mess we find ourselves in, and
that he will tell me Daniel has ruined his life, just as his
father has declared. But he doesn't say anything. He stares
up, glassy-eyed, occupying a place far away and un-
reachable. I pull on a nightshirt, run my fingers through
my hair. I am all at once embarrassed by everything about
me. I want to cover myself up. I want to run.

'Stephen, don't do this,' I say.

'Don't do *what*!' he says.

I have no answer. What shouldn't he do? Be angry? Of
course he should be angry. Anyway, in this new world we've
entered since Daniel's diagnosis there is no emotion that is
out of bounds. But there is something more going on here,
and I don't want to say it and he doesn't want to say it.

Stephen begins to shake and I see now that he is crying.
I realise all at once that I've never actually seen him cry.
I've seen him shout, hit a wall or two, and I saw him
when Daniel was diagnosed, how floored he was. But this
is different. It is as though he has been completely brought
down. I can do nothing to soothe him, although I try. On
my knees, beside our bed, I speak to the back of his neck,
but he will not turn to me, or look at me, or answer.

'Don't blame me,' I say. 'Don't blame yourself.'

* * *

Dear Dr Bettelheim,

Were you there when I rocked my baby to sleep, or held his rattle for him before he could hold it himself? I didn't know I could love so much as I have loved my son, my daughter. Why do you insist this isn't the case? Why do you openly despise me, despise all mothers of children with autism? I am twenty-nine years old. I would give my life publicly if I thought I could lift from my baby this appalling diagnosis. If it were that he could be normal – just ordinary like other children – I would climb the scaffold and tie the noose myself, smiling as I waved away the pain of watching him unable to speak or play or look at people. You would not hear me complain. I would run for the chance. You'd have to beat me away from those steps.

I write this letter and fold it carefully, putting it in an envelope, and pressing it into my jewellery box, an ornamental wooden box lined with crimson velvet that Stephen gave me on our first anniversary along with a pearl necklace. It is hard to remember that he loved me that much, but I'm trying to.

Bettelheim has been dead for many years now, of course. A case of suicide.

I want to be a good wife. A good mother. The glue that keeps a family together, a sign of permanence and peace in our lives. Isn't that what a woman is? What else are we anyway? Lots of professions, lots of titles you can read in the want ads. I lost my first family early and ever since then I've been scrambling to get a new one. Marcus and I were trying to start a family before he died. We weren't married because both his parents and my own mother thought we were too young. So our plan, if you can call it that, was to fake an accidental pregnancy. What kind of idiots fake an accidental pregnancy? But that is what we were doing. And I'm sure we would have succeeded, given our commitment – which went far beyond simple bedroom lovemaking, and included the seasonal shelter of willow trees, cornfields and beach dunes, not to mention several modes of mass transport. But that didn't work, although it might have done if we'd had more time. I try not to think too much about him because if he were still here then certainly Emily and Daniel would not be. It's an awful thing to admit, but if it meant losing Marcus to have my children, then that is a deal I would make.

'This is a completely twisted sort of logic,' says Jacob, wagging his chin back and forth slowly as though to punctuate the sentence. 'Nobody had to be killed in order that you would have your children. I don't understand your meaning.'

'Yes you do,' I tell him. I'm glad I didn't tell him about the letter to Bettelheim. God knows what he'd have made of that.

He looks up at the ceiling, then down to his clipboard where he writes furiously, his lips pressed grimly together.

'I'm a mother. And mothers are like bears,' I say. 'OK, you don't have bears in this country.'

'But you wouldn't actually *kill* Marcus?' Jacob says, his pen angled toward me like a microphone.

'Jacob, stop it. Of course not. No.'

'Then what are we talking about?' he says, his hands outstretched.

'I'm just saying that if he hadn't died I wouldn't have my children. And that I don't allow myself to think of him or miss him or anything because to do so would be like a betrayal of Daniel and Emily.'

'And Stephen?' says Jacob.

'OK, add him in,' I say, rolling my eyes.

Today, as part of being a good mother and wife, I do a survey of all the local dry-cleaners as I can't remember where Stephen's clothes are. He is sure it was me who deposited clothes at the dry-cleaner and did not retain the ticket. OK, so maybe it *was* me, I say. I have to admit it sounds like something I would do. I will find the two suits and three ties he needs right away, yes, I will do that before his business trip to Vienna. No problem. It was a real oversight on my part not to keep that ticket taped up on a cupboard door or strapped onto my person or some-place anyway. A mistake, though if I may say, it would help if the dry-cleaner put the name of their enterprise on their tickets instead of just a number, which one can easily mistake for a raffle ticket or any number of other things, like Lucky Dips or racing stubs.

So I'm going from dry-cleaner to dry-cleaner all morning with Daniel in the pushchair dragging his toes along the pavement so we can't go quickly, that's for sure. Emily is in pre-school so I can focus all my attention on him, but he does not want to include me in whatever fun he finds in his disc-shaped objects. He keeps these objects in his lap, and is particularly attached to the top from a Snapple bottle. Nobody is any help at all finding Stephen's suits. And aren't they an unfriendly bunch, these dry-cleaning people? They want all sorts of very specific information like *when* did I bring them in. Isn't it enough that I brought them in? At least, *may* have brought them in because I have brought other items here before. Of that I am certain.

Another thing – and I'd just like to say this now – is that I think parents with autistic children should have disabled parking badges. No, they should have their own badges that let them park even closer than those with regular disabled parking badges. I think the other disabled people would agree. Certainly this lady in a wheelchair, who my son is now trying to push off the chair so *he* can sit in it, would see the logic in my idea. She is screaming for help, and the race is on now between me and a security guard.

'Just tell me if you found the suits,' says Stephen. I am breastfeeding Daniel, which is annoying Stephen, who feels all babies should be off the breast by nine months. Emily was off the breast by nine months, he often reminds me. But Daniel is different – if one can make such an understatement without begging laughter – and he has a cold coming on. The glands in his neck are up. His nose is running and I can see it is hard for him to turn his head. The only thing I can get him to take is breast milk, so Stephen will just have to live with that.

About finding his suits, I say, 'Not yet.'

'Mel, I need those suits. They cost hundreds and hundreds of pounds. I don't even have time to replace them right now and I need them for this trip.'

'Don't they sell suits in Vienna?'

'Who the hell knows? Yes,' he says impatiently. 'But I want *my* suits.'

I promise I will find them and I set off the next day, doing the rounds once more to all the dry-cleaners, not having a clue when I dropped the suits off but begging them to look anyway. According to the one sensible book I read about teaching autistic children, you are meant to spend the whole of the day distracting the autistic child away from their autism, their odd obsessions with objects, for example. But today is a total loss. Feeling ill, stuck in his pushchair, forced to charge around with me looking for Stephen's suits, Daniel is getting no help out of this crisis at all. Not today anyway.

'Did you find them?' asks Stephen, calling me from the train platform around dinner time.

'Yes,' I say.

'And where were they?'

'In the closet,' I state flatly.

'In the wardrobe?' he says, immediately translating my American 'closet' to his British 'wardrobe', a mild correction I choose to ignore. Then he starts to laugh. He says, 'They were in the wardrobe the whole time? Oh, Melanie! You banana!'

But I'm not laughing. I'm actually very upset. Daniel has his face pressed up against the front of the television and Emily is sulking because her Febo Dumbo has broken. Earlier in the day Daniel turned off the washing machine mid-cycle, which I didn't notice, so when I went to open it gallons of water poured on to our kitchen floor. I haven't had more than two hours' sleep in a row since Daniel caught this new virus and, generally speaking, I am not in a good mood. But I have to make myself laugh along with Stephen – I know I do – because the man hasn't touched me in three weeks and because I am beginning to think he's never going to again.

And I'm feeling scared. Sleepless, tearful. I can't concentrate or think straight. I race through the house adjusting curtains, organising toys, scrubbing a stainless-steel pan until it is surgically clean. Veena asked if I wanted her to babysit the children so that Stephen and I could go out to dinner tonight before he leaves for his business trip, but I said no. I couldn't do it. Couldn't sit that long in a chair.

'Whatever you are taking, stop taking it,' said Veena.

'I'm not taking anything,' I said. 'I do it all on Nescafé.'

But I guess I ought to have gone out with him. Once again, I'm the idiot. Because the next morning, after he leaves for the airport, I find a Hamleys bag with a present for Daniel's third birthday – a shaggy Elmo glove puppet which you might call 'life-size' if Elmo were an actual living thing, which I am sure he is not despite how life-like he seems, certainly more lifelike than my husband, who for the past few weeks is always on the telephone, in the office, or typing emails on his laptop. There is a card with Thomas the Tank Engine on the cover, a button saying 'I am 3' and a roll of bills inside a rubber band. A thousand pounds. A thousand pounds is way too much if he is planning to return in a few days, as he told me he would. And it's pitifully little if he's never coming back. Which is my new, and not unfounded, fear.

9

The speech therapist is pregnant – I'd say about six months, judging by the look of her. She has an intelligent, lively face and a jolly American voice. She turns in her office chair, Daniel's file in front of her, and hikes her legs up under her skirt. With no hesitation whatsoever she speaks to me directly about the problem, my son, before her.

'Moderate, but not severe,' she says, squinting through her rimless glasses. She wears a half-dozen studs in her left ear, has a cloud of curly black hair pinned up over her head, and a big smile that overshadows the acne she's acquired during pregnancy. 'Of course, I am perfectly wrong to even *say* he's autistic. It's not in my training. If I were you, however, I'd be thinking about special school and about respite care. You really have no choice.'

This is what Stephen says, that we have no choice. He thinks Daniel must go as soon as possible to a special nursery school for children with learning difficulties. He insists. That is the worst problem he is handing me right now, but not the only one.

'Yes, I do have a choice,' I say.

She laughs. 'You're a tough cookie, but I'm telling you for a fact this is a big one, autism. Regular speech therapists like me can't even touch it. Give me your basic kid with a mild language disorder and I'll fill your ears with good ideas. But your boy?' She shakes her head.

In front of us, Daniel sits with his feet behind him so his legs form a 'w'. He tears the pages of a magazine I've bought him, one featuring Thomas the Tank Engine. He seems completely oblivious to me and the speech therapist, to all the speculation about him. Nothing interests him at all other than the steady ripping sound he makes on the glossy pages of his magazine.

'Why not Daniel?' I say. The speech therapist looks at me, then at Daniel, chewing her lip. I say, 'Just tell me the truth. You cannot possibly make me feel bad.' Of course, this is a lie. She's already made me feel bad. She's telling me no. And she's telling me no because she sees Daniel as unteachable, at least this is how I see it. 'Please,' I urge her. 'I've already been through it all. Just level with me.'

She sighs, shrugs her heavy shoulders, heaves her opulent, pendulous breasts. 'Because he isn't talking,' she says. 'If he was even saying a handful of words I'd give it a shot. But I'm not qualified to treat this kind of thing. You are going to need special help here. Like I said, you might consider a school –'

'He's only three years old.'

'I mean later, when he's a bit older.'

'I don't want to wait until he's older!' I say, perhaps a little too harshly.

The speech therapist opens her mouth to say something

and then, just as quickly, decides not to. She sets her face and I know at once that I've lost this one. Then she says, 'I'd like to help you, Mrs Marsh. Really, I would. But I can't.'

I waited four weeks for this appointment. I'm here instead of at the airport where, according to my watch, Stephen's plane has just landed. He's been away for three days and I haven't gotten a single phone call. I keep waiting for the call that says he's sorry, that he's coming home. When I dial his mobile all I get is voice-mail. I don't know if that's because he can't get his phone to work in Vienna or whether he has decided not to answer it.

'Surely you could help me get started,' I beg the speech therapist. 'To get him talking, I mean.'

'No, ma'am. Really, I don't know how.'

I have pages of questions, an open cheque book, a lot of time. I am ready to do whatever she says he needs – and she says she doesn't know *how*?

'What about this stuff called Applied Behaviour Analysis?' I ask. I have discovered a book called *Let Me Hear Your Voice* by Catherine Maurice, the mother of two autistic children. In it, she claims that ABA brought her children from autism to normality in just over two years. It sounds impossible, but it also sounds like hope.

'ABA is Lovaas,' says the speech therapist, raising her eyebrows. 'I'm from Los Angeles where Lovaas worked. Lovaas kids don't use language in context. They can respond robotically to specific stimuli. Like if I said, "What is your name?" then the child would state his name. But he wouldn't *understand* language.'

'I see.'

She scoots her chair forward a bit, tries to cross her

legs, but finds that is too much effort with her pregnant belly.

'But if Daniel could say his name and a few other words, you would work with him. That's what you said before. A handful of words and you'd try.'

She laughs, points at me. 'You got me,' she says.

'I got you,' I smile back. However exasperating, I am willing to play the game.

'OK, look,' she says, shrugging one shoulder, then the other. 'If he learned them spontaneously, yes, but not if they were drummed into him Lovaas-style,' she says.

'How would you know?' I ask her. 'Can I at least try?'

'I'd know,' she says, gives me a wink. I don't know how she stays so cheerful through this conversation. There is something very abnormal about how happy she is to tell me she can't help. 'And don't even *think* about using that Andy O'Connor. You'll hear of him if you're looking toward the behavioural psychology approach. He's got no qualifications other than an undergraduate degree, no formal training in working with children. He's a maverick. No decent university or health authority would have him. And he charges the moon, too. A cornball rip-off artist, swindler of the first degree. You don't even want to come near him.'

'What does he do, this Andy O'Connor?' I ask.

'Oh, he *claims* he does everything,' she says, rolling her eyes. 'Teach them to talk, get them to play. What a shyster.'

Andy O'Connor. I will not forget that name.

Because Stephen won't ring me back, I go to his office with Daniel. Third floor, end of corridor, corner office, overlooking Hyde Park. I sit in his big office chair swivelling the minutes away, while Daniel climbs over his desk, paws at the computer keys, presses buttons on the phone.

Ten minutes and no Stephen. I switch on his computer, log on to the Internet using his password, which I guess first time: Emily. I then pull up his emails and have a little look through. From his brother I get cricket scores and some boring garbage about team selections. Many emails from others in his office, of course. From me scores of unread posts with headers such as 'Read this PLEASE' and 'SHALL I ALERT THE POLICE?'. I dispatched them from an Internet café on Baker Street. All . . . let's see . . . seventeen of them.

A quarter of an hour goes by. Well, he's probably in a meeting.

Daniel is in the chair now and I'm on the desk. I've kicked off my shoes and am turning Daniel in the chair with my feet. He likes this, his eyes light up. What I am trying to do is to get him to clap, so I turn the chair, stop, clap, then wait for him to do the same before turning it again. But he won't clap. I have pictures of him clapping when he was only twelve months old, but he won't clap now. Why won't he clap?

'Clap,' I tell him. But he doesn't understand. I take his hands and bring his palms together. 'Clap,' I say, then wheel him in the chair again. 'Yeah! You're clapping!' I tell him, which is almost the truth.

Twenty-five minutes. I am breastfeeding Daniel in Stephen's office chair. He would just scream if he saw this.

Forty-minutes. Daniel is asleep.

Fifty-five minutes. Stephen's assistant, a woman, comes into his office with some papers, finding Daniel and me there.

'I'm sorry, Melanie,' she says now. 'But he's not in today. Did no one tell you that?'

No one told me.

'He's working from home,' she says. She looks very confused, a little flustered. Now she leaves quickly, her heels clicking against the floor.

10

One mistake was making all of Stephen's friends my friends. I cosied up to the wives and girlfriends of his chums from school, from university, and now that he has walked out, I am set loose from their circles. They don't know quite what to say to me.

'I'm sure this is only temporary,' is one set piece I hear. But if it is only temporary, and Stephen will return home any minute, why do they avoid me? If, surely, it will all come right, as they suggest?

They turn out to be his friends and not mine at all. Never were.

'We're terribly sorry,' they say. But they do not invite me to see them. Do not want to come here either. Their diaries are full. Their children have nasty colds; their jobs have implacable demands.

'You won't believe what happened yesterday!' says the wife of Stephen's university friend, a couple we've gone on holiday with, who we've exchanged Christmas presents with, who I thought actually liked me. 'I have been asked to do work in Bristol for every weekend until August!'

'Have you?' I say. And no, I don't believe her.

And it seems to me I've burned through all my own friends, the mothers I met at childbirth classes, for example. They have normal children and average problems. Husbands that work late, not enough money, or perhaps a child with grommets in his ears. That's about the extent of their problems. So hard to stay on course around them, asking them important questions about which holiday worked well for them, why they prefer one catchment area over another, how they like the new nanny agency, or the new nanny, or the new job, or the newborn. And they, too, grow weary with my situation. I am living proof that there are no guarantees with our children, that bad things can happen. They see nothing appealing about my child and I see their own children as geniuses simply because they do the amazing, expected, miraculous and completely average feat of developing like normal children.

'It's so cute the way Theo says Mickey Mouse,' says this one here who I know from a postnatal group and who sends her daughter to the same pre-school as I send Emily. Theo is the little brother, just a baby. 'Say it for Melanie, sweetie. Say Mickey Mouse.'

'Icky Owse,' says Theo, then a big smile.

'It's the cutest thing, don't you think?' says Theo's mother. She's supposed to be a friend. Or at least friend-like. Her name is Becca and I've had her over for tea before.

'Adorable,' I say, nodding, forcing a smile. Daniel is asleep in the pushchair, so at least I don't have to listen to his iron silence in contast to Theo's giggling and new, beautiful words.

'He's only sixteen months, you know,' says Becca, who

I might like to kill right now except her baby can talk and he'd probably report me.

'It wasn't the MMR, was it?' asks another of the mothers who wait at the gate, as I do, each afternoon at twelve thirty. It's one of my least favourite moments of the day – not that I can't wait to see Emily – but it is all I can do to stand among the crowd of nannies telling children Daniel's same age to shut up, stop making so much noise, while I try desperately to get Daniel to imitate me as I make faces, or point at a red bus, or laugh when I blow raspberries on his tummy.

'I don't know,' I say honestly.

'They say the doctor who claimed it was the MMR is a fraud, you know,' says another. She's only here because she's waiting with her friend. Her children are older, both at St Paul's Girls' School – the sort of place that makes me shiver.

Now I realise the MMR is a good, solid medical precaution that has nothing to do with autism. That's true and right. I have heard the radio shows, the TV reports, all of which assure me that my feeling the MMR is to blame for Daniel's autism is something I've completely made up. But you know, there is this part of me that understands with absolute certainty that I didn't make it up. I could have been hallucinating and still I wouldn't have missed the signs that after that shot my baby changed.

'I don't think that doctor is a fraud,' I say.

'Oh *please*,' says the St Paul's mother. 'He lied. He joined the parents who just want someone to blame.' She is dressed in blue and white linen and has a beautiful heart-shaped face. She is a woman whose hands have never cleaned her child's excrement from walls, never waited

through hour-long temper tantrums, never hurt for anything, I imagine. But she wants to hurt me. Of that, I'm
positive.

'My son has autism and he has problems with his
bowels,' I say to this lady, who doesn't give a damn.

'Well, it has nothing to do with vaccinations,' she sniffs.
'Vaccinations save children's lives!'

She turns away from me, shoulder to shoulder with the
other mother, looking into the distance at the school,
preparing for the moment it releases dozens of pre-schoolers
to this waiting crowd.

Iris has never heard of Andy O'Connor, but she's heard
of ABA and is sceptical.

'It's probably just another scam,' she says, her voice full
of caution.

'A scam?' I say. My heart sinks. I have come almost to
rely upon the idea that ABA is the answer for Daniel.

Iris says, 'Not to mention expensive. But then my
information is a little old. I'll make some calls.'

And with that, another door shuts.

But a few hours later I hear from Iris again. She has
spent the morning on the telephone, seeking information
about Andy O'Connor. Her voice bubbles over the line,
filling me with hope even before she gets the words out.

'Andy O'Connor is *gold dust*,' she says. 'The few
mothers I've spoke to say he's just amazing! Apparently,
all the kids love him.'

'And he can help me? Help Daniel, I mean?'

'Just get him,' says Iris. Her voice is calm but certain,
delivering the phone number to me as though it is a secret
code. 'Make sure he agrees to see you.'

'I will,' I tell her.

'Don't give up,' she says. When her son was Daniel's age there was no treatment of the sort that Andy O'Connor can provide. Not in England anyway. If I were her, I'd be bitter about this, but Iris only wants to help me, to help my son.

'What can I do for *you*?' I ask her genuinely.

'Make that call,' she says. Then she has to ring off. Her son wants to go on the Internet – again – and they only have one phone line.

I call Andy O'Connor a dozen times and all I get is his voicemail.

'Hello, you've reached Andy O'Connor. I'm not able to take on any new clients at the moment, but if you would like to leave your name . . .' He has an Irish accent, a quick and friendly voice. But does he call me back? No.

I've left polite messages, curt messages, messages in which I apologise for leaving so many messages. I've left messages adding to and correcting other messages. In my most urgent voice I've asked him to please telephone me right away. In my most pleading voice I've insisted he call me. I even pretended to be a reporter from the *Daily Telegraph* interested in doing an article on him, but I think he might have recognised my voice by then from all those other times I called. Still nothing.

I guess it is the 'not able to take on any new clients' part of his voicemail that is the reason for him not calling back.

This last message is my final one. 'Hello, Andy. What do you say to a girl with an undergraduate degree in English from Tufts and a postgraduate degree from Oxford? Give up? You say, "I'll have that burger with fries, please."'

It's an old joke, but the next morning he rings.

'I'll have that burger with fries, please,' he laughs.

While Emily is at pre-school, I go through exercises that I've learned from a book about Applied Behaviour Analysis, this stuff Andy O'Connor does and which the speech therapist claims is deceitful, a waste of time. Andy can't see us for several weeks. 'Too many children right now,' he tells me on the phone. 'These mothers are running me ragged! I barely get to sleep at night!'

'Well, why should *you* sleep when all the rest of us aren't allowed to sleep?' I tease.

'Why, indeed!' he says. He sounds a good-natured man, gentle, optimistic. He knows how hard it is to live with a non-verbal child. He will come as soon as he can.

'You're American?' he says. 'I like Americans. Well, the girls.'

And I like Andy. Can't help it. He's the only one holding any useful cards right now, and I really don't care how much I have to pay him. Stephen is convinced we have to get Daniel into some sort of programme right away. He believes that special school is the answer. He calls me from the office to tell me so. My answer to him is that we haven't even tried yet. If he would just come home and read some of these books with me, he'd see autistic kids have more scope than he realises.

'I can't come right now,' he says.

'What on earth prevents you!' I ask.

'Your temper for one thing. That prevents me.'

'Oh, right.' I can't take him seriously, behaving like this. 'Big scary me!' I say.

'There are schools –'

'If he goes into one of those schools we'll never get him

115

out,' I say. 'Anyway, we can always put him in a special school if we don't succeed at this other thing. You're throwing in the towel before the fight even begins!'

'I'm tired of fighting with you,' he says.

'So what is the story? You won't come home unless I agree to put Daniel in special school?'

'No, that's not it,' he begins.

'Then *why* won't you come home!' I say this quite loudly. OK, maybe I'm yelling.

But it doesn't matter. He's already off the line, having taken another call.

'Where's Daddy?' Emily asks. She asks every day after school, like clockwork.

'At the office, of course,' I tell her, trying to sound cheerful. She holds a picture of a caterpillar and a butterfly. The caterpillar has been drawn by making a rectangle and then adding eyes. The butterfly is a number 8 that has been turned on its side, then coloured. If the school had let her do it in her own way they'd have been more successful, but even so the colouring is good. 'Hey, that's a really good picture!' I tell Emily.

Emily slaps the picture onto my stomach. Then she says, 'When is Daddy coming home?'

'He's coming to take you to the park,' I tell her. She doesn't look satisfied with this answer, which isn't really an answer at all, as she well knows. 'Come on, let's skip!' I say. She holds my hand while I balance Daniel's pushchair with the other. In this manner we manage to skip along the sidewalk – well, mostly skip. It's a miracle we don't all fall down.

'Which *day* is he coming home?' Emily says. She concentrates on skipping, her hand clasping mine. 'Today?'

'Soon,' I tell her. 'That's good skipping.'

'But *when*?'

'Let's hop!' I say. 'Ready now? One foot!' I say, hopping. But Emily stops suddenly, nearly pulling Daniel and me over. She is not going to hop or skip. She is going to cry.

'He's coming on Saturday,' I tell her, scooping her up in my arms. 'And maybe even earlier if we're lucky.'

The book I have on this bizarre therapy for autistic children emphasises the need to get kids talking as soon as possible. So, Daniel must learn to talk. He has to learn the names of objects, which means he has to listen as I tell him the name of an object. The only way I can get him to pay any attention to me at all is by stealing his Thomas the Tank Engine and holding it above my head. When finally he stops screaming and lunging for Thomas, I put a car on the little plastic table in front of us, and say, 'Car,' and put his hand on it. Then I let his hand go and I give him the train as a reward.

The first time I tried this he threw himself on the floor, banging his head against the cupboard door and flailing his arms and legs for about four minutes as I stood above him, waiting. I found it very difficult not to immediately scoop him into my arms and give him back the train. Every instinct said do something – anything – to make him stop crying like this. But I had to get his attention somehow, and confiscating his train – though difficult and painful – seemed to be the only thing that worked. He soon stopped whacking his head but was determined not to have anything to do with me, the table, the car – none of it. Eventually I managed to catch hold of his hand, placing it on the car. I said, 'Car!' and then handed over Thomas.

The second time he did not throw himself on the ground but just screamed. I put his hand on the car, said the word 'car' and then let him have his train.

The third time he put his hand on the car himself.

'Car!' I said, and for a moment he let his hand linger.

That was worth a dance around the kitchen, he and Thomas and I. It was Prince on the radio, a song I hadn't heard in too long . . . *I just want your extra time and your . . . kiss.*

Stephen has been living at Cath's now for just over two weeks, seeing the children on weekends. This is totally insane, but I cannot convince him that it is totally insane. He visits his own house to play with his own children, takes them to the park, kicks a ball around with Emily. Everything just as he used to do, except then he leaves to sleep at his sister's house. Two weeks of this and I've really had enough.

'Right, fine, you've made your point, Stephen,' I say. 'But please –'

For my benefit he always arrives at the house in horrible clothes, his grey tracksuit bottoms and an ugly sweatshirt, his hair dirty, needing a shave. He's trying to look ugly, but he must know that men like him only look sexy when they do this. If he wanted to look ugly he'd have to slap on some black leather trousers three sizes too small, push his neck into one of those long, clinging turtlenecks that ride around the jawbone, grow a bushy beard that hangs like moss off his chin, and shave his head. If he did that, maybe I could relax. But not if he's going to saunter into the house looking like he just crawled out of bed. That will not work.

I miss him kissing me goodbye in the early morning,

his face smelling of soap. I miss him sitting at the end of the couch with his laptop, stabbing at the keyboard replying to messages. I miss seeing his favourite beer in the fridge, the way he used to bring me tea in the mornings and we'd all climb under the covers to cuddle. And I miss him in bed.

So I try to imagine him with the mossy beard and no hair and the turtleneck from hell and the matador trousers. Oh sure, it works for a few minutes. Until I see his real face smiling out of the photograph I keep on the mantel of the four of us at the primitive little cottage we have in Wales. Then I lose it.

'I'm so sorry about this, Mel,' says Cath, speaking to me from her surgery. 'What do you want me to do, throw him out? Would he go back home if I did? I can tell you he's miserable anyway. Just sits up at night watching TV and drinking beer.'

'No, that's normal for him,' I say.

'Is that what married people do?' says Cath. 'God, I'm glad I'm single. The only other thing he does is play with his sodding computer or his phone. All communication is strictly limited to machines.'

'Hmm. Again, normal,' I sigh.

'Look, I know you're going to ask me if he talks about you at all, but the answer is no. He doesn't say a word. Nor does he tell me when he's going to move out, which is too bad, because I'm rather looking forward to that day. He certainly isn't *happy*, I can tell you. He just hangs about on a Saturday night turning channels on the TV with his thumb.'

'That's who he is,' I say. 'The man I married.'

'Crikey, you can have him back, I tell you.'

'Well, just keep me posted, OK?' I say.

'Yes of course. And let me know – about Daniel, I mean. I feel responsible.'

Why would Cath feel responsible for my child?

'I ought to have seen it. Being a GP,' she says. 'It's just that we hardly get any training in developmental delays or autism. The only kids I ever saw who were autistic were much older and quite severe. Not at all like Daniel,' she says.

And this brightens my whole evening. *Quite severe, not at all like Daniel! Not at all like Daniel!*

One thing I cannot live without is a VCR. This one is broken and so I go immediately to John Lewis and get a new one.

'But your first one is still under warranty,' says the salesman.

'How long will you need to repair it?' I ask.

He shrugs his shoulders.

'Right there is the problem,' I say. 'You're telling me it could be days.'

'Well, actually, it could be weeks,' says the salesman.

I shake my head. I hold out the money. 'Just get a new one in a box,' I tell him.

In the evenings I am so lonely that I call my brother. My brother, older than me, is mostly on one army base or another. When he's not on a base, he lives with a woman who regresses to past lives and thinks she used to be a Gregorian monk, a Roman soldier, a handmaiden to Queen Elizabeth, and also a victim of the sinking of the *Titanic*. She is roughly twenty years older than he is, nearly at the menopause, and has spent her present life being a kind of freak, rehabilitating traumatised parrots and living in a trailer in Maine, where often you will find my brother, if he's not out on some useless evening course investigating aspects of his inner being or just getting wasted on reefer.

'You were so hot when you were young,' says Larry now. 'I mean, I'd show your picture to all the guys and they would just go *Shiiiiit*.'

You have to be desperate to want to speak to my brother. If you can hear him, that is. Those parrots make one hell of a racket, and he says he's come close to cooking one of them, who sits in a corner pulling out its feathers and saying 'Life is sweet' over and over again.

I am learning a useful trick with Daniel. What I do is use his obsessions to my advantage. For example, while he is sleeping I take his Thomas train, stick it high up on the curtains that Veena hates so much, and then wait for him to wake up and go searching for it. When he can't find it, I point to it on the curtain pelmet. He eventually figures out that pointing means he has to look. He spies the train, and then – just as he sees it – I reach up and get it for him. I do this several times a day, putting Thomas on the tops of picture frames, or tied to the light-pull in the loo, or up on a high shelf in the cupboard. The minute Daniel actually looks to where I am pointing, he gets his train.

And then, one day, I have an even better idea. I put the train up on the curtain rail and take Daniel's hand, arrange it into a pointing shape and get him to point at the train himself. As soon as he points, I give him the train. It works every time. Soon he's pointing for biscuits, milk, his disc-shaped objects, which I plant all over the house in high places.

'Car,' I say, and he touches the car.

'Dumbo,' Emily says, and he touches Dumbo. 'Don't break his ears,' says Emily, snatching Dumbo away.

Here is one that takes my breath away. Armed with a plastic jar of bubbles and a yellow wand, I swipe a bit of bubble fluid, hold the wand in front of my lips and say, 'Ready, steady g-g-g-g –'

'O,' says Daniel.

And I blow, and blow, and blow.

We have a game in the pushchair. Emily and I run behind it, pushing it along the wide paths in Hyde Park, and then we suddenly stop.

'Say GO, Daniel,' says Emily.

Daniel does his best, which is 'Gah!'

And we're off again, another sprint. Then a sudden stop while we catch our breath. Daniel sits in the pushchair impatient for more.

'Gah!' he says, and on that cue we take off, beating the ground with our trainers, laughing as we glide past dozens of disapproving faces, who have perhaps forgotten the joy of hearing their child's first words.

'How exactly do parrots get traumatised?' I ask Wanda, who is Larry's 'lady friend', as she calls herself. I am stuck with her because Larry is not there and she has answered the phone and gets a kind of kick out of the fact I am calling from England.

'People buy 'em, don't want 'em, get rid of 'em. Then they don't settle, so they come to me,' she says. I can hear the parrots in the background, screeching. It's so loud I have to hold the phone away from my ear. 'So, you're calling from England, huh? Why don't you have

Daniel Isn't Talking

no English accent, then, if you're calling from England?'
says Wanda.

'Because I'm Larry's sister, Wanda,' I say. Duh. 'I grew
up with him.'

'But he's not English!' she says.

It's too much trouble to explain.

I say, 'Wanda, why don't the parrots settle? Why do
they come to you in the end?'

'Because they're psychologically abnormal. Can't you
hear them? They're psycho loser parrots. Nobody wants
them.'

'But why not?'

'Are you telling me you cannot hear this *blaring* noise
over here?!' she shouts.

She puts the phone nearer the birds and it sounds as
though there is a screaming mob taking over the nation.
I wish she'd have warned me before doing this. Then
Wanda comes back to the phone and says, 'They destroy
things, shriek, freak out and break their wings against the
cage bars. They bond with *one* person. So if that one
person lets them down, they go psycho. What about your
kiddies, then? Do they have English accents?'

'The talking one does,' I say, thinking about Wanda's
'loser parrots'. What she describes sounds a little like
Bettelheim's theory of how children become autistic, or
more precisely what is called 'institutionalised autism',
which is when you take a child and refuse to give it any
parenting, any love, toys, or stimulation that tells the child
who he is. They withdraw and fail to develop.

'So the parrots start out normal, then?' I ask her.

'Yessirree. It's the hand of man's done it to them,' she
says. 'Hand of fucking man.'

'But they get better?'

'Well, it can take some time, I tell you.'

'What if you never left them?' I ask. 'Would they become traumatised?'

'Not if they stay with the first owner, no. Then they're happy parrots. Parrots with a smile.'

'If you loved them and cuddled them and played with them from the time they were born?' I ask. I know this is what I did with Daniel. I cannot remember a day away from him. And then suddenly I realise I have sunk to a new low in my life. I am seeking reassurance from Wanda, who believes she was once an Iroquois squaw.

'You looking for a parrot, honey?' says Wanda. 'Because if that's what you'll give him, that kind of love, he'll be your buddy for life! But don't take one of these psycho birds! My birds are a BIG disappointment.'

When Stephen comes this morning we have a surprise for him. He looks a little impatient, wanting as he does to take the children to the Princess Diana Memorial Playground, which they love. He cooperates with me because I beg him, and because I am hoping things might turn around.

'OK, stand here and watch this,' I say. I then get the bubble jar, find Daniel and bring him by the hand over to where Stephen is. He's interested at once, bubbles being round, and round being his favourite shape. He stands beside me as I kneel on the floor with my bubbles and all my hopes.

'Ready, steady . . .' I say.

'Go!' says Daniel.

Stephen can't believe it. He watches as Daniel swats at the bubbles, stamps them with his feet, turns around, his fists balled, putting his face into the ones that still float.

'That is amazing!' Stephen says, his face alight. 'Do it again!'

And so, once more, just for Daddy, I get the bubbles out and give Daniel his cue. 'Ready, steady . . .'

'Go!' says Daniel.

Stephen is so excited. He kisses Daniel all over his face, turns to me and hugs me hard. I cannot remember anything feeling so good as this hug. He wraps his arms around me and I cling to him, fold my arms over his shoulders and wish more than anything he'd kiss me, really kiss me. That he'd claim me as his all over again. He's still wearing his ring, after all, we're still married.

'How did you do this?' he asks. His eyes are full of love; he thinks I'm a genius. So I tell him about ABA, about how I read this book and then I got on the Internet and downloaded instructions and examples and all sorts of stories about kids who couldn't talk but learned how through this method.

'You motivate them by using whatever they like: chocolate, toys, whatever. And you break down every goal into tiny chunks.'

'You're remarkable,' he says. 'You're brilliant.'

I'm waiting for him to kiss me, as surely he will. Kiss me and come back and be here with us again. 'We miss you so much,' I whisper to him now.

But he looks down, then away from me.

'Stephen? Can't we do something?'

'Do what?' he says. And there it is, his indifference, like an iron lid clamping down on top of me. It seems to me I even hear a thump.

Emily is watching the Muppets on television and turning the dials on her Etch-A-Sketch at the same time. Daniel has returned to his train. I take Stephen's hand and lead

him out to the garden. There's a bench there by the ornamental pond, which now looks like a fizzy green pool of
slime beneath layers of chicken wire. Sitting on the bench
I ask him, please, to come home.

'I know I was a little crazy . . . and maybe I still am. I
know I neglected you, but I'm getting much better at
coping now that I know what I have to cope *with*. Stephen,
I'd do anything for this family. I love us,' I say. '*Us*. You
and me and Emily and Daniel.'

He doesn't say anything. He looks pale and very tired.
He's put on some weight, I see, and from the way it hangs
on him I think it's probably all beer.

'Well, yeah, I need to talk to you about us,' he says.

Us. I don't like the way it sounds coming from his lips.

'No, don't,' I tell him. In my mind I've floated up, away
from Stephen, hovering in the air above like a departing
soul of the newly dead. 'No, don't say what you're going
to say. Daniel is talking now – let's just think about that.'

'One word,' says Stephen. 'I still think he needs to go
to some sort of school. Not that what you are doing isn't
important. Not that I'm ungrateful –'

'But you *are* ungrateful,' I say. I cannot believe this is
happening. Not now, not after how many times I've played
this scene over in my mind. In my imagined version of this
moment, when Stephen saw that Daniel wasn't so hopeless,
he came back and we made a fresh start, and everything
worked. I even imagined Daniel a couple of years older than
he is now, speaking in sentences, playing with toys, being
part of a group of laughing children. I should never have
let myself dream like that, or at least I ought to have reminded
myself it was only in my head, and that it would never really
happen.

Now I touch Stephen's chin, turning his head so he'll

look at me. I've done the same thing with Daniel count-less times. I'm not quite ready to give up, however grim things seem right now, so I say firmly, confidently, what I truly believe. I say, 'If he can say "go", he can say anything.'

Stephen licks his lips nervously. 'I understand what you are telling me,' he says. 'And I will support you through this . . . whatever it is . . . you are doing, to a *degree* –'

'You'll come back?' I say.

He shakes his head.

'You can't live with your sister for ever,' I say.

'I'm not living with Cath any more,' says Stephen. 'I'm sorry. I'm . . . I've been seeing Penelope again.'

And now I have nothing to say, no way to say it anyway, because I cannot breathe.

'What happened to the famous French ethnomusico-logist?' I manage finally, gulping. 'I mean, surely *he* has something to say about all this.'

'Penelope turned him out for sleeping with his students,' says Stephen. 'She was pretty cut up about it.'

'Oh, *was* she?' I say. '*Poor* Penelope. She wasn't so cut up when she was the student he was sleeping with, now was she? And I suppose he didn't do anything so thoughtful as marry her or have a family with her, so maybe she's a little impatient as well. Is that it? Maybe she's thinking tick-tock, time for finding a man who likes kids. Oh, and look, here comes Stephen!'

Stephen takes a long breath. 'You know, your sarcasm is very unattractive,' he says.

'Tell me she isn't talking to you about having a baby,' I say.

He says nothing. And now I'm even more upset. Because I realise that I am exactly right and that at some point – maybe next year, maybe the year after – Stephen will have started himself a whole new family. Through the glass doors I see Emily, her curly hair, her pink cotton shirt. I think it is seeing her there, so innocently doing her drawing, laughing at the Cookie Monster, perched on the papier mâché chair we made, that makes me feel as I do. I want to take her in my arms and tell her everything will be OK. I will make it all right for her again: a brother who will play with her, a father who is with her every evening. The only thing the child has is me, and what am I? Not much, judging by the way Stephen is looking at me now. A bit of skin over some long bones, a marked-up body, a woman with a mentally handicapped son and no career. Not much more than that.

11

There are certain times in your life when you better take stock, and that is what I did right away. We had what we called 'the cottage', a dilapidated stone bungalow with an attic we always meant to convert and no central heating. We stayed there weekends in the summer when London got too hot, hacking back the small lawn which grew like a hayfield from March to September and turned into a kind of muddy yellow hash all through winter. The cottage, which was really only one step up from camping, had been a rash purchase while on holiday in South Wales. I bought it outright with money left to me by my mother. We spent quite a bit getting the water sorted out so we could use the rusted little sink in the kitchen, and patching the roof with slate we'd managed to buy locally. But it also had four damp walls and structural subsidence. The soil around it was more conditioned to grow nettles than grass, and there was also this little issue regarding the drainage – it seemed we were creating a bog in the back garden. The cottage had always been a kind of pending project we meant to get to, but couldn't due to our immense fertility and the typical manner in which life in London swallows you whole.

The cottage did have one advantage, however: it was entirely in my name. I am aware of the fact I once stood at an altar and vowed to share all my worldly goods with Stephen, but then he vowed to love me until death parted us, which is not quite the same as until things went a little off-kilter and the ex-girlfriend with all the exotic music decided she'd have him back now, thank you. So the cottage went on the market and I began looking around the house for things to sell. It wasn't that Stephen refused to pay the mortgage now, or that he wouldn't give me grocery money – that stayed the same. But for all her good manners and whimsical appeal, Penelope was a practical girl who expected Stephen to pay half the rent, the food bill and the petrol. Oh yes, that's another reason I had to sell the cottage. Stephen took his car one night, stashing it God knows where in this car-hating city. Getting to the cottage was now nearly impossible as it was four miles away from the nearest village – which consisted of only a post office and a tackle shop – and involved driving through a permitted path and crossing the cement yard of a goat farm. So one thing I sold – illegally, of course – was our permit sticker, which I saw no use for now that I had no car. I sold it to a man with a cockney accent and the word 'HATE' tattooed across the knuckles of his hand. That paid for a half-day with Andy O'Connor, this guy who specialises in play therapy and says he wants to show me how to get Daniel interested in playing like a 'typical' child.

When I first meet Andy, I think him little more than a child himself. He is about my height with a schoolboy's mop of dark chestnut hair, and a less-than-average amount of facial hair for a full-grown man. Nonetheless, he carries a briefcase, dresses in a suit, and smiles as though he sees treasure the moment he lays eyes on Daniel.

'Clever bugger,' says Andy, who hails from County Cork. He holds out his hand for me to shake, but keeps his focus on Daniel the whole time. Right now Daniel is running his eyes along the countertops, squinting. This is one of his favourite activities. Whole hours pass with Daniel squinting at venetian blinds, at shafts of light across a floor, even at the broad end of a shiny spoon. Now Daniel pulls a chair to the sink so he can climb up to the window and lick the condensation at the corners. 'Not MR, no,' says Andy. 'Look at him, sticking his tongue out. He won't be slurring too badly then. Once he's talking, I mean.'

MR is mentally retarded. I asked the paediatrician who assessed Daniel initially whether 'developmentally delayed' really just meant mentally retarded. She was hesitant to tell me that the answer was yes, and showed me a number of charts which indicated that 80 per cent of autistic people were also mentally retarded. I don't know if I expected to be shown so conclusively that my son was retarded and remember feeling a little dizzy as I took this in. We'd gone that morning from a family with two healthy, beautiful children (we thought) to one with a mentally retarded, autistic child. It seemed impossible that we'd suddenly moved into such territory and it was at that point that the panic set in and I could no longer speak. 'Delayed' meant retarded, and my son was delayed in every single area of development.

'How do you know he's not retarded?' I ask Andy.

'I just know right away. All these stupid tests they give

you are shit,' he says, throwing his briefcase onto the seat of an armchair, taking off the earphones to his music player.

'I spent four hundred pounds on those tests,' I tell him. 'He scored an IQ of 49. The educational psychologist says he's functionally retarded. Now you say he's not?'

'No, love, he's not,' says Andy. The guy is just about the most self-assured, cocky young man I've ever laid eyes on, hanging his jacket on the high end of a door, stripping his shirt of its tie. He unclips his cuff links and rolls them across the table like dice. Then he kicks his shoes off, pulls his shirt-tails out of his trousers, undoes the button at his collar.

'What are you doing?' I ask him. I've got him for three hours and I'm paying him more than brain surgeons get, so he'd better not make himself too comfortable here. One more button comes loose and the man is going out the door, cute green eyes or not.

He laughs. 'You want me to play with this kid or get out the British Ability Scales?' I turn my head, indicating with my eyes his discarded jacket, his flipped-off shoes. 'I've just come from an educational tribunal,' he explains. 'I'm helping on a case in Reading where they won't release the kid from special school so he can do a home-based programme. His mother has set the whole thing up, but does the school care? It's her kid and they won't let her help him. It's a fockin' sham.'

His face is dead serious but I can't help but smile. Five and a half feet of Irish hero is my man, Andy. In his socks, his sleeves rolled up, he gets out the wooden Brio track and expertly aligns all the bits to make a figure of eight, including a bridge and a tunnel. Then he rifles through the toy box, finding Annie and Clarabel, the two passenger cars that Thomas always pulls, at least on the videos anyway. He takes out another blue engine, which he knows from years of experience is called Edward, and makes persuasive steam-train noises as the train goes barrelling around the track. All of this has Daniel interested. He steps toward Andy, looking shyly at the track.

'Oh nooooo!' Andy shouts playfully. 'Crash!'

The track is broken up, has to be repaired. Annie has to be put back with Thomas, Clarabel needs her wheels sorted out.

'Back on the track!' says Andy, then around the track again until the bridge, which Andy knocks with his knee. 'Crash!' he says, and the whole sequence starts again.

At some point – and I couldn't say exactly when – Andy puts the trains together and then backs away from the track, an invitation for Daniel to have a go. Daniel puts his finger out and touches the train, pushing it gently so that it moves a centimetre, no more.

'Choo! CHOO!' Andy calls, pushing the train toward another crash site. As the train nears the bridge Daniel jumps in the air, anticipating the crash.

'Crash!' calls Andy, then connects the train again, waiting for Daniel to push it a centimetre, maybe two centimetres.

It isn't long before Daniel himself is pushing along Thomas, Andy blocking him every so often and calling 'Crash!' which Daniel loves. You can see a light in the child's eyes, a kind of recognition. I cannot describe what it does for my heart, seeing him on the floor with his new pal, Andy.

'What about all these other therapies?' I ask Andy. There's art therapy, music therapy, sound therapy, therapies that involve brushing the child in order to help with 'sensory' issues, not to mention many highly structured teaching practices that happen in schools.

He's setting out a new track, one that finishes at the edge of a seat cushion so that the train will crash to the floor. He looks at me, then back down to the track again. He says, 'You can try other things. Mostly they won't hurt him.'

'But will they help him?'

He shrugs. 'I'm a play therapist. And I like the behavioural approach.' A flat statement, a non-comment. But it feels to me he is saying much more, that I am speaking to someone in the trenches, who has been in the trenches for a long time, who is battle-weary but full of wisdom. It is as though he is saying, 'Here is the only gun that fires. Pick up the bloody gun.'

Later, we walk to the school to fetch Emily. I show Andy how I get Daniel to say 'Go!' while seated in the pushchair.

'Brilliant,' says Andy, and winks at me. 'You're a natural, sister,' he says. 'You want a job?'

The mothers and nannies at the school gate all notice Andy. Maybe they think I've gone in for him, and frankly you could do a lot worse than hitch yourself to Mr O'Connor here, who taught Daniel to say 'Mama' today by raising him up in a tiny blue chair like a rocket launching into space every time Daniel got his lips into the shape to make a 'mmm' sound. He then raced him like that across the room holding up the chair with Daniel in it whenever Daniel made a 'ah' sound. I could hardly watch, thinking both were going to crash into the wall at any second. But Andy knows how to motivate Daniel, that's for sure. Clownlike, he'd skip across Trafalgar Square in a pink tutu and a garter belt if that's what it took to get my boy to speak.

'It's that lass, isn't it?' he says now, pointing out Emily.
'How did you know?' I ask.

'Look likes you, and miserable in that school, I see.'

'She says she likes break times . . . and, uh, I'm sure it's good for her to be around other children.'

'Keep her home one day, Melanie Marsh,' he says, stringing his words together into one long one. 'It'd be good crack seeing them play together, don't you think?'

I don't know where he's come from, or what I've done to have the good fortune of this man – a play therapist, who knew there was such a thing? But he's the first professional who has looked favourably on Daniel. When I say that Daniel is autistic, what I mean is that he reaches into his nappy and smears his faeces across the backs of chairs, the glass doors that lead to the garden, the tiles of the fireplace. If I don't engage him in some other activity he will spend hours pulling at the individual strands of wool on our carpet, lying on the floor watching his Thomas two inches from his nose, or pushing his face against the glass of the television. He is dangerous to himself – will slap his head if you get cross at him. He refuses point blank to use a toilet and will scream and hit anything in front of him if you try to convince him to sit on one. If what Andy is promising is that Daniel might one day play with his sister, actually get a toy and do something with it that includes another child, I will do *whatever* it takes to keep him in my employ. At home I look for more to sell. If I pull up the carpets, I reckon the Hoover can go, for one thing.

12

Veena tells me a soldier has been looking for me.

'He came to the house this evening while I was cleaning the cutlery,' she says. It astonishes me to think Veena can stand in the middle of my house – which is covered in dried oatmeal, dropped crusts of toast, candy wrappers and discarded toys – and serenely polish the cutlery, but I try not to register this. 'I took with me to the door a long knife, just in case. He was a very clipped fellow, his hair shaven here and here, and a diamond of fur just across the top of him.'

'Veena, that is a vivid description, but his name would be of more use,' I say.

'He left some presents,' she says.

Behind her, on the kitchen counter, I see a large Sears bag. I haven't seen a Sears bag since I left America and the sight of it turns something inside me – homesickness, I imagine.

'It wasn't my brother, was it?' I say. 'He didn't look like a cross between Brad Pitt and a large black rhino by any chance?'

Veena waves me away. 'He was a soldier, that's all I know. I don't speak to soldiers. What is *bratpit*?'

'So you didn't actually open the door?'

'Of course not,' she says, like *that* is a question?

We investigate the presents. I have to do this because it would not be entirely out of character for my brother to give a three-year-old boy live ammunition and a budding five-year-old girl a collection of thongs. That's just the kind of guy he is. But the presents turn out to be nothing like that. He has put real care into choosing toys that are appropriate for Emily and Daniel's ages, and he's wrapped them beautifully in pastel paper and ribbons. For Emily there is a shimmering mermaid costume, which I know she will adore. For Daniel, a small soft football and a tiny-sized football helmet. It touches me that Larry would send someone by with these gifts, because even if it was Wanda who chose the gifts and wrapped them, it must have been Larry who convinced his army buddy to carry them all the way across the Atlantic to my door.

'So now you know they aren't pornography, we wrap them up again, is that it?' says Veena wearily. She thinks it is complete nonsense to vet gifts from relatives.

'Yes,' I say. 'We have to make it look like nobody opened them.'

'This is like working for the government,' she says, 'all this covert wrapping and unwrapping.' But she sets about refolding the paper, bringing the tape back to where it was before so that the pattern on the paper is perfect.

'You have lovely children,' she says now. 'I will miss cleaning their toys.'

It's the last time Veena is here to clean for me. I can't afford to pay her any longer and I won't let her take any less, which she has offered to do several times now. I am going to miss her. I always look forward to Thursdays when she arrives with her handmade radiator duster, her hair tied back with an army of clips. Each afternoon when she finishes, she tells me the house looks no better at all. Standing in the middle of the room, she frowns as though the room has personally insulted her. When I pay her she shakes her head as though to say it is wrong to pay for jobs that are incomplete, or perhaps to say that the money isn't enough. Either way, she would be correct. I wish she weren't going.

'Ah well, I should be reading my Walter Benjamin anyway,' she said when I gave her the news. 'And watching you starve yourself has been no fun at all.'

Now she is on her way out. It feels to me like everyone is leaving my life, one at a time, as though through an invisible door. 'Come over whenever you like,' I tell Veena.

'I leave you my duster,' she says, slipping her cloth bag over her shoulder, touching my cheek with her delicate, brown hand.

Veena is not correct that I am starving. At the Italian pastry shop they fill my arms with biblical-looking loaves of *pane toscano*, with glazed plaits of polenta bread sprinkled with pine nuts, with focaccia dimpled with the fingerprints of Max's sons, who knock back the bread dough and wheel it on their fists.

'My wife has made you some dinner,' says Max. He passes me a brown bag of home-made ravioli, its top daintily folded. Through the paper I can feel the warmth of his wife's tomato sauce, the hard glass of the jar. 'You are looking better, we think,' says Max.

I feel better. Life isn't perfect, no, but this one thing is going well and it's enough: Daniel is talking. All over the house he's invented crash sites for his trains, which may not seem like much but is a heck of an improvement on rolling them one inch one way and one inch the other in front of his face. Now the trains fly off the edges of window sills, the corners of the dining table, the flat top of the television casing, the rim of the bath. 'Crash!' he says, and there the trains tumble. 'Go!' he says, and off they shoot. He must say 'Mama' if he wants my attention. Tugging at my hand without the essential word will get him nowhere. When he says Mama, however, I pick him up, twirl him, let him lead me wherever he cares to go. I'm his pesky friend, always invading his games, his happy dog nosing behind. He has a new word almost every day, taught to him deliberately, methodically, but it is still a new word. For this reason I feel great. I smile at Max and tell him so.

'More healthy,' Max says, and puts his fist up in the air, shakes his short, muscular arm. Then he cups his hands around his cheeks and says, 'And in the face. More colour.'

'You need bosoms,' says the youngest, whose name is Paolo.

I go to him now, to Paolo who stands outside the rather crematorial-looking bread ovens with their blackened interiors, their clattering trays. I put my mouth next to the ear of this boy of fifteen, whose father is going to hit him, he says, if he cannot shut his mouth.

'Paolo,' I coo. His brothers are staring. Their eyes, filled with expectation and amusement, fix on the two of us. 'I *have* bosoms.'

And now they are laughing, even Paolo, who sinks down under the weight of his own chagrin and cannot look at me without giggling for many days.

*   *   *

The other person I have to say goodbye to is Jacob the Shrink. He leans back in his leather chair, his legs stretched forward, crossed at the ankle. He holds his pen at each end with the tips of his fingers, blows through his lips so that his cheeks fill with air, then lie flatly once more, two burnished brown planes. He studies me hard through his thick lenses.

'Why don't you come for a reduced fee?' he suggests. 'You're really not ready to quit therapy altogether.'

'What's it going to help?' I say. The weather is warmer now. I have on last year's rather grungy sandals, a pair of cropped jeans. My hair, which defies elastic and metal slides, wags below my chin in chunks of newly sunburned blonde. 'Not to be insulting, Jacob, it's just that I know now what my problem is and it's not going to go away no matter how much we dig up memories while I sit on your nice Conran sofa here.'

'Is that what Daniel is? A problem?'

'Screw you, Jacob,' I say, and he laughs.

'You are so young,' he says. 'You think you're all grown up, but when I see you I think you are awfully young to be out on your own like this.'

'I'm not so young,' I say.

He waves his fingers through the air in a manner that means he does not agree but also will not argue. 'I'm concerned about you,' he says. 'And I do have my reservations about this ABA thing. What happens if it doesn't work?'

Jacob is not a fan of this new therapy idea for Daniel. Behavioural psychology conjures up for him the idea of mild electrical currents and boxed rats. He keeps asking me how this is going to affect Daniel's emotional health if his mother is constantly challenging him to produce sounds, holding out a chip of chocolate as a reward for his efforts. Better than what his emotional state will be if he goes through the world unable to speak or understand, is my fast reply.

'I might be able to help you to come to terms with what has happened,' Jacob says.

I consider that. 'Well, you know something? I am not sure I *want* to come to terms with what's happened. I feel like my unwillingness to see this as a closed deal somehow helps Daniel. I know he is autistic, of course, but what I am thinking is that if I work tirelessly to move him away from the autism, then maybe he'll end up some-place closer to normal than he otherwise would have been.'

I know what Jacob is thinking: that I'm wasting my time. And he may, too, be thinking I've got some nerve to believe that other mothers just didn't 'work' hard enough for their children. I don't believe that, of course. I don't think I'm more clever or more diligent. Other mothers have worked hard and have moved their children just that little bit further along – I keep hearing stories in which this is the case. It was the other mothers who got me Andy O'Connor's phone number. Another mother who stopped me in the supermarket and told me my son was lovely.

They are the ones that tell me to try. And what is so *wrong* with trying?

Jacob says, 'And we need to talk about Stephen. It sounds as though you will have to come to terms with that as well.'

Stephen, I do not want to think about. 'I've got a different agenda than he does,' I say. Pictured in my mind is an image of myself as one of these tough, stout women with broad calves and strong, rough hands, a woman who runs her house with coarse efficiency, claiming Monday as washing day, Tuesday for the polishing of all surfaces.

Someone in control, in charge, a woman not even Stephen could challenge. But of course, I am not like that. I put on a brave front for Jacob, but really I am just all mush inside. Scratch me and my misery rises like sea foam.

'You want to know what I worry about now?' I say.

He raises his eyebrows, fingers his moustache like he always does.

'I worry that I'll get Daniel just so far, you know, and he'll be a young guy out there in the world, but not entirely normal, right? Not normal at all, really. And then one night he's hanging out on a city street, maybe running his eye along an iron railing the way he does – what they call 'stimming' – and some policemen see him and think he's acting like he's on drugs. So they stop him and he yells and tries to run. They think he's being violent, and so they hurt him. He's calling for me and I can't stop them shoving him around and hurting him because I'm not there and he's helpless.' I stop speaking and all at once I am shocked by what I've said. I've spooked myself and I feel a little sick inside. 'Do you know what I mean?' I ask quietly.

Jacob says, 'Please don't stop therapy.'

'What on earth is *therapy* going to do when the police are holding my son?'

Jacob clasps his brow, moves his face back and forth across his palm. 'Melanie,' he says.

'Anyway, I can't afford you,' I tell him.

'Forget this month's bill. It's paid!'

'It isn't paid!' I say.

'*I* say it is paid.'

And now we look at each other, each as stubborn as the other.

He says, 'Melanie, listen to me. You're not wrong to worry about that, what you're describing.' He leans forward, his hands raised, fingers stretched toward the ceiling. 'I have a boy myself, nineteen years old, art student in Camberwell, living in Woolwich. And I have a fear that one day he'll get cornered by the wrong group of kids and they will beat the life out of him. And when I'm not worried about that, I'm worried about the police who might pick him up and what *they* will do to him!'

'Why would they do anything to him?' I say.

'Because he's black,' says Jacob slowly, as though he's talking to an idiot, which I guess he is. 'And if that weren't enough, he's also gay.'

I try to imagine Jacob's son, who bought his father those strange yellow trainers he wore to my house that one day, and who I discover now sculpts statues of people from cold steel.

'They are beautiful,' says Jacob. 'He's gifted. And we worry about him all the time. You would be very interested in what I say during *my* sessions,' he tells me.

And then we are looking at each other, and maybe laughing. There's some sort of emotion coming here, but I don't know what you'd call it. A kind of acknowledgement. A kind of instant love.

I say to Jacob, 'I like you. But I don't want to come unless I pay you for your time. What kind of shrink are you if you don't drive a Rover?'

'I drive a BMW,' he says.

I tell him the truth is that inside myself I don't really believe that therapy will make any difference to me. I gesture around the room, at his plush furniture, his shelves of books with titles like *Self and Others*, *The Crisis of Loss*. 'It's not what I need,' I tell him.

'What do you need?' asks Jacob.

What I really need, I think, is to get back home. Stephen wasn't so thrilled about looking after the kids tonight, and he'll be wanting to get back to Penelope. I'm still getting used to that. No, I'm actually not getting used to it at all.

On the way back home I anticipate all of Stephen's questions. He has probably spent the whole of the evening being kind to Emily, reading her books, arranging fairy cakes for her Disney characters, sailing Dumbo through the air. She is suffering without him. Some evenings she weeps, pounding her fists against my belly, asking when he will return home, demanding that I bring him to her. For her sake I would be willing to try on Stephen any ploy or mild treachery, any sexual favour. If I could manoeuvre Stephen's heart by writing him poetry or pole dancing in our living room, do you think I would even hesitate? I'd set into iambic pentameter the longing of my heart while raising my naked leg over my shoulder like a spear.

I mean to have him back is the point. No argument about his shoddy response to Daniel's autism, about marital treason, about his general aloofness can shelter me from the yearning I have to return to my children their father.

When I come into the house I see the glow of Daniel's musical lamp shining from the children's bedroom. It taps out a lullaby while turning slowly round, projecting images of coloured animals across the blank walls. I love this lamp. I have photographs of the children staring into it, amazed at its mystical qualities, how it brings alive their whole room with the dreamy images of giraffes and toucans. Removing my shoes, I tiptoe into the bedroom,

finding Stephen in the wicker armchair set in the centre
of the room between the twin beds. His arms are folded
across his chest, his chin resting on them; perhaps he is
asleep. I think how he will be some day, an old man in a
chair. Who will sit beside him then? Surely it is not an
insignificant thing that I have promised to be that person,
who will not need him to be handsome or young. But will
need him.

'You are late,' he says.

I say, 'Have the children been happy – happy to see
you, I mean?'

'I thought perhaps you'd decided to go on one of your
midnight jaunts,' says Stephen.

'Only for a minute. I went to a bookshop, to the medical
section. I want to know more about how the brain
develops.'

'It won't matter what you learn,' he says. 'It's not going
to make a difference.'

'I couldn't afford the book anyway. It was eighty
pounds.'

'You can't go around buying eighty-pound *books*,
Melanie,' he says.

'Well, I didn't. And your shirt costs eighty pounds,' I
tell him.

In the Bible somewhere – is it the Book of James? –
we are warned about the words that we speak. *Consider
what a great forest is set on fire by a small spark*. Quickly,
before it is too late, I change the subject. I say, 'I do not,
of course, leave them in the middle of the night on their
own.'

'I should think not,' says Stephen. He knows perfectly
well I'd never leave them. I won't even leave them at the
supermarket crèche.

'Daniel says the word "crash." And he plays with his trains,' says Stephen. 'Plays, not just holds one in front of his eyes. I want to meet this man who you say is teaching him.'

I nod.

He says, 'Cath gave me a book on child development and it says he should have several hundred words in his vocabulary by now. Full sentences, questions that begin "Who", "What", "How".'

'One step at a time,' I say.

He stands. His hair is pushed back so that it flops to one side. His chin is thick with stubble. It appears that among the new changes in his appearance, a different way of combing his hair, a new shirt, Stephen is now going in for facial hair. So perhaps he *will* some day turn up with clinging clothes and a mossy beard. Chuck in a few tattoos and put a bull ring through his nose and I would be most happy never to touch him again. Unfortunately, he looks good in his new facial hair. Doesn't that just take the piss?

He says, 'I can't help but think we are holding him back by not allowing him to go to a special school. And that you cannot continue as you are. At this rate we will most certainly go bankrupt. And for what? We have been told he cannot attend regular school, or be like a regular child.'

I shake my head dumbly. I wonder, has Stephen ever *been* to a special school? Has he seen how impossible it is to learn language in a group setting, surrounded by others who either cannot speak at all or repeat the same dismal, senseless phrase over and over? Does he not realise there is no way to model your own behaviour on normality when there is nothing normal happening around you? Has Stephen looked at the rate of improvement among these children who get so-called 'special' help? Because the morning I went along to check out the special school that the Local Education Authority would like Daniel to attend, I thought to myself he could be there all his life and never learn a single word.

'You're out of your mind,' I tell him.

He stands close to me, too close. His face is menacing. With this expression in his eyes and his new beard, he looks plain mean. I don't know what happened to the guy who taught me how to waltz, laughing as I clambered all over his toes, who sat patiently – and really, rather bravely – in the passenger's seat as I screeched through London in his car, trying to figure out how to drive on the left side of the street. This man, towering above me, is nothing like the one who made me a record player out of a rose-wood box, told me in his perfect French that my body was like a garden – he saw in it everything beautiful. Now he looks at me with a mixture of pity and disdain. He says, 'You just came back from your psychiatrist and *I* am out of my mind?'

In my dream I am walking down a street on a wet night. Winter leaves form clumps at the kerb; the trees have that skeletal look, as though they could never again bud flowers. Suddenly I remember that I have left the children in the house alone. It is impossible that I would ever do such a thing, but in my dream I have suddenly remembered that they are all alone in that house. I rush through the city now, panic rising in my chest. It seems the streets are all tangled up; I cannot find my home. Then all at once I am there, running for the door.

Inside there is a man I think I recognise. Bettelheim. He's small, weasel-like, with heavy glasses. He sits in the armchair – Stephen's favourite chair – and points to Daniel, who stands in a corner turning round and round, focusing on nothing. Daniel doesn't even look fully alive as he spins slowly in a circle.

'Look what you've done!' shouts Bettelheim. His face is the mask of an accuser. I recognise him more by this fact about him than any other, and the thought that I am to blame stuns me, silences me.

I rush for Daniel, the blood pounding in my ears, but when I reach him he feels like wood in my arms.

'Look what you've done!' Bettelheim taunts once more.

When I wake there is orange light flooding through the window. I have forgotten to draw the curtain, so the street lamp shines through the window in the manner of the glowing bulbs of certain terrariums and fish tanks. I feel I am being observed. Outside, the morning sun is hovering low in the sky. When I open the window, the air smells like coal and it smells like rain. The man in my dream is gone now, as is the man in my life.

13

I have a book of all Daniel's new words. Among others, he can say ball, Thomas, egg, button and balloon. Except he doesn't say the whole word, of course. That would be too hard for him. 'Balloon', for example, is more like 'bah-ooh', but that's fine. That's beautiful. At first I was afraid to keep a record of his words, for fear he would lose them. That is what seems to have happened all through his babyhood, which I am at pains to remember is over now. At three and three months he is a little boy.

'We have time,' Andy assures me, but all I can think is that Stephen will insist Daniel go to nursery school by four. And where will he go if he cannot speak?

'He *can* speak, woman,' says Andy, then swigs back some tea. He drinks his tea sweet and strong, 'the way the brickies like it' is what he has said. His two brothers, who also work in London, build walls all over the city. 'What are you writing in your book about him if not all his good words?'

On the days that Andy is here, I find myself a bit simpering, a bit quiet. I rely on him to reassure me that

Daniel won't return to mute, won't become one of these children who must move from nappies to adult diapers, the sort that go round as incontinent old men. No, he will develop into a boy who pulls on his jeans and races shirtless to the garden with a bat and ball. He will find friends to compete with on hillsides, battle on playgrounds. Easter will bring egg hunts; he will dream of racing cars and piloting hot-air balloons. He will be normal – or close enough. He will be happy.

Andy tells me that Daniel's progress is steady, controlled. He says it's magic compared with that of other children he has, and that I am lucky. Lucky, the word sticks in my throat, but as Andy speaks I begin to understand why he says that, and why it is true. One of the children Andy works with, an eight-year-old, used to run through the house repeating, 'Have a Break. Have a Kit Kat. Have a Break. Have a Kit Kat.' Hundreds and hundreds of times he uttered this same slogan, often under his breath until it was only a hoarse whisper. Yesterday he came out with 'Have you been hurt in an accident? Call 0800 treble five treble nine. That's 0800, treble five, treble nine.' And he hasn't mentioned KitKats since.

'Verbal stimming,' says Andy. 'Worst kind of stim.'

I ask him if he can help this child, wait for his answer to be no, some cases are well out of his ability.

'Oh, sure,' says Andy, snapping a rolling paper from its cardboard wallet. He dumps in a clump of tobacco that smells wet to me, like freshly cut summer grass mixed with leather. Rolling the paper back and forth in his fingers, he says, 'It's best, however, not to let a child get that old without useful language.'

As though he has to convince me.

'Will you help my friend Iris? She has a teenager. He

can talk, but I get the impression there are other problems. Quite bad ones.'

The trouble with Iris's son, among other things, is the fact he has become a grumpy adolescent. 'If there is anything worse than a teenager,' she told me, smiling, 'it's an autistic teenager.' He storms through the house, stomps out to the garden, paces and swings his arms. He wants to go out in the middle of the night. He seems to be fascinated by the lighted windows of people's homes, by the gleaming colours of Piccadilly Circus, the abrupt, moving brightness of night buses. Midnight, one or two in the morning, the later the better. Iris has placed complicated locks on every door and every window. She makes no apology for making her house into a prison from which, sadly, her son is clever enough to escape.

Andy nods, smiles. He can help, he says. But he only has so much time.

Now he shows me how to get Daniel to use language while doing a puzzle. The theme of the puzzle is, of course, Thomas the Tank Engine. It's a wooden one, from the Early Learning Centre, with pull-out pieces. Daniel has the empty wooden tray with the missing pieces. Andy has figures of all the trains, plus the Fat Controller. Daniel has to make a sound like 'Thom' to get Thomas, a 'Puh' sound to get Percy, an 'Eh' to get Edward, etc. Then I have to put my hand over his hand to help guide the pieces into position. It doesn't take him long to figure out the idea, and I am thrilled because I've never gotten him to complete a puzzle before. He usually just tips the puzzle over and watches the pieces fall, then walks over them as though they weren't there, or he's forgotten they are there. What has changed is that we direct every movement, loudly praising him for each effort. And when he completes the entire puzzle, out comes a battery-operated Thomas with a headlamp, which goes like blazes across the wooden floor. This battery-powered version only comes out at the end of the puzzle – it's a 'reinforcer', which means that it is only used during therapy sessions. Daniel loves it. He grins with anticipation throughout the whole process of making the puzzle.

'Five minutes every two hours until I see you next,' Andy tells me. 'Before he gets bored with that puzzle, get him a new puzzle. Keep him talking, every day, all the time.'

'This will work?' I ask hesitantly.

'This will work,' Andy says. And I believe him.

Before he leaves he tells me, 'If you see Daniel stimming, distract him. I don't care what you are doing – hanging the laundry, making the tea – stop what you are doing and redirect him so he doesn't just sit there and stim.'

A 'stim' is whatever someone is doing to distract themselves. Jumping up and down, nodding the head back and forth, or humming continually. These are stims you see in autistic people. But we all have stims, of course. I bite the ends of pens, for example.

'Nose-picking, tapping, biting fingernails, hair-twirling, licking your lips. And eating pens like you're doing now,' Andy explains. 'And that's my pen, by the way.'

I whip the pen out of my mouth, holding it toward Andy. But I see that I've gnawed off the blue cap, put my teeth marks on the transluscent plastic casing.

'Put it back in your mouth, Melanie,' says Andy, waving away the slobbered-on pen. 'I don't want it!'

He makes me laugh and he fixes my kid. In his rucksack he carries clipboards and developmental charts, note cards and dozens of small gadgets: a top that spins and throws sparks, a wind-up frog that hops across tables, a speaking turtle with a string-pull, lots and lots of things that light up or buzz, plus a great number of trains.

He promises Daniel will enlarge his interest in trains and, just as predicted, a few weeks later I find Daniel latched on to more than just Thomas. He's gotten Annie and Clarabel out of the box on his own, connected them on to the back of Thomas, and is pushing them along the wooden floor. I don't care what the speech therapist said about Andy having no professional qualifications, he seems to understand how to make Daniel more and more like a typical child. Daniel cries less these days; he has things to do other than haul around disc-shaped objects. The discs are useful for teaching Daniel to learn the concept of big and small; a coin next to the lid of a mayonnaise jar. When he gets it right Andy showers him with pieces of round, coloured confetti he's made with a hole-punch. For Daniel it is ecstasy to have a cascade of these circles pouring over him. If he could, he'd wade in a river of geometric shapes.

The Hoover fetched ninety pounds and I really don't miss the carpet at all.

14

Cath says she wants to see the children, wants to see me. She meets me at the school gate and we find her car. Strapping Emily and Daniel into the back, I feel the thrill of an adventure. To my delight, she insists we go to the zoo.

'My treat,' she says, which is a good thing. A visit to the zoo for the three of us costs the same as one hour of Andy's time or half a week of groceries or the blazer for Emily's school uniform come autumn. Well, I don't have to worry about the blazer – Stephen will pay for that, I'm sure – but he's made it very clear he thinks Andy O'Connor costs too much and that he doesn't believe anyone should be paid that much for playing with a child. But then, he's never seen first-hand what Andy can get out of Daniel, and he doesn't understand that there's a lot more to it than playing.

'Every Easter holiday my parents took us to the zoo,' says Cath. 'It was the same routine each year. Saturday was zoo day, Sunday was Easter. I cannot imagine that London Zoo exists in hot weather like this. I always associate it with Lent. Whenever I hear "When I Survey the Wondrous Cross", the image of barking seals comes into my mind.'

For Emily's sake we are going straight to the elephants, marching along the warm, white pavement at a brisk pace that has Cath puffing. It amuses me she thinks today is hot. In Virginia even early in spring the heat is a suffocating and invisible spectre that you have to walk through. I can remember summer days when it felt exactly as though steaming wool was being held over your face as you breathed, the sun stabbing at your skull so you felt it was too much trouble to go anywhere. Certainly the pace with which we arrive at the elephants would be impossible during a Virginia summer. You'd stay indoors with the air conditioning and iced tea – a drink you simply cannot get hold of here in Britain – battling to keep the insects out of the house. Silverfish crawled up through the drains, wasps appeared from nowhere. We lived in a clapboard house surrounded by toads that buried in the earth to stay cool, snakes that without any particular worry spread themselves on the warm rocks in the evening. By dusk the mosquitoes had you slapping your skin, and I wonder sometimes if it was all the poisons I sprayed on my body to repel them that made me give birth to a child with autism. That or the pesticides they dumped into neighbouring fields, dispersed by single-engine planes that flew low like geese and made you hunch your shoulders and cringe as they sped over the land. As a child I waded in streams, drank from any flowing water I found. My brother and I traversed whole woodlands in flip-flops and baseball caps, picking wild blueberries off the vines, wild strawberries from under their cheerful green leaves. *Wash* them? We didn't think about such things. We fished and didn't wonder about the state of the water. Popped rasp-berries we stole from next door into our mouths without a thought about how they grew so beautifully in a land infested with every kind of pest.

'I want you to know that I never liked Penelope,' says Cath. We are standing outside the elephant enclosure, watching Emily as she delights in a baby elephant, tiny compared with his mother, about the size of a London taxi and covered in waxy-looking grey skin. Daniel is less interested, but is definitely looking in the same general direction, even if he does gnaw at the collar of his shirt, making a damp patch the shape of a crescent moon. I spent a few minutes on my knees beside him, helping him point and say, 'Big elephant! Little elephant!' but I couldn't really conduct a therapy session and speak to Cath at the same time.

'She's very pleased with herself, a little spoilt,' Cath says now. 'Very attractive in her own way – don't get me wrong – but I was relieved he didn't marry her. And I was always quite proud to have you as a sister-in-law.'

Emily moves along the enclosure. We trail, not too close. We don't want her to hear.

'Why are you speaking in the past tense?' I say. 'I'm still your sister-in-law. Or is there something you know that I don't know?'

Cath looks at me, then away.

'Oh fuck, Cath, please tell me.'

Later we go to the sea lion show, sitting among the crowd that gathers on marine-green seats, listening to a lady with a microphone strapped to her head and a pouch of fish lashed to her belt. In front of us is a pool of unsteady water, bobbing like a tray of shaken jelly. Daniel would like to go swimming in it; I have his shirt in my fist, supporting him as he leans forward, his arms flailing as though he might fly if he could only get up enough speed.

Cath says, 'I agree with you that he's still in shock – there's something about the abruptness with which he left you that makes no sense at all. He may come to his senses. But I know Penelope. She's got some sort of plan. I'm only allowed to use his mobile number or else she goes spare.'

'I don't like Penelope either,' I say. 'But she wasn't the one who stood before God and man and told the world she'd be my husband. That was Stephen.'

'Like I say, I don't really understand him,' says Cath.

Our conversation is conducted in whispers and close, small movements. Around us are shouts of surprise at the sea lions, who can hop backwards in the tremulous water, sail through hoops with their backs arched, catch beach balls with their noses.

'This is Salt,' calls the lady with the microphone. She tosses a silvery fish in the direction of a sleek grey female sea lion, ploughing through the pool.

I have Daniel up close against me, comforting him when the crowd makes a big noise. He hates sudden loud sounds; puts his hands over his ears and howls when Salt tosses a ball back and forth with her trainer, causing the audience to cheer. But he is watching, definitely, and that is a good thing. Emily, springing up and down in her seat, could be attached to a pneumatic drill she bounces so fast, laughing and pointing all the while. Everything is going great until Daniel gets splashed. Suddenly, as though he's been shot by a gun, he howls and twists against me, scrambling to get away, and now he is running toward the back of the audience, his knees pointed out, his arms above his head. And I am running after him. I don't allow myself to think of what this might be like when he is older, taller than me, faster. I will not be one of those people who have to keep their grown autistic child fastened to their wrist by means of a coiled rope, a kind of handcuff, something I saw earlier at the owl enclosure as a team of staff from one or another special school moved reluctant autistic teenagers from one exhibit to the next, much as one might move recalcitrant cattle.

The tiger is pacing back and forth, back and forth. His stripes mirror the metal bars of his enclosure. His eyes seem to focus on everything and nothing. It is a look that turns inward, attending to some biological need: to hunt, to mate, to shit. I've seen this same expression in my son, a fact that visits me with alarm. To watch the tiger, feeling as familiar as I do with his state of internal concern, requires a kind of self-control that does violence to my spirit. I will myself to remain, still and standing.

Emily is enchanted, quietly leaning on my legs. The big cat is only a few feet from us. You can see his loose skin, his dense pelt, the yellow of his canines as he pants. Daniel, standing with us, ignores the tiger altogether. Six hundred pounds of exotic animal straight out of the Indian jungle apparently does nothing for him. Instead, he focuses on a sparrow that is taking a dust bath in the tiger's enclosure. 'Bird,' I tell him. And after some prompting he says, 'Burr.' This word will be added to my book when we get home. And we will practise it along with every other word, purchase models of birds and draw pictures of birds, spread our arms and pretend to fly like birds. I will make wings from card, tie string so that we can wear them on our backs like angels. At the pond in Regent's Park we will point at seagulls and imitate their swoops and dives.

This I do for every word he picks up. And I am determined to do it until he has full use of the English language.

Cath says, 'I don't think my parents helped matters much. They're very powerful people, you know. Mother looks innocent enough, carrying in the jam jars for church sales, always making time to look after David's and Tricia's boys, but whatever Dad wanted always had to go. She would defend his wishes against her own children a hundred per cent. That is what she thought one did as a mother, presenting a united front at all times. Stephen cried himself to sleep all the first term of boarding school, at the age of eight. Back then they didn't allow parents to speak to the boys for the entire first month, thinking it would only contribute to homesickness. There was none of this email or use of a dormitory payphone. When Stephen came home at exeat he begged Mum and Dad not to send him back – literally, begged them on his knees, crying. But Dad would hear none of it.'

This information pains me. With her upper-class vowels and her Liberty print shirt-dress, her delicate Russell & Bromley pumps with little brass snaffles at each toe, Cath is nonetheless a very unguarded individual, which is why I've always liked her so much. I know she is telling me the truth. And Stephen is still someone I love and wish for. Our son looks exactly like him, with his dark eyes and broad cheeks, and it tears at something inside me to imagine such a boy on his knees, at the mercy of parents who think there is only one way to raise a child and that is to send him away.

'It must be awful for you to be continually scrutinised over everything you do and have done for Daniel,' whispers Cath. Emily is asleep on the sofa. Daniel is asleep in my arms. The sun and all the walking has worn them out. Cath and I are recovering with large glasses of lemonade, happy with our zoo day.

'I've had some people come around trying to get me to enrol him in a special school for moderate learning disabilities,' I say now, remembering a horrible pair who came by with their clipboards and their raincoats, looking more like spies than anybody who should be near children. They regarded Daniel as one might a wild animal, admiring him from a safe distance as we did the tiger who paced his enclosure. I try not to think how Daniel sometimes paces our back garden as I say, 'I told them to get lost, and yes, they probably thought I wasn't doing right by Daniel. But they don't see the progress I see. They think he's in terrible shape because he only knows fifty or sixty words. But I see fifty words as fifty times what he had before we started.'

Cath says, 'I've watched you with him, with both of your children. Don't let people upset you or condemn you or say it was your fault. There are more and more kids with autism these days, and I don't know why.'

'I don't think it is my fault,' I tell her. I don't tell her I am haunted by Bettelheim, who attacks me in my dreams, that I'm routinely hurt by the mothers at Emily's school gate, that the nights are the worst, just waiting on my own. 'And I do think his vaccinations were tough on him, each one, not just the MMR.'

'Every day I authorise vaccinations,' says Cath.

'I'm not blaming you,' I say. I've begun to understand that once you are a mother there is just no safe place to cast a vote. Everything you do, the consequences of every action, you will take to the grave. And there is no point in assigning blame.

Cath says, 'And I'm telling you not to let anyone put you down. Because they will, you know. I had a woman in my surgery yesterday concerned because her husband, who does contracts for the council, had to have a wall cleaned and repainted for a flat in Maida Vale. It seems the teenage boy, who is autistic, smears his faeces at night. The woman went on and on about how the boy should be locked up, how her husband shouldn't have to do this sort of work, how it was dangerous for his health, how it's the parents that she blames.'

'What did you say to her?' I ask. I have a lump in my chest as though I've swallowed a light bulb, like the glass is shattering and sliding toward my heart.

'I handed her the box of latex disposable gloves I have on my desk,' says Cath, looking at me with a conspiratorial half-smile, 'and I told her, "This is the medical answer to your problem. Doctors use these every day."'

I laugh with her, hug her. 'I'll be your friend whatever,' she says to me.

I nod, knowing she cannot bring herself to tell me Stephen is planning a divorce.

15

Here is a photograph of Daniel, sitting on the steps with his sister. In it he is smiling broadly, eyes to the camera. His face is full of the radiant, expectant joy of any normal child. I often look at this picture and wonder what was going right that day – what food he'd eaten or not eaten, what chemical change in his brain made that such a good day. At a lecture I attended, a doctor who has taken an interest in the biology of autism explained that food seems to affect autistic kids. E numbers, sugar, aspartame, corn, monosodium glutamate, anything with a lot of colouring in it even if it is natural, even certain fruits. The worst thing is gluten and milk, which is all Daniel wants to eat. And gluten appears to be in everything: Carr's water biscuits, McVitie's digestives, not to mention all the Italian bread that flows through our house. I can understand that these are not essential items of nutrition – and we can live without gluten – but it feels completely wrong to me not to let Daniel have his milk. Having spent so long now getting him on to a cup, I now find all I can put in the cup is water or watered-down juice. He wants my breasts, lifts my shirt, his mouth open. I move him away, gesturing to the cup. 'Gul,' he says. It's his word for milk. And then, plucking the word from the air, he says, 'Milk,' and points at my chest.

But I have to direct him to the cup.

The other idea this doctor gave is to allow raw goat's milk and give Daniel a special enzyme to help him digest it. The raw goat's milk is from Wales. I have it brought by courier every week, costing me over twenty pounds. Twenty pounds a week seems an awful lot for milk. Twenty pounds a week is also about the same amount Daniel gets from the government for being a disabled child. So the government is paying for Daniel's milk. That's their one big effort for my little boy.

As for the enzymes, I have to plump for them, and they aren't a giveaway, I can tell you.

At night, because I am lonely and because Daniel wakes up so often that I become unable to go back to sleep myself, I ring my brother.

'Why don't you watch TV?' he says. 'Don't you have cable? Cable, twenty-four-hour supermarkets, chat rooms, casinos, airport lounges, all these things were made for people like you.'

'But what I actually *want* to do is sleep,' I tell him.

'OK,' he says, like that's no problem. 'Valium, Ativan, Tranxene, Xanax, Buspirone. Just get it off the Internet. God knows, you have *time*.'

His other suggestion is that I speed-date. 'Isn't that the latest craze in Britain?' he says. 'Man, that's what I'd do if I were in your shoes.'

I try to explain to him that I am married, that the last

thing I want is a three-minute date, and there is nothing whatsoever attractive to me in this notion.

He makes a sound, *Mmmmmm,* as though what I've just told him is very, very wrong. 'Mmm,' he says. 'All what you just said there, don't mention it on the date. Just smile and tell them you like sex. That's the way to do it.'

Another phone call with Larry. It is five in the morning. The sun is an orange lollipop hanging low behind shadowed buildings. Larry's voice on the phone is wide awake, however. It's eleven at night his time.

'Wait a second! I don't believe it!' he is saying.

'Well, it's true!' I tell him.

'But what you are saying is just not *possible* in the twenty-first century! You are telling me that the best-loved soap in that country where you live is on the *radio*?' he says.

'*The Archers,*' I tell him, exhaling a breath of smoke against the receiver. I've copped a cigarette Andy left behind by accident. Out in the garden, of course, in the seat by the belching dead water of our pond.

'On the *radio*?' says my brother, flabbergasted. 'During the *day*?'

When things are going well I count up Daniel's words. He has over a hundred now and is beginning to put them together. Having not been able to get a word out of him for three years I now find that if I am inventive enough, he will try for me every time. He likes it, this talking game. I teach him to play ball, rewarding him for every effort he makes to catch or throw.

'Nice catch,' I say, standing an arm's length from him.

When I tried this months ago, Daniel just let the ball hit him in the face or body, wherever it might land. When I gave him the ball he held it to his eye, squinting. Or he cast it up, never looking where it went, then walked away. Now he can catch. Now he makes some kind of effort to toss it my way. Well, most days he makes an effort.

We wheel down the pavement on his tricycle, shout 'Duck!' at the mallards that crowd Regent's Park. I hold the swing seat, pressing my weight against the tension of the heavy chains, and say, 'Ready?'

'Ready, steady, GO!' says Daniel, and I release him so he flies.

On a bad day I feel like crap, looking for a switch that I can flip or something that will remove me from this life. When Daniel isn't talking or looking at anything, and none of the people I want to talk to return my messages. Everything is bad and my shoes don't fit. At the grocery store I am injuring myself by staring at the mothers with boys Daniel's age – boys who shoot sentences from their young mouths effortlessly, holding sophisticated negotiations with their mothers over such matters as how much chocolate they can buy. They seem to shine, these children. They seem covered in some sort of gloss that both protects them and attracts light. Meanwhile, Daniel slouches in the seat of the shopping trolley, staring blankly or pushing his tongue around and around the edges of his mouth until he forms a bright pink oval of skin beneath his lower lip. He might point and call out a word, but mostly he will remain silent until I speak to him, prodding him into conversation. It is as though he is one of those old-fashioned cars you have to crank into working. However, once he's talking he can say quite a bit. And these days he doesn't need to have a pack of chocolate biscuits just to stay seated. The strategy I learned from Andy was to feed him a huge meal before we went shopping, bring along chocolate biscuits that are gluten-free, and keep rewarding him for sitting in the trolley. It works – though it didn't the first time. The first time Daniel screamed so much that he made himself sick, then tried running away. Andy stopped him, so Daniel threw himself down on the floor, writhing and crying. All of this sent me into agony, but Andy just worked through it.

'We have the whole morning,' he reassured me, his voice measured, controlled. Somehow he even managed to grin. 'Forget everyone in the shop. It's just you and me and Daniel. Stay calm and we'll make it.'

I stayed calm. Daniel eventually slowed down his crying. Andy picked him up and walked him along the aisle by putting his feet under Daniel's feet and half carrying him, talking with him all the while. I put jam, eggs, a loaf of bread in the trolley, hardly noticing, as I watched Andy and Daniel ahead of me.

'Fantastic walking!' Andy said, even though it was Andy who was doing all the work. 'Keep going, mate!'

When Daniel began to walk himself, Andy turned his head and winked at me. Then he gave Daniel a biscuit. We managed five minutes like that, then left the shop without buying a thing.

'But you can't just leave a trolley with stuff in it like that!' I said, as we slipped out the door.

Andy laughed, thumped my arm. 'Oh, I think we can,' he said. He got out Daniel's favourite battery-operated Thomas train. 'Every day, maybe twice a day, until I see you next.'

'So when will I see you next?' I asked.

Now Daniel has new requests, more sophisticated, not to mention articulated.

'More trains,' he says, and it is a command, not a question.

But there is the increasing problem of my poverty. I'm wishing the cottage would sell – and fast – because Stephen thinks I am irresponsible with money. All these doctors' bills, homeopath bills, kinesiologist bills. OK, they might have been a waste of time, but how did I know before I tried? And certainly what we pay Andy is not a waste. He is as necessary as water, the heartbeat of Daniel's recovery. But Stephen won't give me any cash at all and is warning me about the credit card.

I'm running out of things to put through the free ads, through *Loot* and *AdTrader*, to pin up with a colourful 'FOR SALE' at the newsagents. And there are specialists I mean to see with Daniel.

Autism turns out to be an expensive condition. That is, if you treat it.

When Stephen finds out that I have taken up the carpets, sold his favourite chair, sold the antique maritime clock we once had on the mantel above the fireplace, the Persian rug we had beneath our glass coffee table (also gone), not to mention his collection of *Wisden Cricketers' Almanack*s, he looks like a fire that has been stoked and fed until it gathers its fury and comes at you, hissing. I think he may hit me. I've never stood in front of a person who is going to hit me, and I find it requires a mixture of courage, foolishness and quiet denial. Not unlike what it takes to try to help your autistic child, I note, stepping back as Stephen shouts.

'Well, this is what I get for marrying a crazy person!' His teeth flash as he yells. There's a scowl line like a dark canyon, separating his eyes. I see the veins in his neck, in his forehead. He seems to grow in height and breadth, all at once too big for this near empty room, which he moves through like a giant, swatting the air.

Strangely, selling all our possessions has little effect on me at all. It's not that our things held no value for me, only that value is relative. I will trade all these possessions for a few new words from Daniel. I am in a different market than the rest of the world.

'You can shout all you want. It doesn't touch me,' I tell Stephen.

He warns me that if I keep destroying our children's home he will expect them to come and stay with him, even though he has only a single large room with a kitchenette and even though Penelope is there.

And now it is my turn to explode.

'If you are issuing threats, I might remind you they have American passports,' I tell him. 'And that no judge in the land will give the father permission to extract his children from their mother to go live with his girlfriend!'

'Unless she has a psychiatric history,' he says. He's so quick, Stephen. He didn't go to business school without learning how to wield power. Didn't get whizzed through the ranks of management for nothing.

'There are no records,' I tell him. 'In fact, it is on record that I am *not* receiving psychiatric help. At Daniel's assessment the paediatrician *wrote it down*!'

'I have financial records,' counters Stephen.

'Would you listen to yourself, you fuck?' I say.

'Would you stop swearing?'

'Would you get out of my fucking house?'

Which he does, very quickly, without saying goodbye to the children who are in the garden now. Emily is there with her bucket and spade, sitting in the green plastic sandbox shaped as a frog. She is looking in the direction of the house, frowning beneath her straw sunhat, wondering no doubt what is going on inside, why her parents argue and never kiss any more, never make up.

On Fridays, to the last minute he is here, Andy works like a plough horse in a wet field. In his torn jeans, his chestnut hair all askew, he holds up a pad and writes furiously with a marker. He is all energy, bounding through the house chasing Daniel, who squeals and giggles and runs, his head turned to watch as Andy trails after him. Andy pretends to be a cruel diesel truck bent on attacking the innocent engine, Daniel, as he travels his branch line. With a cape and hat he is a conjuror of magic, able to make Daniel invisible for ever! Grabbing him round the middle, he hauls Daniel gently to the ground, tickling him until Daniel says, in the shattering high notes of a choirboy, 'Let go!'

And now they are off again.

In the middle of all this the phone rings. I am laughing as I answer it. I have so loved watching Daniel charging around the house with Andy that I've forgotten everything else for the moment.

But the phone call reminds me. It is Stephen. 'We shouldn't be arguing right now,' he says flatly.

Andy is standing in the living room with Stephen. He is wearing a Live 8 T-shirt and what my brother would call 'pickle' trousers – that is, army issue. Stephen, in a summer suit, is wilting in the heat. He takes off his jacket, rolls up his sleeves. He has left the office early for this, wants to learn what Andy does that works so well. I am very grateful.

'You have to make it fun, the zanier the better,' says Andy. 'So you hold the chocolate. When you call "Daniel!", he has to call "Daddy!"'

I can hardly believe we've gotten this far, to have Stephen actually taking instruction, but we have. It's a wonderful day, a day I ought to celebrate, except Stephen is again in a rotten mood. He's mad because I will not go to see the special school he has made an appointment with. I will not countenance putting Daniel in school at all. Any school. It's not that I think special schools are so terrible, only that we are busy with him now at home and he is learning so much. Eventually – if it is at all possible – I'd like Daniel to go to regular school, perhaps with an aide, someone there to help him. For some reason Stephen disagrees. And yet here he is, so perhaps there is hope.

'So remember,' says Andy, 'make it all seem like great fun. You hold the chocolate. When you call "Daniel!", he has to call "Daddy!"'

Stephen looks in Daniel's direction. 'Daniel,' he says. Then he coughs.

'OK, er . . .' says Andy to Stephen. 'The tone is, may I say it, a little businesslike. Probably because you've just come from the office. Put a little . . . uh . . . joy into your voice. You know, like you've got a great surprise for him.'

Stephen nods, then squares his shoulders. 'Daniel!' he calls.

'Definitely better,' says Andy. 'But if I'm terribly honest, Stephen, you sound a little cross when you say it that way. Try this: "Daaaaanieeeeel!"'

'Oh, I get it now,' Stephen says. He takes a few steps closer to us in the garden and says, 'Daaaaanieeel!' in a sing-song voice, loud and clear.

I am sitting on the bench with Daniel. When Stephen calls his name I say, 'Daddy!' which Daniel will repeat. 'Daddy!' he says, and now Stephen brings him the chocolate.

'A little faster on the chocolate,' I tell Stephen, 'so that he connects the reward with what he has done, which is to answer his name.'

'Oh, for fucksake,' he says.

Striding toward us now is Andy. 'Brilliant, the both of you,' he says. 'Not to mention our little star here.'

He kisses Daniel's hair while Stephen frowns.

Because I am so broke, I ask my brother to please-please-please lend me some money. My brother is not concerned about pollution, has no nagging conscience about the environment, is not interested in green issues of international importance. He has established what he calls a 'Vice Fund', which is to say he pours all his money into companies that produce cigarettes, alcohol, gambling casinos, weapons. He's a jerk but not poor. His investment slogan is 'Bet on vice to win, place or show'.

'It's all tied up,' he explains to me. 'And anyway, money isn't going to help you.'

Of course. Why do I bother asking him? He thinks autism is incurable and hopeless, like everyone else. And anyway, he lacks empathy, a condition Daniel is supposed to have, but does not. If someone cries, Daniel cries. It's almost as though he has too much empathy. So I try to keep Emily from ever crying by plying her with sweets. If I feel a tear coming on, I run to the sink to splash water on my face. Meanwhile, my brother who is, I suppose, perfectly normal – this man who lives with shouting parrots and believes with all his heart that no matter how bad the economy is people will still buy everything they need to kill themselves – says he has no money to help out his only nephew.

However, one night I get a call from Larry. This is most unusual because he is too cheap to phone overseas. He tells me that the Chinese, due to a shortage of grain, have decided to save their grain by killing all their sparrows. Something he has heard about or read or perhaps been notified about through one of the millions of user groups he's on. He calls while I am reading a story to Daniel, or trying to read it. Keeping him still is the first part.

'What?' I say.

Larry says nothing.

'What?' I say again. All I hear is miles of empty silence.

Larry says, 'I can't tell you. I'm speechless. I don't have words to describe . . . language doesn't have the capacity to hold the depths of . . . *what is it?* Anger, frustration, shock, a feeling of *intense* betrayal . . .'

'You're doing very well, actually, but *why* do you feel like that?' I ask. Has Wanda left him? Has a parrot amputated his ear?

'Birds,' he says. 'Are. Being. Gassed.'

We sit in a circle and I say, 'Mummy!' Andy says, 'Andy!' Daniel says, 'Daniel!'

'You *are* Daniel!' I say, tickling him, delighted, laughing, proud of him in a way you cannot know unless you've lived with a child who cannot say his own name at three years old, and at times during those years seemed to have no identity at all.

But Andy shakes his head violently, telling me to stop. 'Don't use pronouns. He's not ready for pronouns.'

'OK,' I say, committing this information to memory as I do everything Andy says. 'I won't do it again.'

He begins to speak again, then stops, touches my shoulder. His eyes hold a tenderness that makes me turn away. 'Don't worry so much,' he whispers.

'Andy!'

'Mummy!'

'Daniel!'

Later, I ask if I can try to teach Daniel to say 'I am Daniel'.

'You can try,' says Andy. He's lying on the floor catching his breath after a particularly taxing session during which he had to fly Daniel around in the blue plastic child's chair again. 'But he's got to get two words together solidly before he will get three.'

I nod, standing above him. He puts his hand out; I take it and he rises up. For a moment we remain there, standing hand in hand. His fingers are warm in mine. His eyes are the colour of sage. Emily is drawing a picture of Donald Duck, which Daniel notices. 'Duck,' he says, which makes Andy wheel round and congratulate him.

'Donald Duck!' says Andy.

'Duck!' says Daniel.

'*Donald* Duck!' says Andy slowly.

'Donna Duck,' says Daniel. Andy takes him by the hands and whirls him around.

'What about me?' says Emily, holding out her arms. I clasp her wrists and twirl her as she laughs, my little girl, my pal.

With so little furniture in the downstairs of our house,

there is more room for toys and games and tossing children into the air.

The speech therapist is even bigger this time, her belly hanging on her like a cannon ball she's slung onto her waist. I've come back because she told me if Daniel could speak – even a few words – she would work with him. But all I can think about since coming into the office is how pregnant she is. I keep staring at her belly, at her hand that lingers there, at her swollen ankles, her jolly, expectant shape.

'When is the baby due?' I ask.

'Two months,' is her shocking reply. I was thinking she might go into labour any second. It crosses my mind that she might be having twins. She notices my wide-eyed silence, glancing down at her bump. 'This is number four,' she says. 'When you get to number four the muscles collapse the minute you read the pregnancy test. If they see a dot, they just give up and dive toward your shoes.'

I nod, jealous as hell of this big woman, who for some reason I imagine with a burly, bearded husband, and all her children just perfect. I would love to be pregnant again, to feel the soft kicking, to lie in bed and hold the edges of my belly, feeling for my baby, counting the weeks.

On a red yoga mat, pushing his train along the edge of the mat, is Daniel. The speech therapist heaves the copious folds of her skirt around her and kneels down next to him. 'Hi there, Daniel,' she says in cheerful American parlance. 'How're you doing?'

Already I am thinking she is using too much language. Saying 'Hi' would have been enough. With so much dialogue to take in, Daniel ignores her, preferring his train.

'So you got a train there, that's pretty neat,' says the speech therapist. Still Daniel will not reply.

'Do you mind if I just show you?' I say gently. 'Just to give you some idea of what he can do if he sets his mind to it?'

The speech therapist is not so sure. She pulls off her eyeglasses and rubs her forehead with the back of her hand. 'All right,' she agrees. She has a mask of freckles across each cheek the same way I did when I was pregnant. And her fingers are a little swollen – yes, I remember that, too. She says, 'But I still think we're wasting our time here.'

I go to the mat, sit down next to Daniel, and stare hard at Thomas, the train. Then I take two fingers, and walk them up Daniel's leg, opening my mouth as though I am astonished at what these naughty fingers are doing, walking up his leg! Walking across his stomach! And now they are tickling him! When he looks at me I retreat, pretend I wasn't even involved with this tickling business. Then I start again, slowly walking my fingers up his calf, his thigh. This time he's ready for it. Before I tickle his tummy, he shoots his attention my way. 'Hi, Daniel,' I say.

'Hi, Mummy,' says Daniel.

I start singing the tune to *Thomas the Tank Engine*. 'Thomas the Tank Engine . . .' I sing, and nod my head quickly, indicating he must continue.

'Rolling along,' says Daniel.

'Rolling along!' I sing.

'Rolling along!'

The speech therapist watches this, a look on her face that tells me my ideas are not welcome here.

'Daniel, how old are you?' she asks. He doesn't answer. He's watching my fingers, which may at any second shoot up his leg to tickle him on the belly once more.

I say, 'I am twenty-nine!'

Daniel says, 'I am three!'

He holds his hand up, trying to get three fingers to stick up in the air, which he cannot manage.

'Good boy!' I say, and help him with his fingers so he's got three pointing up, his thumb and little finger bending across his palm.

'I don't think you quite understand how to be a speech therapist,' says the speech therapist, a woman whose three children smile from a photo on her desk, and whose fourth child sits quietly inside her. 'You seem to be playing tricks on him to get him to speak.'

Playing tricks? I don't understand.

'Daniel, what is your favourite toy? Is it that train? What's the train called?' she says.

Three questions all at once. He cannot cope. He doesn't know which one to answer and which ones to leave.

'I cannot teach this child,' says the speech therapist. On that we both agree.

I want to see an eighty-pound-per-hour occupational therapist because the NHS has nobody available and Daniel needs help with his vestibular system, whatever that is. There is a ninety-pound orthopaedic surgeon I want to check out because Daniel seems to find it difficult to walk for any distance. Then there is the fifty-pound podiatrist who may or may not have some kind of orthotic sole for Daniel's shoes that will discourage Daniel from walking on his toes all the time. Plus I want to see this rather clever doctor who suggested the gluten-free diet and says that sugar is extremely bad for autistic children.

'What do you want to use for primary reinforcers,

then?' asks Andy when I tell him that we can't use Smarties any more to motivate Daniel. If he were an Englishman he'd give me a look of exasperation, but because he's Irish he looks amused, interested, wants to hear all about my new-found suspicion that sugar is like heroin for autistic kids.

'I don't know,' is my honest reply. I am out of answers.

This morning, while Andy works with Daniel, I take the train to Hatton Garden to hock my engagement ring, a square diamond set in white gold. It's a day full of the liveliness of spring. Around me are couples heady with the thought of their own impending weddings, old ladies whose gnarled hands are stocked with gold and stones, tourists looking for bargains. It is not hard to find what you are looking for in Hatton Garden. Even the pawn shops are easily identified, distinguished by the age-old sign: three brass balls hanging above the door.

What I think about as the jeweller examines my ring with his circular eyeglass is not what it means to lose my lover, my husband, the man onto whom I hung every hope, but that I am damned glad I didn't let Stephen give me that ring his mother had. If I'd taken the sapphire and diamond she offered, one that has been in the family for many generations, I'd have had to give it back.

The jeweller is not so impressed with my ring. He tips the spyglass up from his eye, purses his lips, and makes me an offer which I am forced to accept. It's the best one I've had this morning, and I've been up and down this road. I am cross with myself, however. I should have brought the pearl necklace as well.

And now I go home to make my phone calls, set up the appointments, continue with my life.

*   *   *

'You don't have any beer, do you?' asks Andy. Friday. 4 p.m. He's been worn to a frazzle trying to get Daniel and Emily to play hide-and-seek together. It involves me hiding with Emily, and Daniel being guided by Andy to find us. If he finds us he gets the reward we hold in our hand, a bit of chocolate that must be gluten-free, sugar-free and dairy-free and can only be purchased in specialty shops, of which I have now become an expert. I know three different places you can buy such chocolate within a half-mile of my house.

I shake my head. 'No money for beer. Anyway, it makes you fat.'

'Fat you are not, Mrs Marsh. And yes, I have noticed things keep disappearing round here,' he says. In the place we used to have Stephen's armchair Emily and I have put a new papier mâché chair, drying now on newsprint beside an open window.

'If you took credit cards this would be easier,' I say. 'He's not yet cancelled my Visa, which is how we eat. Stephen's strategy, I believe, is to starve me of money so that I file for divorce. Some clever lawyer must have suggested it. If I file, then we have to start negotiating. I'll have to compromise, set in writing his rights of access to the children, for example. Right now he doesn't really have any rights, you see.'

'And you don't have any money,' says Andy. He takes my left hand and studies my fingers. In the spot beside my wedding ring, in the place where the engagement ring used to be, is a waxy-looking circle of pale skin.

'Oh, he's a sly one,' says Andy, smiling, still holding my hand. 'Why don't you do the right thing then, and make an honest man out of him?'

'What? Divorce him?' I laugh. It's how I cope, turning it all into a joke. 'Why should I be so nice?'

'Oh, you're tough,' says Andy, his finger pointed at me. 'I have to admit I like a tough woman.'

The next week Andy arrives with three bags of groceries, an electronic children's book that sounds out the words when you press it with a special tool, and a case of Guinness in bottles.

'Don't you put those things in my cupboard, Andy. I don't need them!'

'I should say you don't, Mrs Marsh! Look over there at the candelabra on your mantelpiece. You could melt it down to an ingot, you could! And what about the fireplace surround? Architectural salvage will have it, I'm sure! Don't forget all the brass on your door handles, Mrs Marsh. Surely they'll fetch a few bob.'

And God, isn't this pathetic. I actually think he's got a point. That candelabra is probably *silver*.

I go to the counter where he is unloading the shopping, humming a tune as he sets out each item. He looks so natural in my house, as though he belongs. But I grab his wrist and shake my head no. 'Under no circumstances are you to bring food or drink into my house,' I say.

He cocks his head, looks at my hand on his wrist, smiles brazenly. 'This beer here is top dollar, Mrs Marsh, and you might like to have some to make you relax a bit, if you don't mind me saying.'

'Stop calling me Mrs Marsh,' I say, trying to hold on to my small petal of anger, trying not to let the great weight of Andy's generosity squash it. In the wake of such unasked-for kindness I find myself unsure what to do. I want to thank him, but then, at the same time I am struggling to hinder the mild annoyance – no, the embarrassment – I feel for appearing to require the charity of another.

'You know what you need here?' says Andy. He steps toward me, scoops his hand under my chin, holds it there. 'You know what you need other than your husband, Mrs Marsh? You need a friend or two, do you know?'

I say nothing. I look down.

'Have I made a mistake bringing you something nice, then?' he asks. He has not made a mistake. I feel drawn to him, with his hair going every which way, with his sweatshirt frayed at the sleeves, his faded collar. He has probably skipped lunch to bring me these things. He says he's my age, but he doesn't look more than nineteen. He says he wants to be my friend, but I'm not sure I have any room in my heart right now. Still, he hasn't made a mistake, no.

'Andy, I like you. But don't be an eejit,' I say, a word I know means 'idiot' but that Andy uses affectionately, in the same tone I'm using it now. It's one of those Irish things he does, like rolling his own cigarettes, which he smokes in our garden beside the pond that I've bound in wire and ruined for the birds.

'Would you kiss me, Melanie?' he asks. His voice is music, his eyes are soft, loamy. 'If I was ever so quick about it? Would you let me?' he says.

There is nothing I would like more. Now that it's a possibility, now that he's said it. 'Not in front of the children,' I whisper.

16

Daniel is three and a half and the Local Education Authority are asking – rather insisting – that I register him with a nursery school for children with special needs so that he has a place for when he is four. I cannot help but think Stephen is behind this.

'It will free up some time for *you*,' says a lady with her eyeglasses on a chain round her neck, her hand-knit cardigan floppy around her sinking bosom, her sleeves extending untidily over her arthritic wrists. They have sent this sweet, motherly lady to pat my hand and tell me what a good job I've done for Daniel, but also to suggest that denying him access to other children now, at this critical point in his life, may actually weaken his chances of assimilating into a classroom.

'We are all thinking of what is best for him,' she says. 'For Daniel.'

But I don't want to put him in a classroom. What is so great about a classroom anyway? It holds no magic. How will it help him, to be with children whose behaviour is abnormal? It's not as though these children look at each other and say, 'Oh, I see you have special needs like me. Let's be friends.' All he will do is imitate children who aren't acting like ordinary children in the first place. I've spent six months teaching him how to imitate and now they want his role models to be children who are not able to attend regular school themselves?

'Some of the children will be even more able than he is right now,' the LEA lady assures me. She speaks in a low, careful, kind manner, as though to a frightened dog. Come to me, she seems to say to the dog: here, girl.

'No,' I say. It seems to me that he hasn't even had a chance yet. Why won't they let me give him a chance?

'You do realise he needs, and will *always* need, very skilled practitioners?'

'No.'

'And we will accommodate the dietary requests you have stipulated. No gluten, that's fine. And you'll provide his special milk?'

'No.'

'Mrs Marsh, I believe you are making a mistake,' she says, but she says it kindly, in a tone that suggests it pains her to see me decide upon something so irrational, so detrimental to my son and myself. 'We have specialists,' she assures me. 'You wouldn't have to pay for speech therapy any more. There's a speech therapist on site.'

But I know all about specialists. I've seen neurologists, paediatricians, orthopaedic surgeons, podiatrists, ophthalmologists, gastroenterologists, speech therapists, music therapists, homeopaths, craniosacral therapists, and every whacked-out practitioner of alternative medicine you can find in this city – and I mean to tell you there are many. Some were mildly helpful, some were no help at all. None of them believes Daniel will ever go to a normal school or lead a normal life.

Except Andy O'Connor, with his notebooks and his charts indicating where we are on Daniel's developmental profile and where we ought to be. He won't take any more money from me now. Says he can't – it would kill him. It turns out that he usually ends up doing most of his work for a greatly reduced fee when people run out of money. There's a guy in Acton living in a tiny flat with no garden. Wife walked out, child with severe autism. Andy didn't even charge him the first time, let alone the hundredth. But the people in Holland Park get the full whack. It's a kind of sliding fee scale, not what you'd expect, and done rather ad hoc, it would seem.

'I'll pay you as soon as I have the money from the cottage,' I told him.

He said, 'Don't even talk about it.'

And he's the only one who was worth his fee.

'When are we going to see Daddy?' says Emily. It's Saturday. She's learned the days of the week by figuring out which days she sees her father and which days she does not. I find this fact of her development almost too terrible to take in. That she doesn't seem to think of Stephen at all on the days he isn't here is equally terrible.

'After breakfast,' I tell her. She's crawled into my bed, her head on my shoulder. Beside us is Daniel, opening and closing his fingers in front of his eyes.

'What's he doing?' Emily says. She climbs over my chest and stares hard at her brother. 'Daniel, *what* are you doing?'

Daniel doesn't answer.

'Daniel,' I tell him, 'say, "I'm playing."'

'I'm playing,' he repeats.

'What are you doing?' I ask him.

'I'm playing,' he says.

It's seven in the morning, but therapy turns out to be an all-day kind of thing. I will give him pudding without a spoon so he has to ask for the spoon in order to eat it. I will make out that I'm putting his shirt on like trousers so he has to say, 'That's not right!' I'll put a sock on my nose, an uncut apple between two slices of bread. 'No, Mummy,' Daniel will say. He speaks because he must, using the language we have taught him, one prized word at a time. His words are like water to a parched throat, I drink them in and am satisfied.

'What's he pretending?' Emily asks now.

God knows. I don't like to think. 'That dust particles are spaceships,' I tell Emily, because I know this will please her.

'See Daddy,' says Daniel.

I am astonished.

'That's right!' I say. 'You will see Daddy! Later today. This morning!'

'Good talking!' says Emily. I look into Emily's face and she smiles at me, really beams, and I don't know if it's because she is going to see her father today or because Daniel is speaking to us. But anyway, she's happy and so am I. I can't wait to tell Andy how Daniel spontaneously spoke of an event in the future, one that he had to anticipate. This is the sort of sophistication of language I've dreamt he might have some day. Of course Andy won't be surprised. 'Have faith,' he'll say. 'Your little boy is smarter than you think.'

Whenever I get the children ready to see Stephen, it is as though I am preparing them for an audition. First I iron their clothes, then I brush their hair. Then I make sure their fingernails are clean, their faces scrubbed, their shoes free of mud. I make sure they eat a big breakfast, that they don't need the toilet, that they are in the right frame of mind. No sulkiness or hyperactivity. No complaining – I've taken care of whatever is required. I pack a little bag with a few toys, some snacks and drinks, sunhats or raincoats, depending on the weather. We meet at the playground and I hand over my children, all perfectly presented. Emily runs to him, holding the corners of drawings she's made. They flap in the breeze, showing colours all the way to the edges. Her best work, the ones for Daddy. It seems to me this habit she has of only showing him what she does best is an ominous sign for the future. How can I stop my little girl from trying too hard for men? How can I show her that the best thing she can ever do is be herself, full of rough edges and the complex logic that is her own?

'Don't trip!' I call to her as she takes off like a gazelle, running to her father's open arms. Don't risk yourself. Don't forget how priceless you are, just as you are. 'Don't run too fast!' I say.

But she doesn't hear me, cannot hear me. Stephen is standing with his arms outstretched, his knees bent, his raincoat trailing on the grass. He is promising her his whole person, every inch of him, right down to his shoes. She cannot turn her attention now from him. And this, I'm afraid, I understand all too well.

Stephen told me on occasion all the little things he thought weren't quite right about me. I swore too much, wore the wrong kind of perfume and needed to do something to get my hair up off my face. When I protested that the perfume was what he bought me, that my hair would never stay entirely off my face as it was two feet long and very fine, such that it slid out of a hair clip no matter what, he sighed. There was also the matter of my American clothes – those annoyed him. He didn't think leather should be any colour other than black or brown, so my lemon-yellow bag with lots of brass buckles was out. He had a problem with dresses that were too short, telling me I looked like Wilma Flintstone in my gauzy summer skirt with a varied yoke. He particularly hated clothes that suggested a Pacific influence or anything with a decorative border. My favourite suede, cowboy-style jacket with a Western fringe was regarded as a kind of relic that needed quiet removal, and he managed not only to persuade me to get rid of it, but to do so unasked. Nothing is so powerful as the English understatement. Wordlessly, it seemed, he'd transformed me, never reducing me to the point of wearing grey skirts with floral patterns, but I found myself looking for more sensible shoes and rather more dowdy colours at Marks & Spencer's, rather than what I'd have preferred to buy, found only in places like Ghost.

I realise upon reflection that it wasn't that Stephen had a problem with my clothes, but rather a problem with my accent, my class, or lack thereof. I think it was a matter of identity. Unlike Penelope, with her trained musical ear, he couldn't quite place me in a particular stratum, and that disarmed him. Penelope, it seemed, could get away with bizarre, unusual clothes – animal-print skirts and clinging chiffon that made you wonder if she was wearing any underwear – but then she was a cousin to the Huxleys and the daughter of a dame. She was *who* she was, regardless of her attire. By contrast, I was nothing. I'd rather fooled him by appearing a serious student, situated as I was at Oxford. But when my mother died, when Marcus died, all I really wanted was a family.

'Well, you have a fair start here,' says Andy, nodding at the children, who are watching a *Spot* video. We are sitting behind them, whispering our conversation as they watch the video on cushions we've placed on the floor. It's sort of like a date, his being here. And sort of like he belongs here anyway.

'You come from a big family?' I ask.

'Not so big,' says Andy. 'I'm number four.'

'That's nice,' I say. 'Four.'

'Of eight,' says Andy. 'There's my three small sisters and one wee brother.'

It is time I got up and did something useful, put away the dishes, do some washing. I cannot remember sitting down for so long. But then, just as I have this thought, I feel Andy's hand on mine. He takes my wrist, turns it over and kisses my palm, watching my eyes as he does so. Then he lets go, touches his finger to my lips, then his own. It is as though he has placed a message inside me, spelling out desire. He will wait for me to turn to him, knows that I will move slowly in his direction, changing as the seasons change. His love lies before me like the new pages of a diary. One day he will fold me in his arms, for he has touched a part of me that was dying and brought it to life once more. This belongs to him.

When I was at university I studied poetry, among other things. It fascinated me how the words looked so dry and lifeless, like seed husks or stringy bits of cut grass, sitting on the page. Almost lonely they were, starkly articulated against a whole page of white. And yet when I read them, they came alive inside my mind. I liked to hear the words in my head, flowing through me in a melody that is not exactly sung. If I read a poem now, for example, I find myself reading a stanza, then turning away from the printed page, listening.

> There are ribbons that hold you together,
> Hooks and eyes, hollows at the collarbone,
>
> As though you dismantle your skeleton
> Before stepping out of the crumpled ring.

I am listening with my eyes turned away, hearing the words, thinking of my own thin frame, my own wedding ring, which I now remove. I should have sold it when I sold my engagement ring, but it's hardly worth much, being just a gold band. And now I am thinking something else, about autism. Autism, of course, because the subject is never far from my mind, hovering as it does at the edge of every thought, squatting on my shoulder like a hideous second head.

I consider that this listening and turning away that I do when reading poetry is because I cannot truly glean the words while staring directly at them. I must consider them in quiet, and so I cast my gaze away from the page. Perhaps this is what Daniel does when he turns away from me as I speak. He cannot hear and look at the same time. He must choose.

So I stop asking him to both listen to me and look at me, which I can see pains him in a mild way, as though staring into a bright light. I think I understand. I promise him, kneeling before my child of three, that I will let him be Daniel, and that I will let him turn away.

With his eyes focused over my left shoulder, he asks for new shoes.

'I want buckle shoes,' he says. Four words together – this is unprecedented. With his eyes toward the ceiling he says, 'I want shoes with buckles.' And now five.

Alone in the living room, drinking the Guinness that Andy left me from its heavy amber bottle, I hold my face still in front of the hand mirror we use to encourage Daniel to make certain facial expressions, or to help him get his mouth into the right shape to create a particular sound. I can see now that my hair is getting thicker, my skin gaining in colour. Every Saturday morning while Stephen takes the children to the park, I go to the pastry shop and they give me a little sack containing the home-made tomato sauce Max's wife has made for me, this woman whom I have never even met. I heap as much sauce as I can on to Daniel's gluten-free pasta, but he is suspicious of it, refusing as he does to eat vegetables. Somehow he knows tomatoes are involved with this sauce, and he eyes the specks of basil with disdain.

'Burger,' he says. He always wants burgers.

'I want a burger,' I say, because if he's going to get what he wants, he's going to have to use as many words as possible to get it.

'I want a burger,' says Daniel.

Pretending I don't understand, I say, 'What do you want?'

Daniel says, 'I want a burger.' So I make him a burger.

Meanwhile, Emily and I gorge ourselves on ravioli so large and rich you can only eat two of them at a sitting, lapping up the sauce that is made with tomatoes so sweet you could drink this sauce and call it dessert.

'Sauce?' I offer Daniel.

'No sauce,' he shakes his head. He understands negatives now, and he pronounces his 'no' with an Irish accent.

'You love *him* more,' says Emily. 'You'd never make me a burger.'

'You didn't ask,' I tell her. 'Would you like me to make you a burger?'

'No, thank you,' smiles Emily. 'I prefer ravioli.'

Emily's accent is like her father's. She will fit into her pre-prep without any difficulty whatsoever, but thank God for these summer holidays we have, during which she is all mine, and I am hers.

'You *do* know how much I love you, Emily?' I say now.

'Yeah,' she says, bored already of the subject.

'And I love you, Daniel, you know that?' I say, leaning toward him. He looks at me for a split second, then away, then back again. But he doesn't speak.

One morning I wake with a terrible backache and I don't know why. The pain is familiar, exhausting, a cramp that seizes me so that I long for a hot bath. When I take off my clothes I realise my periods have started again, and that I haven't had one in almost a year, and that I have gained weight. I am healthy once more.

I phone Veena to tell her that I am well, that I am not starving at all. That Daniel is talking, little by little. That I am alive, alive, alive!

But there's no one by that name at this number. And no, they don't know where Veena has gone. It has been months since I thought of her, since I spoke to her. I collapse onto the floor, realising I have let go of this precious friend. She is shy, thinks people do not like her, fears that her accent and her foreignness make her unwelcome. She would

never have rung me, and must have concluded that I had
no use for her except as a cleaner. How do I tell her it
wasn't the cleaning that I valued? With no forwarding
number and only a dim recollection of how to spell her
complicated surname, how in this blasted city do I find a
lone Indian woman?

Here is Bruno Bettelheim, heavy mouth, aged half-moon
eyes, balding, weak chin. He has tortoiseshell glasses and
an accent I cannot place. 'I said I was sorry. Why blame
me now?' he asks.

I know I am dreaming, but it feels so real. He is a small
man but fierce and quick. The lenses in his glasses are so
thick you cannot tell where exactly he focuses his eyes.
He nods his head as he speaks, as though punctuating
each word.

'I *killed* myself. Isn't that enough? Why do you hound
me? I am no criminal!' he says, spitting the words. Like
a cornered toothless animal, like an assailant who has
been caught and has no weapon now.

When I wake from this dream I find, to my surprise,
that it doesn't frighten me.

17

I can no longer go into a shop and buy whatever the children need. That ended some while ago. I find myself fanatically recapping Emily's markers so that they won't dry out, buying the children clothes that are too big for them so there is more room for growth, hoping they won't need new shoes. When Emily goes on her painting sprees, covering her model animals with poster paint, I find myself watching with a measure of resentment the paint she wastes, and trying in vain to pour it back into a bottle that, because of a design flaw in the packaging, makes this impossible. I hate myself for caring about such small matters – for noticing, even – the wasted paper and broken crayons. And for hurrying Emily past the toy shop lest she should see something she wants, meanwhile buying whatever Daniel needs to help him speak and learn.

The one buyer I had on the cottage pulled out after the survey, and Stephen continues to make it impossible for me. He gives me no cash at all. He says we need to talk – and I know what that means – and he says that he still thinks Daniel should be in special school, which I refuse.

So he punishes me. I cut the children's hair to save money on a hairdresser, can't use the credit card past a certain limit. Stephen is right that I shouldn't need to spend so much each week on groceries, but I am buying organic fruit, raw goat's cheese, goat's butter and grass-fed beef. These are all extremely upmarket items; and then there are all the supplements I need, which have to be specially ordered so they contain no harmful fillers. Daniel's chocolate costs five times what normal chocolate costs; I will not let him eat normal bread, only gluten-free bread which is four pounds a loaf unless I make it myself, which I often do, but even then you are talking about organic eggs at thirty pence a yolk.

Even though there are times I hate him, I do not stop wishing he would return. For Emily's sake, I wish this. For Daniel's, too. Stephen is their father and so I feel I owe it to them to dress him in a robe of benevolence that does not quite suit him now. It is a deliberate action, this reworking of my husband, who will not allow me to call him at his flat, but requires me instead to ring his office or text his mobile. Unless it is an emergency, he has stipulated. He grunts when I tell him that the whole of the past six months has been an emergency. He makes the same face I've seen him use to dismiss a blundering waiter or to instruct the chattering cab driver that he does not wish to talk.

'What do you remember about me that you loved?' I ask him now, meeting him at the Princess Diana Memorial Playground with its impressive ship. The ship, angled to one side and sunk into a bed of sand, is not a real ship of course but an elaborate toy for children. Arriving with Daniel and Emily, I had the thought that our lives had become a little like that ship that will never experience the sea, a kind of marvellous pretend family in a wonderland of the imagination. Looking at us, we appear happy, united. Wouldn't you think so? See the tall man with the loose shirt and crisp khaki trousers beside the woman with the light hair and a summer dress that flows down to her ankles? See their children who play in Hyde Park on a summer's day? Aren't they lovely together? But it's all a trick of the eye. When I ask Stephen what he remembers about me, what he loved about me, what he cherished, he only turns away, distancing himself even more on this wooden bench we share.

So I speak.

'I remember how you tipped an amber bottle and filled your palms with the smell of almonds, then pressed them into my back so that the whole room smelled like an orchard,' I tell him. 'And how when you finished making love it was almost as though you were going to start all over again, those shy kisses, those delicate hands. On Sundays you brought me a mug of tea, the newspaper that of course I would never read. But you read it to me, the bits you thought I ought to know.'

'What are you doing?' he says, his voice sounding as though I've touched some private part of him to which I am no longer allowed access.

'I'm remembering how you swung me round at that party where we met and said, "If you think you're leaving without me, you're kidding." I'm remembering how whenever I took a journey longer than five miles you made me promise I'd call you to tell you I was all right. I'm recalling, not without pleasure, how you watched your children being born.'

'Stop it,' says Stephen. He blinks his eyes rapidly, as though having entered a room full of dust. He turns away, his back hunched. He does not want to hear.

'Stephen, I guess I'm saying that if there is any chance whatsoever that you want me back in your life and your bed, then you better tell me now. Because I'm done scraping myself up against you, and I'm tired of being so poor.'

Across the playground, Daniel chases a starling. Emily climbs the rope ladder of the pirate ship, calling 'Ahoy, matey!' She is not a convincing pirate, dressed as she is in lime-green overalls. Tied to her wrist is a gaudy balloon, shaped as a pink pony.

Stephen reaches behind his back, touches my fingers, and it is as though he has stretched back in time and plucked fruit from last year's withered tree. 'Don't let us go,' I whisper as he removes his hand once more.

'I can't see how we can fit back together,' he says. 'I feel like what's happened to Daniel has just blown us apart for ever. And you are so unwilling to do anything about it.'

'*What?*' I say. 'I am doing *everything* about it! What are *you* doing about it?'

Stephen glowers. I have violated the sacred code to winning his favour, which is never to criticise him. If there is anyone who requires criticism, it is me. Can't I see that?

'He needs special school,' Stephen says. 'The experts all say so.'

'He's learning by the minute. I don't care about these so-called experts. What makes them experts anyway? You can have all the degrees you like, but if you can't help the child talk and play, you're not much of an expert in my view.'

'He'll never be normal,' says Stephen. 'I think we're going to have to accept that. I'll be honest with you, Melanie, I find it hard to live with that fact so up close, all the time. I don't want to.'

Poor Daniel. It seems he must not only struggle to understand a world that, to him, is defiantly elusive, but put back together a grown man's heart. No, he will never be like Emily, who dropped into the world as though she owned it and is always three steps ahead of anyone's expectations. But then he is doing infinitely better than these 'experts' ever imagined. Surely there is hope in that. I say, 'OK, I understand what you are saying. But there are plenty of couples with a child who is autistic. They make it somehow. Maybe we should meet some of them –'

'No,' says Stephen, firmly. He shakes his head back and forth, blows out his cheeks.

From far off, Daniel searches for us, his head like a periscope, turning. I raise my hand and wave.

Stephen says, 'I don't *want* lots of friends with wonky children. I don't want to live in that world. That is not in the plan.'

'*What* plan?' I say.

'You see!' says Stephen, as though that settles it. He rises from the bench, stands over me, a big and commanding man. He does not need to raise his voice to make me think that he is shouting. He *is* shouting, in that he is presenting his thoughts as one might dispatch a warhead. '*This* is what I mean!' he says. 'You can't understand why I might not want to spend my time around people with damaged children. Well, I don't! It's not how I want to live my life, do you understand? It's depressing and hopeless and unattractive. Call me selfish, call me wrong, call me politically incorrect, non-inclusive, uncaring! Call me any crap name you want, but don't call *that* my life!'

'I'm not calling you names,' I say.

'This isn't my fault!' he says. 'It's just the way it is.'

I want to explain to him that he cannot run, and that

there is in any case no point in trying to run. He can no more contain his love for Daniel than alter the flow of blood to his own heart. If I could, I would hold him in my arms and promise him, swear to him, that I will shield him from this hurt with every ounce of strength from my body. I have been given tools to help control the way autism has seized our son. Six months ago Daniel would have come to a playground like this, plopped down on the ground, scooped up sand and let it flow in front of his eyes for hours without any thought of other people around him, of swings or slides or ships that allow for the playful reverie of pirating. But Stephen will not hear this, and has his own invented notion of how things will be in the future. I cannot reach him, though he allows me to touch his arm, to speak softly to him. I say, 'Look across the sand right now, Stephen, and you will see your little boy.'

There, beside the giant pirate ship, Daniel waves.

So now, when the doorbell rings, I think it must be him. Who else would come to my door at ten at night? There ignites inside me a fire of hope, a terrible longing. I fan it by racing for the door, step into the flame itself as I turn the handle.

Then I stop. I think to myself that the Stephen I knew and loved is not exactly the Stephen of today. Or rather, that I have experienced what it feels like to be the object of his scorn and that I will never quite forget that feeling. I think of Jacob, who claims his son can feel the hate upon his back when he walks in certain sections of the city. In Cornwall he'd almost been driven mad by the slightly paranoid, possibly accurate feeling that the people who gave him a bed and breakfast felt he was somehow unclean. As though his blackness might rub off on the furnishings, change the composition of the air in the rooms. I have felt a similar feeling – as though I am considered a contaminant – from my own husband. He blames me for Daniel's condition, not with the fury of Bettelheim, but with the quiet resentment of a punter who feels he's bet on a bad mare. My genetic failing is evident to him. There have been no cases of autism in the entirety of the Marsh family tree.

And so I open the door slowly, with a heaviness inside me; I don't want to seem too eager to see him. I wish it would be Andy with his cocky smile, suggesting we have a little chat now that the children are asleep. 'Five minutes just to sit with you,' he'd say, brushing past me before I had time to object. But instead there is a figure sitting on the stone steps, her hair loose and dark, the colour of the ocean at night, reflecting light in all directions. What worries me is that her fingers hide her eyes. And when she rises it is with the stiff, fragile gait of an accident victim, her cloth bag hanging on her shoulder, its strap tangled with her hair.

'Veena,' I say. She does not talk, but clasps my arm. We walk inside slowly, holding on to each other.

18

When Stephen left, it was like an emptying out of my life, of all our years together. It was as though where once there had been the essential everyday tools of living – cutlery and scissors, car keys and batteries – there was now an empty drawer. But then I discovered something. It seemed there lay buried inside me a different person than the one who had been living with Stephen. Perhaps, through some subtle sleight of hand, love affairs alter you, displace you, transform you into a kind of alternative person. Andy would say they left their mark. The person I had been with Stephen was similar but not identical to the person I became after he left. My yearning for Stephen, my desire to keep him situated here in this home with our children, did not begin with his disappearance. From the start of our marriage it was always me waiting for him: waiting for him to return from work, or return my phone call, or return to bed. I was always struggling to gain his favour – wearing the correct articles of clothing, brushing up on current affairs, changing a word or phrase that had been mine since childhood – no longer calling trousers 'pants', for example. There is that word, 'couple', which can mean to be yoked together, as when hounds are coupled during hunting. In the case of Stephen and me, we were coupled, but he was always slightly ahead of me. I tagged behind, willing him to slow down and wait for me, and not to call it waiting, but call it love.

I tell Veena that perhaps it was the same with her man who has left her now, or rather, whom she has left.

'I thought American men were polite always,' she says, slumped in the chair, head in her arms, her hair spilling over the knotted pine of the table, the rush mat of the seat.

I shake my head. 'They vary,' I say.

'He is always opening the doors for you, not letting you pay for anything. A real clothes-wallah. In his uniform he was ever so correct, and his hair was like carpet, but short.'

'A soldier?' I ask.

'Actually, the one who came to the door that day. He is a friend of your brother's, or so he said. I saw him again after I left, standing at the end of the road outside a pub. His pint glass was overflowing, so he was bending his head carefully to drink from its rim. He saw me. I looked at him, but I have been ignoring men since many years. Obviously, I paid no notice. He followed me, leaving behind his glass. I quickened my pace – I am not so stupid. I *thought* I was not so stupid – oof, what a stupid I am.'

I can imagine perfectly what the young man looked like, the same as my brother might. In clothes with a woodland camouflage pattern, black beret angled on his head with the unit crest on the high side. His trousers would have cargo pockets below the hip, fastened by a flap with two buttons. The boots she remembers are tanker boots, with leather straps instead of laces. Some army liaison

200

officer here on a joint training operation between British and American armies. He could be in the Special Forces on some sort of training exercise, looking to get to know the city in which he will live now for a year or two, before moving on. It is hard to imagine that Veena would allow him near her. She is a woman who does nothing whatsoever to disguise her disdain if a man approaches. I was with her once when a perfectly innocent guy stopped us to ask directions, saw her tip her face from him, refusing to speak so that I had to explain. Afterwards she called me gullible. Called the man who needed directions 'an opportunist'. And yet, this officer captured her attention, her heart. And to that rare offer from this, my good friend, he showed no gratitude.

'He seemed such a very nice fellow,' she says, sighing. 'I am married to him now,' she adds, bringing her hand up from under the table and placing it palm down on the wood, fingers splayed. There, on her third finger, is the soldier's ring. 'I want you to know this is the first and last time,' she says, pointing to her eye.

He's made a perfect target of her left eye, circles of dark bruising emerge from all points surrounding it. I hope this fellow comes here looking for her. My brother, who is a wiry sergeant first class, with a jaw broken twice and knuckles dulled from various punch-outs he's had over the years, taught me a few of what he calls 'dirty' moves that will bring down the toughest of men. All of these involve making sure the victim has no idea you are about to hit him, and require only ordinary household objects. 'You need ice,' I say to Veena, staring at her face.

'It's too late for ice. I was going to ask if I could sleep on your sofa, but you've turned your living room into a gym,' she says. 'Where is the furniture?'

'Sold it,' I say. 'You can have Emily's bed.'

She begins to smile, then winces. She is a tiny woman with dainty, angular bones. In her socks she would fit very nicely into a year six class and not even be the tallest there. 'How are the children?' she asks.

'Daniel can talk. He points and says, "Look, a helicopter. Look, a purple car." But he cannot ask questions yet.'

'That is just as well,' says Veena. 'I don't want a lot of questions.'

In the morning Veena drinks herbal tea in bed, asks me to bring her a book. With her good eye she squints. 'Let me read to you,' I say. Sunday morning, the children are racing back and forth across the bare floors. I would almost say they are playing together, as Andy once promised. He will arrive later, in his loose jeans fraying at the pockets, the knees already shot out from spending so much time on the floor with children. In his Bono T-shirt, with his lean and freckled arms, he will clasp Daniel by the hips and place him like cargo upon his shoulders. My little boy, into whom Andy and I have collected ourselves, who has linked us in a way we cannot explain. Andy carries him for me, and swings him in his arms.

'What shall we read?' Veena asks, sinking back on to the pillow, her dark hair in contrast to the pink and white posies that decorate the walls of Emily's bedroom. 'Can it be a happy story?'

About children who run in fields, and surprises arriving like kittens in spring. About the discovery of a secret shop where all the sweets take you back in time, of friendly dragons and clever, speaking owls. Of brave and true men willing even to risk their lives for ordinary girls who discover, later, that they are princesses with royal blood and kingdoms all their own.

I nod. I promise her this.

Stephen has agreed to a drink. I have tried very hard not to care what I wear to this drink, not to fix my hair just right, not to notice if my make-up is perfect. I don't want to make it appear I am trying too hard. That would be a turn-off. And I don't want it to appear I don't care at all. That wouldn't do, either. So wearing my favourite jeans belted loosely at the hips, a pair of suede boots and a shirt that shows off my eyes, I waltz into the wine bar as nonchalantly as if I meet Stephen here all the time. Nothing to it. I see him seated at the far end punching the buttons on his mobile phone, texting someone. He glances up at me, then back at his phone. I sit down and wait until he is finished. Why do I resent this so much? A few minutes of waiting? Why does it matter?

Our table is a dark circle next to an exposed brick wall. The place is crowded with after-work drinkers and we share the narrow room with a whole slew of people who obviously work together and use this wine bar as a kind of after-work party place. They keep erupting in laughter, which annoys me. I feel like it just punctuates everything wrong between Stephen and me, who do no laughing whatsoever. He's only got time for one drink, so I launch into what I want from him right away.

'Come home,' I urge him. 'Quit this nonsense and come back to your family.'

He winces, makes a face as though I've just said something very, very irritating. It's clear to him that we were having a hard time before the diagnosis. Certainly we cannot recover now.

'Why are you always harping on at me?' he says.
'Shouldn't we be discussing more constructive issues, like
how Daniel is doing?'

I want to say, Stephen, don't even *pretend* you have
Daniel's welfare in the forefront right now. I want to say,
Stephen, when have you even considered what is best for
Daniel? But, of course, I don't say this. I would never say
such a thing. I am a tactician; my testimony is whatever
will help my children. So I glance at the framed pictures
of the Thames that grace the walls of the wine bar, squint
my eyes at the array of twinkly lights that run along the
ceiling, gathering myself together. And then I say, 'Daniel
is playing and speaking at about a two-year-old's level. So
he's made up eighteen months in the space of seven
months. He might be autistic, but he is gaining skills. He's
smart. He'll make it, but only if we keep doing what we're
doing, working very hard for him.'

'Who's *we*?' he says.

'Me,' I tell him. I don't mention Andy. 'And you, if
you'd just –'

'Look, I'm not a therapist, or whatever it is you want
me to be,' he says. His phone beeps and he glances at the
screen. I'd like to throw the phone against the brick here,
but somehow I think that would be interpreted as insanity
rather than longing.

'What about Emily?' I say. 'Don't you think about her?'

'Blackmail,' he says.

'You're their father,' I say.

'I'll always be their father.' That's a fact, sure enough.

'I want you to be with us,' I say.

'But why? It's better this way. Less . . . friction.'

I would tell him because I love him, but I'm not sure
that is the case any more. I don't feel love. But then, this

conversation – the whole thrust of this plea – isn't about me or how I feel at any given minute.

He says, 'We weren't happy.'

And this just really makes me cross. He's talking about being *happy*? Like his being happy is the most important goal right now. Like it matters so much.

I lean forward, whispering, 'They are your *children*. How happy do you need to *be*?'

He moves back in his seat, gazing at me as though constructing some kind of analysis. Then I realise he's looking slightly above the level of my eyes. He's thinking, but not necessarily about anything I am saying.

He sighs. He begins to speak, but then stops himself. He is just waiting now, probably calculating how much longer he has to sit in the chair.

A little longer, I decide.

Picturing my children's faces, I pour out a whole string of reasons why he just has to come home. We need you; we miss you; the day is not complete without you. Regardless of what has passed, we simply must work it out. I say all this and I look at him in what I hope is a loving way, a beseeching way. He allows this, so I continue. I am giving my best; I can hear the strain in my voice and I wish it weren't there, but I cannot help it. I want him back. It is as though I can hold in my chest the hearts of my children along with my own, and I respond to those hearts. But then I realise, all of a sudden, that I am only providing a kind of amusement for Stephen. He doesn't believe a word. And maybe I don't believe it either. Everything about him is a closed door.

The phone rings. It comes alive all at once, suddenly full of lights, echoing a shrill tone, rattling on the table. He reaches for it – I think at first to turn it off – and then

I realise he's going to answer it. He's answering the phone. I slap at it, knocking it to the table once more, and we both stare as it rings and vibrates, shifting across the table like a dying insect. I stand up, shaking with fury. I am turning away now, readying to march out of here. The ringing continues, increasing in volume as my words spill out above the sound of the phone, the laughter of the people around us. 'You're going to regret this, Stephen!' I shout at him. But he isn't listening. He's answered the call.

All the way home I look at men. In their business suits, in their jeans, wearing denim jackets or sweatshirts or no shirt. I look at them and I wonder what's going on, who are these guys? Where's the mother ship or *whateveritis* from which they've come?

When I tell Larry what happened with Veena and his army buddy, do you know what he says? He says, 'Like I had anything to do with it.'

No expression of sympathy, no further information about this guy – his friend – who was so awful to her.

'That's *it*? That's your comment on the matter?'

'Uh, yeah, I guess so. I mean, I don't even know your friend Frieda –'

'Veena!'

'Whatever.'

I tell him he's a loser, a complete loser, and that it's almost unbelievable that he's related to me.

'Uh-huh,' he says lazily. 'Yup. So? I sent the kiddies presents, though, and that was good, wasn't it? So that girl got a black eye. Shit, I've had dozens of those. *Hundreds* even. Sometimes I wake up and my eye is just black and I don't even *know* why.'

Now I'm really cross. 'Larry, I've really had enough of you!' I say.

'Had enough of me, *what*? Look,' he says, 'what did I do, hold a gun to her head and make her marry the guy?'

He's right, of course, but just to punish him anyway I tell him that not only are guns not allowed in England, but since they've banned fox-hunting, the government now feels compelled to ban all gun-related metaphors: *shoot from the hip, right on target, under fire*. None of these are allowed by law.

'When you next arrive in this country, you will be unable to use any of these terms,' I say to him now, using a sorrowful voice as though this is true.

And bingo, I've got him.

'Stop this madness! It's fascism!' he says. I can imagine him clutching his head.

'. . . no more *on the wrong side of the barrel, straight shooter, bring out the heavy artillery . . .*'

'Oh my God! When does this insanity begin?' he says. He's clearly in agony. Behind his voice the whole of the Amazon jungle he lives with call out their inane, senseless chatter. Especially the one bird. *Life is sweet* rings loud and clear across three thousand miles.

'Tomorrow, at noon. There will first be a moment of silence for all people shot by guns over the whole of world history. And then, an end to the metaphors.'

Daniel is naked from the waist down, his slim legs like two drinking straws, his knees splayed out as he sits on the chequered tiles of the bathroom floor. We have brought in the Duplo bricks, hundreds of colours that make a pleasing sound like seashells if you roll them together, and which fall clattering to the hard floor when we tip a tall tower. The base must be wide, so we form a square of bricks across the green Duplo board, its grid of convex circles perfectly in line.

'You watch his willy, I'll do the tower,' says Andy. He squats on the floor in his dirty trainers, no socks, his jeans the colour of the sky on a cloudy day. He's missing a rear pocket, a fact I noticed when he came through the door this morning, looking at him the way I do now, studying his anatomy as a careful student might. I am aware, as a lover might be, of the curling hair along his ankles, thickening as it disappears inside the dark folds of his jeans, the ruby birthmark the size of a thumbprint that begins at the hairline on the back of his neck, the white scar above his right eyebrow, where he has pierced it, then let it heal.

We are teaching Daniel to use a toilet. There is no hope of regular nursery school for him unless he abandons the nappies.

'When you see it rise just a little bit, then get him to the toilet,' he says. 'And be prepared that he might scream.'

Daniel looks at me, then at Andy. 'Nappy,' he says.

'Toilet,' says Andy.

On the ledge at the head of the bath we are armed with chocolate drops and orange juice – both of which are particularly coveted treats. Daniel has been taught using this reward method for so long that he knows the prize reliably arrives with his best effort. He thinks he is meant to make a tall tower, and so focuses all his energy on creating what he thinks we want, a colourful tower as tall as his arms will reach.

'I want juice,' he says.

'Nice try,' says Andy. He looks at the juice, indicates with his finger. 'Can I have some juice please?'

Daniel watches him, considering this example, but turns to me instead. 'I want juice,' he says.

Andy makes it more obvious. More dramatic. With one hand on his hip, the other stretched out, pointing to the glass, he issues his demand. 'Mummy, can I have some juice please!'

Daniel points. 'Mummy, can I have some juice please!'

He gets his juice right away, and a nugget of chocolate, too, for trying so hard.

'Here it comes!' I say.

'Toilet!' cries Andy.

'Nappy!' screams Daniel.

I scoop Daniel up and sit him on the toilet, where he yells at me, grabbing bits of my hair and pulling, kicking so that I have to duck.

'Stop laughing,' I tell Andy.

He smiles, shakes his head. 'You might like a new shirt,' he tells me. Daniel has peed all down my front.

In the kitchen I peel off my shirt and drop it on the floor in front of the washing machine, then move toward the back door to take a dry one from the line in the garden. I'm thinking so much about whether Daniel will ever give up the nappies that I hardly notice I walk through the house in nothing but shorts and a bra. But Veena notices. She and Emily are playing hospital. Emily is the doctor, of course. And poor Veena, the victim, must lie on the table while Emily examines her for heart failure, a plastic stethoscope angled across her sternum.

'You're no longer a skeleton,' says Veena, glancing at my shape. 'You are no longer one of the walking wounded.'

Back in the bathroom we are setting up a garage full

of cars. There are a half-dozen all in their places, but this one, the fire engine, will be the focus of our game. From his pocket Andy produces a votive candle. His lighter, a plastic Bic the colour of Scotch, is fascinating to Daniel, who tips it and puts his eye to the lighter fluid within, as one might stare into a microscope.

'Nineteen, eighteen, seven,' Daniel says.

Andy takes the lighter, flips it in his hand, stares across its shiny surface which is hard, enticing, reminding me of a boiled sweet. 'So you're right, you are,' he tells Daniel.

On the bottom of the lighter, in lettering no larger than a midge fly, are these five numbers which Daniel can read.

Rolling his thumb, Andy scares a flame onto the head of the lighter, places the wick of the candle to the fire, and says, 'FIRE! FIRE! Get the engine!'

And now Daniel rolls the fire engine down the long stretch of the car park's track, making a sound like an engine, heading for the candle which threatens a purple Mini, Daniel's favourite vehicle because purple is his favourite colour. When the fire engine reaches the car he puffs his cheeks and blows the flame.

'Yeah!' we cheer, clapping. Daniel rolls back into a sitting position, smiles at us. 'I blow fire,' he says.

Three hours later we come downstairs. We've played cars, blown bubbles, had picnics with train engines, made Donald Duck play hide-and-seek with Pluto. Daniel has peed twice in the toilet and produced one rather hard poo. Once he realised what was at stake – chocolate – and what was never going to appear – his nappy – he found it less difficult to comply.

'No more nappies,' says Andy, who was witness to it all. Who would think that a relationship could have started like this? With a child who seemed at times as feral as a wolf boy, among intimacies as unappealing as toilet training? And yet here he is, his eyes full of tenderness for me, for my boy. He brought Emily a half-dozen pastel crayons this morning, wrapped in brown paper and string. For Daniel, his favourite orange juice, plus a ladybird that wiggles if you pull a cord. 'I don't ever want another nappy on that child,' he says now.

'Not even at night?' I ask.

'No.'

'Or when we are out shopping and there's no toilet nearby?'

'No. He can pee on the street. I'd rather he did that.'

I say, 'Yeah, well, other people might not like it.'

'Other people,' he says, shaking his head. He has his rolling papers out. He extracts a sheet in a quick movement. He works the tobacco back and forth in his fingers then positions it in the crease and rolls it tenderly, securing the slim log of his cigarette with the fine edge of his tongue. 'Other people don't have children with autism,' he says. 'They are not entitled to an opinion.'

19

Veena and I are going through what used to be her home with the soldier, collecting her things. He isn't in the flat, of course. She never would have come if he'd been here; she even refuses to speak to him on the phone. With a suitcase and a duffel bag we go through the flat like thieves, taking back what is Veena's. She is very quiet during this time, as though we are stealing. She puts her glasses in her shirt pocket, her hair in a knot, pushes her sleeves up, gets down to work.

The flat is in a modern brick building with a stairway that echoes. The banisters are cold steel, painted yellow on one floor, orange on another. The doors are decorated with bright numbers just below the peephole, which is apparently standard in this building.

'Ours was thirteen,' says Veena. 'I should have known then.'

We leave the bags on the street beside the taxi driver, who chews gum and leans against his cab watching us. He doesn't offer to help bring the bags out or even to put them in the taxi. He looks bored, as though it is trouble enough to wait for us. We come first with the clothes, then with the books. There are so many books we dig out some old Tesco bags from what was once Veena's kitchen and place the books inside them, bringing these to the kerb as well.

'What is this, a house move?' says the driver impatiently. His eyes skim his watch. He spits his gum into the road.

Veena glances at him, scowling. 'Have some money,' she says, holding out a bill.

Back in the flat we finish with the books, then go to the CD collection and take from it Veena's music. On a table by the phone is a small picture of the two of them together, Veena and the soldier. I put the picture in my bag, not letting Veena know that I have done so. She would only say she doesn't want it, but she may change her mind later. I will keep it for her, just in case.

When we are finished, the flat looks tidier, but empty. The soldier has papers and clothes and lamps and oddly matched chairs. He has a flat-screen television on a chrome-and-glass stand, a swanky CD player with thin towers for speakers.

'I think we should take something of his,' I tell Veena. 'Something valuable.'

Veena looks at the television, the stereo, telephone and fax machine. The computer, some hi-tech model with a swivelling screen.

'There's nothing of value here,' she says.

It is one of those hazy late summer evenings in which the light stretches on and on. There has been no rain for many days and the air smells bitter, choking, with the sharpness of industry plugged into every breath. It is not warm, however. Over my T-shirt I wear a flannel shirt, unbuttoned; jeans, a pair of socks.

Veena says she cannot study. Her mind has been taken over by the soldier, she says. Occupied, as though in war. So instead she discovers a programme on the radio to listen to and takes the radio to the children's bedroom, where she curls up next to my sleeping daughter, finding her a comfort as I have often found. Children and hot-water bottles, warm cocoa and radios. All these things make it possible to sleep when your mind is whirring. Even though she has her own clothes now, she prefers a nightgown I lent her. It is way too long, of course, trailing behind her like the train of a wedding gown.

Downstairs is Andy. He has fashioned a bed from great-coats and sheets. He has arranged all the toys neatly along the walls, stolen a pillow from my bed, the extra duvet from the top of the closet. His jeans are so threadbare I think I hear them tearing even further at the knees as he moves over this nest he has made, which looks like a place you might give an animal to bed down and is not in the least bit appealing.

'I am not proposing a thing,' he says, when I find him there. 'Just want someplace more comfortable to sit with you other than those hard fockin' chairs you have. And I know you won't let me anywhere near your bed.'

'Daniel is in my bed.'

'Of course he is. And that's fine –' He pauses, lets out a breath. His crosses his jaw, smiling as he does so, shakes his head. He looks both perplexed and wrung out, but also a little amused. 'Look, I've made no vows of celibacy. When I was younger I'd give a girl two chances. If she didn't kiss me the second time, she was out. I just moved on. And if she didn't sleep with me within, say, a week or two, I moved on. Imagine what more of a prick I'd be if I were good-looking like your sodding husband.'

I can't quite picture him as anything but sweet, patient, earthy, himself. When he says 'prick' it comes out 'preck', an accent I've come to adore. He's flustered, uncertain. I've never seen him quite like this. He's always so sure of himself, as though he's got the world in his pocket. 'What are you asking for?' I say.

'I'm wanting you to know I understand . . . the circumstances.'

'You mean that I'm weird, don't you? You mean that I'm strange.'

Now he looks at me squarely, purses his lips in thought the way I've seen Jacob do countless times, speaking slowly, willing me to listen.

He says, 'You're not strange, Melanie. You're an autism mum. I see them all the time. I saw you that first day we met, how you agonised over your boy, mute in his pushchair while all the other pre-schoolers made their clever observations about the world; I see how you worry now over his odd way of walking, the animal noises he will sometimes make instead of words. And I see how no amount of pain in the experience of caring for your son will put to death the fire of love you have for him. It wouldn't matter even if he *couldn't* talk – which he can, and will, I promise he'll speak beautifully. But if he always ignored you, pushed you out of the way, evaded your kisses, ran from your grasp, even so you would be his champion. Autism mums have in common with God this ability to love the unlovable. What the world sees as unlovable. Not that I agree with the world,' says Andy. 'Nothing like that.'

Embarrassed, I turn away.

'Melanie,' he says. He rises, comes toward me, touches my shoulder. Then, as though leading a blind lady, he brings me to the bed he's made on our floor, sits me down, kneels in front of me. He's such a slim man, about my height. I could wear his jeans, I realise. We could swap belts and shoes. As he kneels before me I can see the spidery lines his smile has etched at the corners of his eyes, the dark shadow of his beard stubble just barely visible against his pale, freckled skin. He is not as young as I always think he is. He is a man who has had love affairs and dreams, whose career has been fashioned out of the desire to help fix broken children and who lives, if I am to believe him, in a bedsit not much larger than the inside of a London cab, surrounded by walls of psychology books.

I realise all at once that I would like to see this room. To see his clothes in their drawers or boxes or wherever he keeps them, to see the intimate details of his life: his photographs, his notebooks, what he keeps on his shelves, in his wardrobe, near his bed. Apparently, he spends most of his day doing work for free. There is a father whose wife has died of a rare neurological disease, a kind of early Alzheimer's. This father spends what he has on a mediocre nanny and has nothing left for therapy for his daughter, who is five and autistic. An Asian mother whose husband insists she look after his two parents and produce another child for him, even though the third child has severe attention deficit disorder, is moody and belligerent, and when Andy met him, had no capacity for play. The fourth child, autistic, would only jump on the beds and play killer games on the PlayStation. He could speak but would not follow simple directions, and repeated aloud the schedules for favourite First Great Western trains throughout the day.

Those who can, pay. Those who can't, receive Andy's charity. He makes it easy for them by insisting he is very rich. Nothing could be less true.

'I tell them my dad has a horse farm in West Cork,' he explains to me. 'I tell them that and they think I have money. But the situation is quite the opposite, though we do have a lot of horses.'

'Where I come from, a horse farm would mean you were loaded,' I say.

'Yeah, well. We've got a few things in Ireland. One of them is grass.'

We are stretched out on the makeshift bed. On his back, his hands behind his head, he tells me the horses are a big, thick, hairy sort with patches of black and brown. 'Cobs, they are. With cloddy hooves and bushy tails. Solid as houses, and kind. When I was no older than your daughter, I'd lead around the baby foals, and my brothers would push me on to the two-year-olds, get them used to being ridden. He'd set them to plough, my father, even though of course he had a tractor; we weren't that primitive. If you don't give them work they get simple, he explained to me. Though, frankly, they seem simple to me anyway. He only did it so he could say they were trained to harness at the sales.'

I can imagine Andy in a blue-green field on a summer day, strolling barefoot across the wet grass, finding the poking nose of a spring foal pushing its way through the fence wire. Around him the laughter of his brothers and sisters, enough of them to make up a football side. I picture him on the way to a horse fair, sleeping in the back of his father's truck on feed bags and horse rugs. A life of open air and peat fires. Why on earth would he choose these days to spend his time shut into bathrooms with children and their worried mothers, setting wooden tracks in the cramped living rooms of families in London?

Why? I ask him. I want to know.

He flips onto his side now, touches my cheek, my neck, moves his hand down the space between my breasts and lets it rest upon my stomach.

'When I went to university we studied a man named Bettelheim who set up a school for autistic children in Chicago. He was presented as a hero, this man, like he knew something. I read what he had to say about autistic children, about their mothers. OK, mostly nobody believes him now, but –'

'I know about Bettelheim,' I say.

'My eldest brother, Liam, was autistic. Severe. My earliest memories of him are how he'd run through the house naked, bang his head against the fireplace mantel until his forehead went black and blue,' he says. 'He had a helmet he was meant to wear, but he'd rip that off, make for the mantel.'

In my mind I see a boy not unlike Daniel, but taller, with long, rubbery legs that spring across the floor planks. Across his pale forehead lies a knot the size of your hand, bright red, pulsing beneath the skin like a second heart.

'My mother is like a spring lamb, shyly trusting, obedient to the herd. When they told her to put him in a home she did so, because they said he would harm the other children, the seven of us, who'd learned to walk while dodging Liam. He was unpredictable in his move-ments, bouncing apelike across the furniture even in his teens. So that is what my mother did, because she was told to do so. And my father allowed it, not knowing what else he could do.'

I picture Andy's father, hitching the heel of his wellington into the bootjack and pulling. His hands are red, calloused, scarred across the joints. He looks through the house he has practically taken apart and put back together again from all the repairs he's made. Standing by the fireplace he thinks, with agony, about the boy who is missing from it now.

'He died, my brother did. Epilepsy. He had a fit while coming down the stairs and he fell. That was only a year or two after he went to this place to live, what they called a school but I can't think they taught him anything. My mother always wished she'd had him home. If he was going to die, she said, let him do it in his own house like a member of a family.'

I shake my head. I cover my eyes with my hands.

'You know, it wasn't like I was so upset,' Andy says. 'I was nine, ten. He seemed much older than me and was, anyway, not very communicative, as you can imagine. But my mother. She was never the same. Not seven of us could make up for the boy she lost. She was always sad. Happy for us when things went well, and she did her best always. But inside herself, deep inside, she was sad. You know what that's like, don't you? Don't you, darling?'

I nod. I turn so I lie on top of him, cover him, tuck my face into the crook of his neck and smell the salt on his skin.

'Maybe you will come with me to see my parents one day, hey? They'd love the children, you know. They'd love you.'

In my mind I see again a picture of Andy's father. I have no reason to think he is wearing trousers the colour of burlap, or that his wife has a long neck, a delicate face, creased and bony. But in my imagination there they are, just so. They are welcoming me into their house, welcoming my children. To them Daniel is a particular delight. They see him as a miracle, as Lazarus risen from the tomb, conjured by the hands of their son.

Andy kisses me. It seems incredible, given how much he knows of me, how many bizarre and intimate hours we have spent together, that this is our first kiss.

'I won't ask to stay over tonight,' he says. 'But one day, yes?'

I nod. I try not to think of how to present such a thing to the children, when to do it, whether or not I should tell Stephen. I try not to think of Stephen at all. I've made up this new defence regarding him. Whenever Stephen pops into my mind I say to myself, 'He's gone.' That's all I allow myself to think.

He's gone, I tell myself now. Andy wraps his arms around me, kisses me beautifully, slowly, his hands on my waist.

He's gone. I push my arms over Andy's shoulders, my palms into the soft blanket of his hair.

He's gone. I am discovering somebody I was always meant to discover. He's waited for me, this gift, all of my life. If I allow myself, I can love him. And yet every move in that direction feels a little like I'm betraying my children.

'It seems that lately it has become impossible to feel happy,' I say now to Andy. I am so disappointed in myself. My words sound like an apology, which I guess they are.

'It's ahead of you,' he says. 'Just keep walking.'

*   *   *

Clarks does not do buckle shoes for boys. Velcro or laces, that's it. You cannot get buckles at Start-Rite either, except the girls' shoes, of course. The flimsy-seeming summer shoes, what we used to call party shoes when I was young, *they* have buckles. But not the heavy shoes. Not the boys' shoes.

Daniel is meant to have shoes that support his ankles. That is what the orthopaedic surgeon told me. He was a tall man, completely bald, who reminded me of a pelican with his big smile, his middle-aged paunch, his long, slender legs in their suit trousers. My hundred and twenty pounds bought me a diagnosis of hypotonia, and joint hypermobility. In other words, Daniel is a rubber boy; he bends too easily. Children like Daniel are prone to accidents, falling as they walk ballerina-style on their toes, unable to jump without stumbling as their loose joints are weak, easily injured. Like a tube of toothpaste, they can take only light pressure.

'Will it improve? Is there anything I can do?'

Yes and no. I can buy shoes that support his ankles. I can wait and see if the joints stiffen as he grows.

'Was he a floppy baby?' the orthopaedic surgeon wanted to know. Did I notice anything unusual about how he felt in my arms?

Daniel was a perfect baby. He walked at eleven months, gliding easily through the house in his new shoes. He chased Emily around, giggling. He certainly did not walk on his toes – I would have noticed that. What bothers me with this notion of autism as a genetic condition – other than the fact there is no autism on either side of Daniel's family – is that accompanying symptoms such as hypotonia were not present in babyhood. Hypotonia and hyper-flexive joints ought to have presented themselves right from the start. But Daniel was a perfect baby, passing his eighteen-month check, looking overall very much like other babies. Something happened between the time Daniel was born and the time he was two and starting to look abnormal. Some change to his brain, some insult to his system. The government insists it is not the vaccines, so what was it? To remember your child as normal, to watch him falter as though attacked by some invisible, menacing force, will change you. In the presence of doctors and their unhelpful diagnoses, I am fidgety, unnerved. In the orthopaedic surgeon's office, I have shaking hands, eyes that wander, a voice that catches. When finally I speak it is as though I cannot stop talking. I gush streams of sentences, then am silent again, searching the clean walls of the doctor's surgery, unable to rest my gaze. I stare down – at my hands, my legs, at my son. It is only the sight of Daniel that calms me. He is here, he is getting better. Nobody can deny that, not even doctors.

'You seem very agitated,' the doctor said to me. My hair was still damp. I'd ducked my head in the sink to wash it before leaving the house, balanced Daniel on my shoulders and walked from the Tube as I couldn't afford the cab fare. 'Are you sure you're OK?'

'I've been on the front line for a good while,' I told him. 'You've just told me that you cannot help me, which I understand and accept. It is what I hear all the time. But don't expect me to remain totally calm.'

That was in June. Months have passed before and since; I've spent thousands of pounds on every doctor and alternative practitioner available in the whole of Greater London. Now I think, according to their track record and the fact that my bank account shows no sign of life, that I am on my own.

Here at the shoe shop, I search for buckle shoes because Daniel has asked me so beseechingly for them. Every day he says, 'Please, shoes with buckles,' and claps his hands together, making a little movement as though bowing to a queen. I promised him the shoes and he believed me. His eyes danced. So why don't these shops have any shoes for him, my boy who now regularly puts together four- and five-word sentences?

'Only for girls,' says the lady at Clarks. She has an awfully lovely accent for a shoe clerk, elegantly dressed in a linen suit, her bifocals hanging on a decorated chain round her neck, her own shoes a better brand than Clarks. She says, 'I told you that when you came in earlier.'

'I know,' I say to the lady. 'But he really wants buckle shoes.'

'Velcro is very nice,' she says. 'Convenient.'

'Buckles Ahh! Buckles AHAHAHA!' Daniel is jumping on his toes as though suddenly caught in an electric current. 'I want buckle shoes! Please, buckle shoes!' he cries, his voice rattling.

That is seven words. Andy told me that one day I would stop counting. Does that mean he will be normal some day? I asked. Andy is honest. He always tells me the truth. He said no. It did not mean Daniel will be normal. There is more to it. I know this, of course, but I find I am always bargaining my way out of Daniel's diagnosis, pleading for someone to announce he has Asperger's syndrome as opposed to full-blown autism, that he has a language disorder, but not autism. Anything but autism. Such bargaining will only win you wasted time, Andy told me. Andy, who sees autism as a treatable condition, but only if you face it head on.

'I'm afraid we only have girls' shoes with buckles,' says the woman. Along the wall of the shop is a pretty display of pink shelves, interspersed with Barbie logos and pictures of blonde dolls. In this decorated world of carnation pink lie the shoes that Daniel wants. He sees this. He understands what the woman is reporting. Language is no longer lost on his ears. And so he goes to the dinosaur display on the boys' side of the shop and removes some of the shoes there, those big greenish-black shoes with heavy treads and prehistoric monsters in holographs on the straps, and takes them to the girls' side. He swaps the dinosaur shoes for the pretty patent leather pumps with the buckles, the ones he so desperately wants.

'Excuse me, could you *do* something?' says the sales lady pointedly.

But I am fascinated by what I see before me. How Daniel knows what the trouble is, how he has been separated from his desired object by means of his gender. It seems to him a simple thing to switch the decorations. To make the shoes with the heavy tread and Velcro part of the world of girls and Barbie, and embed the sacred buckled pumps into the masculine surround of dinosaurs and jungle grass.

'Young man, if you would *please* put those shoes down,' says the sales lady, moving toward Daniel. Uh-oh, big mistake. She's made a grab for his shoes, the ones with the buckles, the ones he's waited so long for. Daniel squirms, makes a noise. She steps over him to snag the shoes and he sinks his teeth into her hand.

'AAAHH!' she screams, and turns to me with fury. The bite is nothing, not even any blood. It was a warning bite, really. If he meant anything by it he'd still have the meat of her hand between his teeth. 'Madam, I insist you remove your child!' the sales lady says, holding her damaged hand, looking at me with a mixture of resentment and withering disdain.

'I'm terribly sorry,' I tell her, and that is true. I am. I ought to have intervened faster, explained that Daniel is autistic, that he cannot quite abide by the rules of the world the way we can – we, who have more ordinary neurology, less intrusive thoughts, more facile communication.

'Madam, you must understand,' continues the sales lady, 'that in this country only *girls* wear patent leather. And only *girls* wear pumps. I'm sorry, but that is a fact of our nation.'

A fact of our nation. Like PG Tips and bank holiday Mondays. Like driving on the left side of the road.

It is clear the woman thinks that being American, I will dress my son in high heels and pantyhose, any old thing. For Americans are sexual perverts, even she can see that.

'I know you don't want to do this,' I say slowly – there is no point in explaining – as I get out my credit card. 'But as much as it might kill you, I want you to put those shoes in a box.'

All the way home Daniel is racing forward and back on the pavement, looking at his new shoes, admiring his buckles. It doesn't matter to me that he has particularly wide feet, and that his chubby legs in the feminine shape of the patent leather shoes place him directly into the cross-dresser category. What matters to me is that my boy is happy. While he normally would complain and whine, collapsing on the pavement in a sweaty heap and refusing to budge, demanding to be held the entire journey to the tube, he is too busy for such nonsense today. Admiring his fancy feet, he fairly skips along. Sure, there are a few looks from those on the Tube who notice a boy wearing what must be his sister's shoes, but they are not people I need ever to see again.

'New shoes,' I smile to the woman opposite me on the tube, who is glaring over her John Lewis shopping bag at Daniel's new, shining, delicate party shoes.

'I see,' she states.

We've done her a favour, Daniel and I. Given her something to tell her husband about later.

I come through the door singing a hello to Veena and Emily, who when I left with Daniel for the shoe shop were busy painting the scenery for a play Emily means to put on for us this evening, an enactment of *Beauty and the Beast*, performed mostly by Mickey Mouse. She's dropped Dumbo for now, possibly for ever. Her painted elephants line the window sill, the home-made Dumbo in front, and they haven't moved in weeks. The last time I read her that story I found myself regarding Dumbo's mother with new, almost profound sympathy. They locked her away for defending her baby, tacked a sign saying 'Mad Elephant!' to the bars of her cage.

'Why did they do that, Mummy?' Emily asked me, looking into the book, at the face of the elephant with her trunk raised in trumpet, her desperate and sad eyes.

'Ignorance,' I said.

'What is ignorance?' asked Emily, my clever girl, almost five.

'It means not knowing,' I told her. 'But also, it can mean not wanting to know.'

There's a note on the counter from Veena. They've gone to a park. And a message on the machine from Stephen asking that I call him right away. When I ring him on his mobile, he answers as though underwater. His voice is slow, remote. It seems that his father's depression has taken a toll on his heart. He died this morning unexpectedly, while on the way to hospital.

20

I've attended almost as many funerals as I have weddings. That is an unusual statement for a woman yet in her twenties. I know to expect a quiet welcome, to take without fuss the offered order of service, to sit in silence, await the solemn hymns, the mild reassurances from the vicar, the formal movement of the prayers. Because this is England, I have worn a hat. But as I come through the door I see I have made a terrible mistake in not tying back my hair. Hanging loosely at my shoulders it is an affront, too blonde in this sea of dark jackets and sombre ties.

I have left the children with Andy, who volunteered himself. 'I know how to play with them,' he insisted. 'I understand Daniel's diet. I understand Daniel, and I understand you.' He gave me his mobile phone and touched my cheek and I thought, yes, he is right. He understands me. He understands that I will call half a dozen times during the journey to the service, half a dozen times the minute the service is ended, and will insist on talking to Emily all the way home on the train.

It's who I am. Why fight it?

As I went out the door Emily was sitting on his lap reading *Go, Dog, Go*. Daniel had been set a task of finding things you can write with, a kind of language exercise which would be boring with anybody other than Andy. Andy will end up insisting you can write with chocolate pudding in addition to all the chalk and crayons, pens and pencils that Daniel will fetch from all over the house. He will make it fun, painting the windows in chocolate pudding, making faces that show happiness, sadness, confusion, surprise, as Daniel learns to read these emotions from the glass. He draws now, Daniel. He makes Teletubbies and children. His girls all have curly blonde hair like his sister. The boys have round tummies with big dark belly buttons.

Bernard's funeral takes place in a brick-and-flint chapel set into a sunlit close off the high street. In the church now, alone in a pew, I admire the vaulted ceiling above me, decorated at the edges with mythical figures carved in stone. The heavy pillars reach up past the balcony like ancient and imposing trees, the doors, shaped as arches, are of fat, dark wood with iron hardware fashioned a century or more ago. Stained-glass windows shield us from the busy high street outside, the imposing summer sun. When I entered the church I noticed the stone steps were dished and worn, trodden on by centuries of worshippers and others, not worshippers, but who, like me, have come because they are meant to, and cannot find a trace of God inside this beautiful building with its ornate detail and carved wooden stalls.

Now an organ begins. I panic inside myself a little, feeling the weight of my children's absence, the emptiness at my sides where they should be. I know – of course – that they would not want to sit through such a service.

Daniel, for example, cannot remain still for more than about five minutes, unless it is on a train. He will moan and twist out of his seat, refusing to be amused by the toys I bring, the biscuits and raisins I stash in my bag. Unless the funeral had taken place on an overnight service to Scotland, there was no way for Daniel to come. As for Emily, I gave her the choice, but she opted for an afternoon with Andy. I can't say I blame her. I'm in for a bad time myself. About ten metres ahead of me, in a pew on the left, Daphne and Penelope speak quietly to one another. Penelope's skin is so pale, almost translucent, shining in the light of a ceiling lamp. Daphne, in a velvet hat, sits quietly next to her, like an old friend. When Penelope turns slightly, searching behind her for somebody – Stephen? – I see that she has lost none of her allure. Still the hook nose, still the wide eyes, but beneath the brim of her dark navy hat is also the appealing sexiness of her long eyes, her brilliantly white, only slightly crooked teeth. She sees me. She whispers to Daphne. And now they both turn, staring my direction. I try to smile, to raise a finger to wave. I feel sorry for Daphne. I cannot imagine what it is to lose a partner of forty years. As for Penelope, I can't help feeling a little like I've sold her a slightly un-workable second-hand car, which sooner or later she will discover cannot make long journeys.

I notice him as he comes in with his brother, as he stands for the hymns. As he sits, as he kneels. In his dark suit, his thin, nondescript tie, and hair tamed for the occasion, I notice him. When he sees me, he looks away.

The sermon is given by a retired clergyman who was a good friend of Bernard's. He goes through the usual assurances of life beyond, and then, his expression changing to one of fond remembrance, he tells us he always found

Bernard to be a most lovely and amusing fellow. I have to admit that 'amusing' is not a word I would attribute to Bernard. He was honest, hard-working, and quite popular as you can tell by the number of people who have turned out for his funeral. But when I arrived the first Christmas to the Marshes' house, carrying bags of garishly wrapped presents I'd bought from Harrods, he announced unsmilingly that this is what all Americans do, shop at Harrods; they think that is what is correct. So 'amusing' is not the word I personally would use, even if this retired vicar, with his kind, ripened face, would.

'I remember how Bernard couldn't stand to use a different pen to complete a letter,' the vicar begins. 'He had this idea you could distinguish easily between two shades of pen ink, so if he started with one blue pen, he was not going to switch to another blue pen later. He'd rather rewrite the entire correspondence. This proved to be a terrible nuisance in his life, so Bernard developed what he called the "timed cartridge" approach. He tallied up the number of lines a single blue-ink cartridge could accommodate, and kept track as one might of the petrol in a tank as he set his thoughts on paper . . .'

All around me people are smiling, remembering this timed cartridge idea of which I never knew. It sounds vaguely like obsessive compulsive disorder to me, as does the next point the vicar makes, which concerns a habit Bernard had of keeping every receipt, for every item he ever purchased, for a minimum of seven years.

'But as you all know, Bernard was a great lover of *people*. And a man very easy to befriend. For all of you except *one*, that is. For Bernard was many things but not what one could call a ladies' man. And so, poor Daphne found herself being courted by a fellow whose technique

to attract a woman was to allow the hand of God to inter-
vene and do nothing *whatsoever* otherwise to garner her
attention. I can remember very well the day he told me
he'd met this lovely young lady named Daphne Took. They
met during the intermission of a carol concert and he
wowed her by standing as far away from her as possible
as she ate a mince pie. "How, then, did you meet her?"
I asked him, when he came in bursting with his news.
"Oh," said Bernard, "because when she looked up to
check the time I made sure I was standing just in front of
the clock. Hence she saw me!" I thought about this. "Are
you quite sure she *knows* she saw you?" I asked. He
replied, "Of course I'm sure. I was standing directly in
the way!" Well, he must have had it right, because not
many weeks later they were seen at the same Twelfth Night
celebration. Not together, mind, but as part of a group.
So Bernard had made great progress, no longer having to
block timepieces for attention. However, despite this
portentous beginning it took him four months to ask if
she would like to accompany him to a concert, two years
to consider themselves a couple, and a total of four years
to find themselves finally wed. So it is a great wonder and
really a triumph of Bernard's persistence, as well as
Daphne's patience, that there are so many young people
sitting here today bearing Bernard's surname!'

We are all laughing now, certainly I am. Until I notice
the vicar looking down at the row of young Marshes
seated in the first row. Is it only me, or does the vicar
seem rather puzzled? Perhaps he didn't understand that
there has been a change of cast, that my pencilled-in name
has finally been erased, and that however persistent
Bernard may have been, his son is the opposite. A quitter.
And certainly a ladies' man.

At the reception, which takes place at a local hotel due to there being no suitable church hall, I tell Daphne I am so sorry. I've brought her a photograph of the children framed in sterling. She thanks me for the picture, says they look beautiful, that she would love to see them, and thanks me for attending the service. Then she moves on. Raymond sees me and I go to him. He takes my elbow, moving close to me because his voice is weak; it doesn't carry well in crowds. 'I apologise, dear Melanie,' he says into my ear. 'I promised I'd come to see you.'

'Raymond –' I hug him. I realise all at once how much I've missed him.

'You look marvellous,' he tells me.

'Oh, I don't know.' I'm thinking once again how everything I'm wearing seems wrong and that, despite how much I try to fit in, I always stand out.

'You're a breath of sunshine in this dire place,' he says.

I am puzzled, delighted, unsure what to say. Raymond sighs and I look at his face which is beautiful, like an ancient image, ornamental with lines and folds. His eyes are waxy with age but full of love, compassion. He holds my elbow and I touch his hand. I kiss his cheek. I invite him to spend a day with us. But then Daphne arrives back to take Raymond off to see someone else, so that I cannot finish what I want to say to him, which is that we love him, the children and I.

If there is anything more awkward than going to a funeral, it is going to a funeral for a man who never liked you as the ex of a man who wants nothing more than to divorce you. It's really not terribly pleasant. Still, as freakish as I might feel, scores of those around us have no idea I don't belong.

'So nice to see you, Melanie, how are the children?'

'Oh, Melanie, I haven't seen you in ages!'

'You look absolutely lovely, my dear. What a beautiful hat!'

Stephen's uncles and aunts and cousins, not to mention Bernard's ancient assortment of friends with short-term memory loss, have no idea I am anything but Stephen's faithful wife, and he my doting husband. Although it must seem a tad odd to see Penelope there, standing with Stephen. That might throw them if the fact I stand alone does not.

'I think you're bloody brave,' says Cath, bringing me a glass of wine.

Cath wears an unflattering black skirt that ends mid-calf, a jacket with long sleeves even in this hot weather, and a nondescript blouse which is hidden in all the black of her jacket. Her hat is plain, her bobbed hair crunched beneath it. She wears no make-up. I always marvel at Cath's seemingly purposeful efforts at sabotaging her own good looks. Perhaps it is something you learn to do at boarding school, where the emphasis is on uniformity, fitting in, being correct. I am none of these things. I thought the English always wore long skirts to such occasions, but I see now that there is only one other woman in the room in such a thing and she is a member of the clergy. Mid-calf would have been correct, and also my blouse is too bright and my jacket has short sleeves – very wrong – plus, I should have realised, no lipstick.

'I came for you,' I say to Cath now. She says nothing. 'OK, and for him.'

'And because you are just nice,' says Cath. 'You were always nice. It's not a trait that gets you anywhere in life, but the rest of us appreciate it.'

I smile. 'I'm sorry about your dad. Anyway, it wouldn't be right if I just failed to show up.'

Across the room from me, near where the food is set out buffet-style, Penelope sips her glass of wine and nods at one of Stephen's cousins, a man named Andrew who teaches at Cambridge and whose specialty is kinship among tribal groups in Borneo. I never know what to say to Andrew, who comes across as slightly lewd in his continual referral to the rites and rituals surrounding the role of mothers' brothers. But Penelope seems quite at ease. She knows all of the cousins well, having many times during university holidays accompanied Stephen and his family to a farmhouse in the Peak District, where they spent their time watching village cricket and fishing in the rain. It is really only right and fitting that she is with Stephen now. She suits him. Standing beside Stephen's anthropologist cousin, she can both marvel at the exotic, quaint habits of tribal people and enjoy the cultural exactitudes of her own, precise and metred class. Whenever I've tried to talk to Stephen's cousins they seemed to keep noticing my accent as though its sound released a mildly displeasing scent into the air. Actually, that is a bit of an exaggeration. They are used to me now. And anyway, they are nicer than that, but not Andrew.

'I think I will say hello,' I say now, heading for Penelope.

Penelope is not a stupid woman. She knows exactly where I am in the hotel reception room, her radar no less accurate than my own. As I step toward her she turns to me, her face open and welcoming, placing her wine glass in her left hand and holding out her right. She unzips a smile, beaming at me with big, horsey teeth. She says my name as though it is good news. 'Melanie,' she says, pausing, taking me in. 'I've wanted so much to speak to you!'

Bending her face toward mine, smiling as though I am a great friend, she is gracious and attractive. I can hardly stand it. She is taller than me, even though she has opted for shorter heels. She turns now to Andrew, brushing his cheek with her lips. 'We'll chat later,' she murmurs quietly.

Stephen is suddenly nowhere to be found. He caught a glimpse of me earlier at the church and again as I came into the hotel, so he knows I am here. When he rang to tell me about his father's death, I assumed he wanted me at the funeral, but now I am not so sure. Perhaps he wanted the children here, which would make no sense. If Daniel were in the room right now, they'd have had their circular doilies and napkin rings confiscated for their roundness. He'd likely have run beneath the buffet table and tugged at the tablecloth until it brought down all the food. Certainly nobody would keep him from the trays of cheese and crackers, as he will do anything to eat gluten. He's like an addict, desiring more and more bread. My gluten-free alternatives are shoddy approximations of the real thing. The boy craves cake.

'You must hate me,' says Penelope now.

'No, not hate,' I say. She nods. I don't like to admit it, but she has really a rather appealing face, a kind of regality. Her cheeks are sharp points, her eyes theatrical and large beneath the solid weight of her heavy fringe.

'Do you remember when I met you that day in Camden Town?' she asks me. Her voice is kind. Her attention is all mine.

'Was it Camden Town?' I say. 'I can't see you in Camden Town.'

'And why is that?' she smiles. She is genuinely surprised. She is stunning. Over the past few years she has become more rounded in the hips, a bit chunkier in her upper arms, her thighs, but she is a gracious and commanding woman. A beauty, I have to admit, making me seem by contrast a dry and angular creature no more appealing than a paper fan.

'Never mind,' I say.

'Now look, you need to speak to Stephen. We would *both* like to talk with you. Don't you think it's time?' she says.

Perhaps it is. I don't know. All I can think is that I am looking at my children's future stepmother and that she seems an awful lot more engaging than their real mother. I can picture Emily and Penelope exchanging tales of head-mistresses and hockey teams, discussing the pressures of GCSE exams and Christmas balls. My daughter, whose colicky newborn stomach required me to pace for hours every evening, for whom I played patient to her doctor, pony to her rider, who I taught to pedal a bicycle by holding on to her seat and running, over and over again, until I had no more breath. It seems somehow unfair that Penelope is so well mannered and so English, and so every-thing that I am not. Still, here she is. There is no escape from her. Not by me. Not by Emily.

'I think you should babysit Daniel,' I tell Penelope now.

'Oh,' she says, a little taken aback. I've never let the children near her. 'What a lovely idea,' she says flatly.

'We *think* he can use a toilet now,' I say, as though this is a grand, scientific discovery. 'But then again, maybe not.'

'I see,' she says, fingering her pearls.

'You just have to watch his willy,' I say. She swallows, coughs softly, tries to smile. 'But as for number two, you have to get there before his hands do, that is my advice. Unless, of course, you have a lot of time and disinfectant.'

She has no answer to this. I spot Stephen coming through the doors from the hotel's reception. 'Excuse me,' I say, and Penelope steps aside.

Stephen's tie has come slightly loose. His eyes have a heaviness to them as though he has not been sleeping well. He runs his hands through his hair and I see, through the cascade of sandy locks, the scar from a rugby game a dozen years or more ago, and I notice, too, that his hair is thinning. Still, he is a beautiful man.

'Very nice,' he says. 'Very nice of you to come.'

'I'm sorry about your father.'

'Doctors didn't give him the right heart medicine. I blame them, you know. He was on that rat poison but not beta blockers. I can't remember what excuse they gave. Something about a stroke.'

He looks away from me, over my shoulder. It occurs to me, now that I notice such things, that he has not looked me fully in the eye for many months.

'Where are the children?' he asks.

'With Veena. With Andy.'

'You mean that guy who helps Daniel to play? That Andy?'

I nod.

Stephen lets out a long breath. 'He seems to know what he's doing,' he says.

'He's Irish,' I say, just for something to say.

'Yes, I think I remember that,' says Stephen tartly, and I realise my statement is not so innocent as I would like to think. Stephen hasn't been married to me for five years without picking up on the habits of my thoughts, the meaning of isolated tones in my voice that others would scarcely notice. What I meant was, He is Irish, not like you, Stephen. He is with the children, not like you. He is good at playing with kids, not like you. He is in my life, not like you. None of this is lost on Stephen, who is at times a cantankerous and insular man, but not stupid.

I say, 'Stephen, I would like to take the children on a holiday somewhere. Summer is almost over and all we've done is hang around London.'

'What about Ireland?' he says now. 'Ireland in your plans at all?'

'I would like just a little bit of money, you know? Just to take them to the beach?'

'I'll take them to the beach,' says Stephen. 'If that is where you'd like them to go.'

He leaves me there and I feel like shit. He walks off in long, confident strides back to Penelope who glances into his face as though she's seen something holy there, something glorious and sacred. Perhaps she has.

When I feel I can finally leave, having said something to David, to Cath, again to Daphne, who this afternoon looks suddenly older, suddenly frail, after I have chatted at least briefly with those who knew me and who made their best efforts to incorporate me into their family – for some of them did – I go to Stephen and say goodbye. I hope not to upset him, or disturb him, or anger him, or annoy him. Just to say goodbye. I find him beside his brother, talking about the cricket.

'Goodbye,' I say, nodding. He nods back, murmurs, 'Bye,' then with hesitation and a hardness in his eyes, he leans forward and kisses me drily on the cheek. The kiss is performed quickly, dispatched. This kiss is meant to be, *what*? Polite? It is an affront, painful in its isolating effect, like a slap on the face. I have been dismissed. I stumble away from him out through heavy double doors which have been propped open, leading into the hotel foyer. I am wishing I'd never come, wishing I weren't so 'nice' as Cath says, wishing I were someone else entirely. I pass a pair of mustard-coloured tassled ropes connected to slim, silver stands. I pass the lifts, pass the reception area with its tidy employees in their uniforms. I am thinking, Just Go Home. Then I hear a voice behind me. I hear Stephen call my name, hear the muffled clap of his hard shoes against the hotel's carpet, which I realise all at once is the exact same carpet that covers Daphne's living room.

'Wait,' says Stephen. He touches my elbow, turns me gently toward him. It is exactly the same gesture he made the first night I met him, when he told me how I must not, under any circumstances, leave without him.

'Here,' he says now, pulling money from his wallet, note after note, twenties and fifties. 'Take them to the beach, Melanie,' he says, his face looking slightly crumpled, not like him at all. 'Tell them I love them, OK?'

21

The Welsh cottage is not what you'd call a holiday destination. Formerly a sheep shed, it was converted sometime in the seventies during what must have been a dizzy moment for interior decorating. The kitchen's linoleum floor has been laid across several previous linoleum floors, and is a brown-and-orange pattern that repeats so often you cannot look at it without feeling your pulse rise. The carpet is a dull green, high-pile affair that is faded where the bay window – OK, the pane of ordinary glass looking like what you'd find in a shopfront – lets in the alarmingly infrequent Welsh sun. The bathroom fixtures are a deep brown, which I must point out is very useful at disguising the need to clean it, and the fireplace is a brick monster that looks something like a cross between a beehive and a bread oven, and suffers from an overload of what can only be described as decorative cement. Then there is the garden, its beauty spot. The garden is described in the estate agent's details as 'a patch of native grasses and wild flowers', but what is really at work here is an overgrown patch of unkempt grass strewn with poppies, enhanced in its fertility by a dodgy septic tank that appears to leak, judging from the boggy soakaway at the edges of the back wall, and that at certain times of year gives off the scent of sulphur.

'Well,' Stephen had said when he first observed the cottage, which I have to admit was a bit of a purchasing error on my part. 'Now we know what primitive man endured.'

But the reason I have my attention drawn to the cottage now is that the estate agent has rung me with what is not exactly good news.

'Mrs Marsh, I'm sorry to tell you, but it seems that someone has deposited a whole pile of unauthorised dung in the back of your cottage. We're not sure how or why, but we can't show the cottage with all the dung like it is, so perhaps you or your husband could come down and sort it out for us.'

A pile of dung? Cow dung? Horse? Sheep? Dung from the stinking goat farm adjacent to the cottage? Dung doesn't come from nowhere. And what does he mean by unauthorised? Would it be possible to get authorisation for this dung, in which case, would that make it all right?

'What kind of dung?' I ask. It turns out that nobody is quite sure what kind of dung it is, though smells have been reported and steam has been seen rising from it.

'You really need to sort it out,' insists the estate agent, a man named Robert who has what I'm sure his mother finds an endearing stutter. When he tells me about the dung he says it's a 'who-ho-ho-hole pile of dung'. But he also warns me that it would not help matters on his side if the parish council got involved with the cottage. 'You're at the end of the selling season as it is, Mrs Marsh. This manure is not w-w-w-working in your favour.'

I promise him I will do something about it, get off the phone and drop on to the floor with Daniel and Andy, who are watching a video that shows you how to make robots out of paper bags. On the television, the camera focuses on a pale table on which rest a pencil, some crayons, a set of bright red buttons, some shiny paper, glue and of course the bag. And now, a pair of human hands which I recognise immediately as Andy's hands. While we listen to the voice – Andy's voice – explaining what needs to be done to make a robot puppet, the hands go about cutting shapes, positioning, gluing down, all of which leads us eventually to the creation of a convincing robot.

'First, we will make the robot's eyes,' says the voice. 'We will use buttons for that. And we will need glue . . .'

It's what Andy calls a 'play video'. Because Daniel learns more easily from things he sees on television, Andy has put on to the television the thing he wants him to learn, which is craft-making, normal kids' stuff, paste and glitter and googly eyes. 'When did you do this?' I ask him.

'While you were out,' he says. Nobody is allowed to say funeral any more. Emily gets a little too weird with her Mickey Mouse, having it die and brought back to life again, when we mention Bernard's funeral.

The play video works a treat. Daniel watches it, mesmerised by the creation of the puppet, then turns to discover that the exact same materials that are in the video are now here, on our table at home.

'We will use buttons for eyes,' says Daniel, parroting the video.

Andy will not allow Daniel simply to memorise and repeat. So he asks Daniel, 'What kind of buttons should we use?'

'Red buttons,' says Daniel, 'for the eyes.'

'Perfect,' says Andy.

But wait a second. There is something that requires explanation. I touch Andy on the arm and he looks at me, his face bright with the success of the play video. 'Andy, *where* did you find the video camera?' I ask. It's about the only thing of value I haven't sold, and I keep it secreted away in case a burglar comes.

'In your underwear drawer,' says Andy without a moment of hesitation.

'And what – what *exactly* – were you doing in my underwear drawer?'

'Looking for the video camera,' he says, trying not to laugh.

Veena, coming to me now with a mug of tea, says, 'I was telling him I thought you had one, but might have sold it. It's my fault.'

I look at Veena, then at Andy, who seems so innocent standing there, a pair of blue plastic child's scissors in his hand.

'Anyway,' Andy whispers to me now, 'I wanted to know if you were a thong girl or a panties girl.'

And then he turns away, cutting as Daniel directs him, and won't be disturbed or even interrupted as I swat at his back, pull the ends of his T-shirt until it makes a bell shape round his waist, or even when I reach under the belt line of his jeans and yank the elastic band of his shorts until it snaps against him.

Late one night, just after I have finally fallen asleep, the phone rings. I think it's my brother so I pick it up and say, 'Larry, what disaster has struck such that you are willing to spend actual real live money to call me?'

'It's not Larry,' says the voice. It is Stephen.

I sit up in bed, hug my knees to my chest. Months ago I'd have given anything for him to call me late at night. Now I'm not even sure what to say to him. 'You miss your dad?' I say.

'Yeah, that.' There's a pause. Then, 'You never liked him.'

I sigh. 'This is the worst time. It will get better. After my mother died I kept dialling her phone number and then I'd remember all over again that she wasn't there. And I kept seeing people who looked like her. But over a few months that faded. About a year later I was more or less OK again.'

'You don't miss her now?'

I consider this. It sounds so awful to say you get over something as dreadful and final as a parent's death. But you do. The only time I've missed her in recent years was when Daniel was diagnosed. She'd have loved Daniel just as he is, autistic or not. I tell Stephen, 'I think of her but it doesn't hurt any more.'

'I keep thinking about Daniel,' he says.

'Yeah, well.'

'You don't get over that, do you?' he says.

No, you don't get over that. Daniel has his good days; he has his bad days. Yesterday morning Andy and I took the children to a big adventure playground and lost him. I was helping Emily out of the swing. Andy was answering one of the many SOS calls he gets from autism mothers on a daily basis. I looked up and couldn't see Daniel, motioned to Andy to look for him. He circled the playground and came up with nothing. Within minutes I was running all over screaming Daniel's name. Andy charged over to a groundskeeper to ask him for help. We rounded up several mothers to help search for him. While giving them a description of him – brown eyes, blond hair, green shorts and a yellow T-shirt – I had a sudden moment of nausea as I realised it was like giving a missing person's report to the police. It all felt so hopeless. I burst into tears and looked to Andy but found he couldn't really comfort me. All he could do was what we were doing right then, asking people to help.

'You think he's getting much better, right?' says Stephen. I know that tone of voice so well and all the feelings behind it. It's usually me who asks this kind of thing, begging a particular kind of answer. Stephen wants me to say yes, of course he's getting better. It will all be fine. There's nothing to worry about.

'You bet,' I tell him. I don't tell him that Andy and I were both hysterical by the time we finally found Daniel. He was sitting inside a play tunnel tapping a stick against its side. There had been a half-dozen people screaming his name all around him, and yet he had not answered or even seemed to notice.

After Stephen hangs up I call Andy. It is after midnight so, of course, Andy doesn't answer. All I get is his voicemail asking me to please leave a message.

On Andy's voicemail I say, 'I was just thinking of you. Thought I'd say hello.'

Andy is here most evenings now, stopping by after work. He arrives in jeans and trainers, a rucksack slung over his shoulder, his hair standing up. He seems always to be smiling. Emily plays a game where she ties his laces to a kitchen chair and he pretends not to notice, then falls down comically when he stands. Daniel brings him trains and says, 'Play with me,' just as we've taught him. Andy is a part of the household. A nice part, I think.

'Not so bad,' is Veena's estimation. I think it's the nicest comment she's ever made about a man.

Tonight, after the children have fallen asleep, we are having a discussion about religion – well, as close as you can get to religion in my household.

'We weren't really religious. My father was Jewish but my mother was an atheist,' I tell Andy and Veena.

'Didn't that pose a problem, your parents having different religions?' asks Andy. 'Near where I come from they'd have to kill each other.'

'Well, no. The two positions are strangely compatible. After Dad died my mother's one concession to Judaism was to hate anything that was definitely not Jewish while not actually teaching us about Judaism either. Because, of course, she didn't know. So, for example, if she saw a statue of a Virgin Mary in someone's garden, which is not so unusual a sight where I come from, she would say something mildly disapproving about it. But at Hanukkah and Passover she merely announced the day and then proceeded to ignore it. I think she gave us a dreidel once, but no one knew how to play.'

'We get Lent,' says Andy. 'You have to give something up.'

'What do you give up?' Veena asks him.

'Not a damn thing,' he says.

'So I take it you're not a practising Catholic?' Veena deadpans. To me she says, 'Were your mother's parents atheists?'

'Quakers,' I say.

'That sounds like a person with a palsy,' says Veena.

'I think it just means you're nice to people.'

'Hindus are nice to people,' says Veena. 'Unless the people are Muslims.'

'Nice to cows,' says Andy.

'What do you know about Hinduism?' Veena says, looking at him as though the notion that he could know anything at all was utterly impossible.

'Nothing,' says Andy, 'except they like cows.'

'What do you believe?' Veena asks him now. She looks at him squarely. She is a woman who thinks only uneducated people believe in God. Only cretins. She says such people are happier than she is, such people are blessed.

Andy flushes, then meets her challenge. 'I believe in the Father, the Son and the Holy Spirit,' he says. 'In the whole Holy Works. I believe it all, but not the Pope. The Pope can kiss my arse.'

Veena turns to me now. 'And what about you, Melanie? Any leaders of world religions you feel ought to make contact with your arse?'

I shake my head as though declining an offer of tea. 'No,' I say. 'I'm good.'

'She doesn't like the Pope either,' Andy says to Veena, watching me as he does so. 'She told me that, you know, secretly,' he says.

'Oh, so now we have secrets, do we?' says Veena.

Another night, just as we are about to eat dinner, I hear Stephen's voice from the answering machine. 'Look, Melanie, I think you should call me,' he says.

He speaks in a kind of office tone and I think I know what *you should call me* is all about. He's obviously heard from the estate agent about the dung pile that is preventing the sale of the cottage, which he didn't know was on the market. So now he's figured out what I'm up to and he undoubtedly has his opinions on the matter.

'Don't pick up the phone at all tonight,' I say. We are taking our food out to the garden for a picnic. All five of us carry plates or spoons or glasses. Even Daniel carries something, a single straw. 'Stephen must have been informed about the dung situation.'

'The dung situation?' Veena says.

Andy says, 'Did you just say dung?'

22

To ask a person to do nothing for their child or to do very little is unfair. For them to do nothing means they have to fight the overwhelming desire to push away the danger, to run through the flames, to slay the dragon. However hopeless the situation might appear, it is infinitely more difficult to do nothing than even an ill-considered something. I knew a man whose teenage son was stabbed to death in the early hours of a Saturday night by kids his own age who wanted his trainers. This was some years ago. His father had repeated dreams – the day and night dreams that I came to be familiar with after Daniel's diagnosis – in which he was there when it happened, just behind the gang as they circled his boy. There, hidden in the luxuriant green of unkempt bushes, he would be crouching. Or he stepped off the bus just in time to reach over and pluck his son, vibrant and alive, from the hands of his attackers. In his dreams the five-inch steel blade that pierced his son's chest never so much as scratched his skin. Instead, he took his child in his arms as he had as a baby, running at a supernatural speed, flying even, not knowing where he was going but knowing it was away. Away from threat and danger and harm, away from four youths and their deadly, sharpened blade.

But the dreams were only dreams. The reality was the boy died. The father slept.

My reality is that my child lives peacefully within a dysfunctional brain while I search madly – tear myself apart – trying to think for the both of us how to get out of the burning building of autism. Even using this method – this play therapy mixed with applied behaviour therapy and whatever else Andy brings to bear – there are limitations. With every learned word or spontaneous moment of play, I see Daniel becoming more like any other child, less 'autistic'-seeming, and I know that if he will interact with others as he is now interacting with Andy, with me and with Emily, his life will not be entirely ruined by the condition. But there is also a time factor. As he develops so do all the other children around him. He has to race to catch up or never catch up at all. I understand this very well. It is almost as though someone has told me, 'If he is going to escape the fire, he must do so early before the roof caves in.'

Daniel plays with Teletubbies and Tweenies, with cars, with trains (of course). He runs with Emily, chasing her with good-heartedness and smiles. He can talk and he can tell me what he likes and doesn't like. He will listen to stories if you present them with enough animation and will draw pictures if you bribe him with chocolate. All of this shows enormous progress; impressive, extraordinary strides. I don't mean to trivialise this progress or make it count for nothing. But he hasn't left the burning building.

The doctors have a way of speaking to me that is unnerving, strange. It used to be, for example, that when

I went to see doctors they asked me what the trouble was. But now they have a mildly pitying look in their eyes. 'Why do you think you are here?' says this one, who is supposed to be a specialist in neurological conditions.

By accident? By abduction? Is this a philosophical question? I have to play it straight. Part of being the parent of an autistic child means humouring the same people you pay great sums to.

'He doesn't walk at all well and he says his legs hurt.'

The doctor looks down at Daniel, who is seated on the floor with his trains. If we wait long enough Daniel will look up, rub his knee and say, 'Leg hurts. My leg hurts.' He's been telling me this every day for a week.

'That is because he's autistic,' says the doctor, a man with a coat, a stethoscope, a Physicians' Desk Reference, a computer and an examination table. So I guess he is a doctor.

'What would the autism affect? The legs or the complaint that the legs hurt?' I ask.

The doctor considers this.

'Well, either, really. It may not be his legs per se which are bothering him. It may be that something hurts him but he says it is the leg, even though the pain is from elsewhere.'

'He knows what a leg is,' I say.

The doctor looks at me as though I am a bit of a problem myself. Nothing like his own wife, who smiles from the polished frames of several photographs, along with his children, all girls.

He says, 'I look after the primary care of a residential school for autistic children. They say whatever pops into their heads or nothing at all.'

It occurs to me that you might as well say nothing at

all if whatever you do say is interpreted as gibberish. And I know the "school" he means. They call it a school because the residents in it are under eighteen.

Ten minutes later this same consultant is telling me Daniel can only be very literal. He can only say what he sees factually and that he cannot make things up. Cannot lie or interpret abstract concepts. This is because he is autistic. The doctor informs me also that Daniel does not feel pain like other children, normal children.

'Wait, let me tell this to you once more,' I say to the doctor. 'Let me start again because I truly believe you have the ability to understand.'

The doctor's face grows dark. He's dealt with autism mothers before. 'Yes,' he says sharply.

Pointing to Daniel I say, very slowly, 'He *says* his legs *hurt.*'

But the doctor is uninterested, already checking the next patient file, feeling no concern at all about anything Daniel says.

That same doctor told me that in the school over which he presides the children drink cow's milk by the bucket, can spin without becoming dizzy, and don't feel pain. I tried to tell him about a theory that autistic children have an intestinal problem and cannot digest cow's milk. That the milk does something to them that seems to make them more 'autistic', and that removal of the milk may help. Not in all cases, but in some cases. Perhaps they ought to try getting rid of the milk?

'Use goat's milk,' I said. 'Raw, unpasteurised. Or if that doesn't work, use rice milk.'

'They'd taste the difference,' said the doctor. 'If you take away their milk, these children will starve.'

'OK, OK,' I said. I understand the trouble with getting autistic kids to eat. I spend hours every day grating courgettes to hide in burgers, stirring organic egg yolks into dairy-free yogurt. 'Then put one-tenth goat's milk into nine-tenths cow's milk. Every week add more goat's milk and less cow's milk. Then eventually get rid of the cow's milk. This works. I've seen it work.'

'Your child is not so badly autistic,' said the doctor.

There was no point in telling this doctor that Daniel's initial diagnosis was moderate autism, not mild autism. Not Asperger's. Or about all the other kids I've heard of who have improved. So I said, 'That may be true, Doctor. But to a mother there is no such thing as a hopeless case. Maybe you could just try –'

'No,' he said, clearly annoyed. I'd touched a nerve with him. Perhaps another autism mother had suggested the same thing. He looked at me with the coldness of a tanker, set his eyes on Daniel and then on me again. 'We don't have time for experiments.'

So they spin, all the children in his care. I'll never forget how the doctor said, just before we left, 'They spin and they don't get dizzy!' as though this personal trait of autistic children was wonderful, exciting, something to build upon.

Today is a little exhausting. Daniel hops all over the furniture, running into the walls on purpose, not talking much. He visits me as I make his special muffins in the kitchen, colliding into me like a chuckling tornado. I am pleased when he grows dizzy and has to sit down. Normal, I tell myself. Stop fretting. He comes to me, his lips pursed like two sides of a peeled banana, giving me what looks like a monkey kiss. 'I love you,' I tell him.

'I love you,' he says. Is he repeating what I say as an echo, the way a parrot might? Or does he mean it?

'Why do you love me?' I ask him. An inane question no child can answer.

'You like trains,' he says. Does he have the pronouns correct? Or does he mean that *he* likes trains?

I point to my chest. 'Me?' I ask. My heart lights up as he nods.

It seems to me I see autistic children everywhere now, at parks, at railway stations, in supermarkets, or just walking down the road. Some of the mothers, like me, are a bit preoccupied, a bit nervy. We have an instant affinity, a common ground. We waste no time, allowing for only the briefest of introductions. From such mothers I have learned that Daniel needs more zinc, more magnesium, more vitamin B than other children. I have learned that Disneyland allows autistic children special passes so they do not have to wait in line, which will be great if I ever have the money to take the children there. I learn about free swimming at the local public pool, about ideas for how to teach language. They are big-hearted, open-handed. They are lovely.

Sometimes, however, even the parents annoy me. They say, 'The hardest part is . . .' and then fill in the blank with something that isn't the hardest part at all. When others stare at you in public places or say some small insulting thing is not the hardest part. When relatives fail to understand or to help out is not the hardest part. The hardest part is what you think and feel privately in your own home, usually at night, often when alone. But we don't talk about that, the hardest part. Nor do we talk about the number of autistic children who drown annually, or get killed running across roads or by swallowing wrong objects. We don't talk about our marriages, or our hopes for the future. We don't like to think of the future.

Some mothers appear to make a badge out of autism, behaving as though it is not a disability but a 'difference' and that we shouldn't be seeking to cure these children. Understanding is what is in order, they cry, a broader mind, an enlightened perspective. What you know about such people is that they have a child who functions very well, who may have Asperger's syndrome and not full-blown autism, and that they have probably not scrubbed faeces from their carpet, or watched their child cry and rock in what looks like agony because he cannot speak. These people annoy me a little, although I admire how they cope, admire their presence of mind, their fearless defences of their children. But we've walked different paths, and they are talking about mine as though they've been there, which they have not, and will not. Because having a child with autism – at least the type of autism I have experienced – is less like walking a path than hacking at a jungle with a scythe, not able to see much in front of you at all except more stuff you have to clear or step over, or around, or through.

Still, Daniel has told me he loves me. If I allow myself, I can see that Daniel has begun to clear his own path, has taken up his own scythe. One day he will ask me what autism is and I will be tempted to hold it up like a badge and tell him it is a difference. Only a difference.

Tonight, for the first time since Stephen left me, I go out at night wandering the city in a haze of insomnia. I wake Veena before I leave, telling her I am going out, to please listen for the children, and that I will be back in a few hours. They are asleep; they will not miss me, or know I've gone. She looks up from the bed, her hair splashed like ink across the crisp white sheets. She nods. Then she raises her hand to touch the side of my face, moving her head back and forth like a slow pendulum. She cannot understand why I am not afraid to be on my own, alone in the city, why I do not worry about myself but instead about others, always others. About my little girl who must go to school for some absurd number of hours the moment she turns five years old, about my marvellous son who spins and flaps his hands beside his eyes and must work a thousand times harder than other children just to understand the world. About her, even. Yes. Because I don't know who will value this flower of a woman whose brain consumes the works of Benjamin and Derrida while all around her people expect she has no real intelligence, being not only Indian but small, female, with a darker complexion than most others from her country.

This summer night is no proper colour for midnight, the stars hidden by clouds reflecting the moony orange glow of street lamps. This is London: you never see the real night sky but live beneath this nocturnal haze. The Underground entrance is full of cigarette butts and rolling cans. Down on the platform there are no bins, due to bomb scares, so crisp packets and sandwich wrappers scatter through open places, collecting in corners. The breeze is cool, a balm across my hot cheeks, like the breath of a parent who blows against the fever of their child, soothingly. I walk through the disparate groups that hang about such places, young people clubbing, couples hanging over each other, heading to one bed or another, businessmen late from important dinners, standing kerbside just outside the station, hailing cabs. In my pocket is the money that Stephen gave me rolled in a band, thick as a cigar. A newspaper skids across the dirty station tiles, the headlines turning like a flip book's pages. I might walk now to the Italian pastry shop, except it wouldn't be open. And anyway, I know where I am heading. Standing in front of the turnstile, eyeing the slot for my railcard, I realise I am not here to wander aimlessly, to observe the world in my ruined state, to flee from my bruised heart, the desperation, the fear. I am no longer that woman; and I'm not in the least bit afraid. I put away the railcard, get out the money once more. When I turn now, it is as though I've split my life like a soft melon, into two opposing halves.

It is an easy drive, straight over Vauxhall Bridge.

The taxi driver is not talkative, not friendly. He pulls away from the kerb with a jolt and I steady myself in my seat. Leaning my head against the window, I feel the vibration of the taxi's engine, the swift swells and isolated potholes of the London streets. It is a city I would compare only to itself, majestic and impoverished, full of feverish lights, garish and improbable against the elegant backdrop of splendid buildings, of lurid advertisements that change every minute as the billboards exchange one set of women's breasts for another. There is traffic all the time, as in New York, but it is more lovely. With chains of lights across the river, bridges that stretch for miles if you stand at the railings and search, with parks deep green and undulating, and people from every nation, skin of every shade, like so many colours in a tray of chocolates.

South of the river there is the Oval, no less grimy for all the impressive cricket that is played there. And here, in a backstreet of Camberwell, an anonymous sort of street filled with identical Victorian houses, with their cement front porches, windows of thin glass, some of them boarded up, some of them lit by single hanging bulbs. At the end of the road, beside a dry-cleaner's that has had its security doors decorated with every imaginable type of graffiti, is the place where Andy lives. I've never been here before, of course, but London taxi drivers know their maps well, and therefore I have been able to enjoy the ride without overdue concern about arriving at my destination.

I give the driver one of Stephen's twenties, fish out another ten. I was right to take a cab. Veena would approve.

His room is at the back of the house, ground floor, what would be the sitting room if it were a proper house instead of converted into flats. He has described for me the neighbour's cat which he spies in the mornings when he wakes, stalking birds in the small garden. Through a narrow, dark alley, past bicycles fastened with many chains to a metal drainpipe, I tiptoe around the house, looking for clues to Andy's whereabouts. All at once I am worried, what if he isn't home? Then a new feeling creeps over me, of jealousy, of regret. What right do I have to expect him to be alone?

There is no light on, but the curtain is left open. I can see by moonlight a room lined with books. He has stacked these books on shelves made of plywood and brick, and above each row of texts are volumes of loose paper, folders, videos stacked on their sides. I know this is Andy's room, not just because the titles are all about child development, about language, about autism, but because his presence is everywhere. His bed is a mattress on the floor, and he sleeps with the window open. The window is flung high, like an open mouth. It is easy to glide through. In a single swift movement, as I lean into the open space of the window, the house seems to contract like a muscle and pull me inside. I stand before Andy's bed, blinking. He is not there.

Then I hear something, the sound of someone walking through grass. I turn and peer through the open window out into the garden. I see him now, gliding across the lawn in his boxer shorts and bare feet, a cigarette in his mouth. He sees me here – in his room, beside his bed, unannounced. I watch as the breeze filters through his hair, as he drags on the cigarette, which answers with a strong, orange glow. His face is serious, contained. Somehow I've entered his life and left him like a visitor peering in. He might not know this yet, but I do.

'How long do I have you for?' he says now. He is not asking how many hours tonight. So I answer the question I think he is asking.

'I don't know. I don't think it's up to me.'

Andy puts the cigarette to his mouth, inhales, holds the smoke in a sigh, and then releases it all at once. 'Is it up to him, then?' he says. He means Stephen, of course.

I wish I could give myself to Andy. Nothing could be more natural. I'd like to tell him I am his, that he can write his name on me if he likes. But I don't belong just to myself; I belong to others as well. To Emily and to Daniel. There are no decisions that are mine alone.

Suddenly, I am ashamed. For being here I am ashamed, and for not being able to give Andy the answer he wants I am equally ashamed.

'He'll come back,' Andy says. He flicks his cigarette on the ground. 'Then he'll go again. When something else happens.'

'How do you know?' I ask.

He shrugs, takes in a breath. 'I've seen it before. I see it all the time. In and out of people's lives, their houses and their children's games. I know what is coming, but it's no use talking.'

He looks at me, smiles sadly. Then he climbs through the open window, pushes his face into my neck, his hands on my hips. 'Even so, I'm glad you're here,' he says.

23

At the bus stop there is a group of girls. One has lavender hair, which is dead straight and reflects light in an odd manner, as though it has a kind of internal light of its own, phosphorescent and very weird against her young face. She wears a nose stud and several other piercings that seem artlessly placed, randomly it appears to me, as though carved into her skin by a drunken man. Another, with pale skin and hair like Wednesday Addams, wears her skirt two sizes too small, slashed to the hip, revealing a tattoo of a malicious-looking long-stemmed rose. A third, hunkered down on the pavement with her back to a street lamp, is a plump girl in a miniskirt, whose thick legs resemble the armour of a heavy machine. Inside the bus stop, shielded from the August sun, is a boy less than Daniel's age asleep in a pushchair.

The girls chat together, digging out their cigarettes, wrestling with slippery purse straps that slide from their naked shoulders, with mobile phones that look like small toads squatting in their palms. The boy dreams on. I wonder which one is his mother.

At home, Andy is teaching Daniel how to cut with scissors. That is the whole of the plan for him today: to take scissors and dig them through colourful sheets of sugar paper. It is all part of the effort to prepare him so he can go to a regular nursery, instead of one for children with special needs. I cannot remember ever having to teach Emily how to use scissors. She just knew. Emily, with me, has brought her hobby horse, a palomino head with dark plastic eyes attached to a varnished stick, which she uses to trot around the bus stop as we wait for the number 10. We are headed for the rental car agency so that we can drive to Wales, a trip she is so excited about she rings the bus stop with scuttering legs and giddy cries of 'To the beach! To the beach!' as her hobby horse bobs and scrapes along the pavement.

'Careful!' I call to her. I worry some whimsical turn of the game will bring her out into the street, where she would last exactly one second before a car took her away. Away from me and the world and her future, from her palomino pony and her dollhouse full of small, grey mice with beady eyes and Victorian clothes, their tails poking through gingham aprons and pale breeches. It is everything I can do to stop myself from insisting she stay here, with me, holding my hand, for it is only when she is physically attached to me that I can relax. But she wants to play, insists she will be careful, so I watch her, anticipating every move, my back to the street, my eyes fixed on her blonde head, her exuberant, pink and happy face.

The boy in the pushchair has hair the colour of recently ploughed earth, and much of it. He sits stiffly, his legs not bending over the edge of the chair as you would expect them to at this age. Casting my glance toward him now, I realise that there is a great deal not right with this child.

His nose is not centred in his face. The lobes of his ears seem to melt into this cheeks, continuing in tiny bumps down toward his chin. There is more, something not quite correct with his breathing; perhaps his nose doesn't do what it ought to do. He sleeps with his mouth open, a pool of mucus along the groove that runs between his nose and upper lip, like a slow-moving glacier. When he awakens, as he does now, he does not move. The girls by the street lamp are laughing, telling jokes with the mild, mindless swearing you would expect. They seem to be planning to meet up with others, almost surely men, and they laugh with the slightly lewd intoxication of promised love.

Then, just as the boy stirs, the girl with lavender hair goes perfectly still, like a deer who has heard the faint sound of hunters' boots. She hands her mobile phone to the dark-haired girl and moves in long strides to the pushchair, where the boy raises his arm. I see, attached to his wrist, the plastic loop of a hospital band. His fingers do not bend, but stand straight out in a horrid and unnatural fan. As his mother reaches down to him, you can see her lacy underwear, sexy against her white, blossoming hips. She picks up her child, a boy whose tragic collision of DNA means he will most certainly never speak or play or kiss or sing, who it would appear must spend his time mostly in hospital, and who, given his condition as I see it, cannot grow normally in any way whatsoever. As Emily circles the bus stop, calling out her beach dreams, this mother, with her lavender hair and casual piercings to her pretty face, nestles her baby against her cheek, coos to him, and loves him, and looks for all the earth like a saint, like someone from another, better, more loving world. I want to say something to her. I want to tell her that she is a woman of great virtue. A woman of grace. That I admire her. And that I see her differently than perhaps she sees herself. Now that I have truly seen her, now that I have taken notice. But this woman who I suddenly admire and care about is also someone I cannot reach. For like so many others in these circumstances I am silenced by the inequity of her condition, and that of her baby, who might have been my own.

Daniel and Emily are playing a game where the ponies have to jump over a course of hurdles as fast as possible without knocking them down. The hurdles are bundled socks. The timer is a stopwatch. Daniel likes the stopwatch. Emily likes the ponies. I am videoing it because Andy wants to present the video to the Local Education Authority to persuade them to provide funds for autistic children of pre-school age. He wants to train others to work with these young children. That's his life's ambition, clear and simple. And I think it's a good one. Another reason, I suppose, that I love him.

'Ready, Emily? You got your pony all set?' Andy says.

Emily nods, smiles up at Andy.

'Daniel, you got *your* pony? Daniel?'

Daniel looks but doesn't say anything. Andy nods vigorously, and Daniel takes the cue, begins to nod. Now they are off, the ponies flying over the socks, the stopwatch ticking like a metronome.

'I saw this boy at the bus stop,' I tell Andy later. 'He was so . . .' I shake my head. 'I thought, what could anyone do?'

Andy nods. He kisses my forehead. He tells me next time I'll talk to the girl. Next time I'll know that there are no fences between us.

'Wait a second,' I say. I pull him back to me. I want him close.

My brother doesn't know how to spell *ingenious*. For this reason, and this reason alone, he's called me tonight. No hello, no introduction. Any normal person would not have answered the phone, not at this exact time. But my senses are heightened as one who has been hunted like a live animal. I've become overly alert for danger. When the phone rings, I jump.

'How do you spell ingenious?' Larry asks. Beside me, in bed, is Andy. His pale chest is inches from my own. He is propped on an elbow, his lips wet from my kisses, his cheeks rosy and hot. The expression on his face says put down the phone. Hang it up, hurl it out the window, flush it down the toilet, but get rid of it. Now.

'How do you spell ingenious? *I* don't know. I'll tell you tomorrow,' I say to Larry. The children are both asleep – at present anyway – and there is little time to do what I want to do, which includes many things, but does not include speaking to Larry. 'Oh wait, I *can't* tell you tomorrow, can I? I'm going to Wales for a few days. Listen, don't worry if you call and I'm not here, OK?'

'I'm not worried,' Larry says. 'I never worry about you. It's me I worry about. I've got so many responsibilities.'

I'm trying to think of any one responsibility my brother has. The trailer is Wanda's, the parrots are Wanda's. Apparently he drives Wanda's car. Perhaps the US Army gives him responsibilities. A frightening thought.

Andy has figured out what is what. He gets out of bed, strides across the room to where his jeans, his sweatshirt, his socks, his sack of toys and notepads, folders of developmental charts and graphs are, and gets a pen and paper.

From across the room he writes out the word and holds it up for me to read.

Meanwhile, Larry is talking, 'I'm trying to write, "I've got an ingenious idea,"' he says. 'But I can't spell ingenious.'

I consider this. Then I say, 'Then maybe you shouldn't?'

An hour later I am leaning against Andy's chest, his chin resting on my head. The breeze blows gently at the curtain; outside I can see the moon high and marbled in a starless sky. I listen carefully for the stirrings of Daniel and Emily in the next room. When I've satisfied myself that they are both asleep, I relax.

'We would hear their footsteps if they woke,' Andy says. How does he know what I am thinking?

'Emily always sleeps through the night. It would be Daniel,' I tell him.

'If he wakes up I'll go get him, bring him to you. Until then, I'd like to stay, if that is what you want.'

'Of course you can stay.'

He lowers his hands, fishing among the bedclothes, pulling them high up, covering us. 'I'm asking what you *want*,' he says. 'I want to know, even if I don't like the answer.'

His eyes are serious. He speaks beseechingly, touching my face, my lips, as though trying to memorise me with his hands. 'Tell me,' he says, 'the truth.'

There are so many things I could tell him. That it feels perfectly natural to have him in my house, in my bed. That no matter how close I am to him, it is not close enough, I want more. I want to hide in him as though in a cave. I want to wear him like a second skin. But all I can manage – me, who is so full of words – is 'I want you'. And even then my voice is barely a whisper.

A car passes below our window. From far off an urban fox calls in hoarse yowls across the city.

'You're not going to change your mind, then?' he says. 'I couldn't blame you for it.'

'I won't change my mind.'

He says, 'When I first fell for you I wanted to rub your husband's face from that family portrait you have on the mantel. Now I just feel sorry for him.'

'Don't feel all that sorry for him,' I say.

'I've had this other thought. I can't quite describe it. Like I've narrowly escaped a terrible event – a plane crash, a sinking ferry. Because that's how it would feel to me if I hadn't met you.'

I want to tell Andy that I daydream about him. I see his smile and I walk down the road feeling happy. He seems to understand something inside me, the way I think, who I am. When he sees me fretting over Daniel, trying to get him to join the other children in a game of tag or speak to a child who has approached him in a playground, he doesn't become agitated or impatient or mocking or angry. He understands and hears me out, reassures me, tells me it is something we will work on and that we have time.

Now he says, 'If what you are after in me is some magic that will make Daniel completely normal, as though autism has never touched him, then you will be disappointed.'

'That's not why,' I say, perhaps a little too quickly.

'Be sure of that, Melanie,' he says. 'Because I can't do it. If what you are asking for is to see a typically developing boy, you won't find it in your son. I hope that is not so terrible for you, because I see something in Daniel that is wonderful, unique. It's him, with or without the autism, that I see. And though I will try my hardest for you, for you both, for us all, I cannot produce for you a normal child. You know that, right?'

I nod, taking this in.

'And anyway, you know everything you need already to do it yourself. You play with him for hours every day and you do as good a job as I do.'

'You're better at it,' I say.

He bends around me so that I can see his eyes. 'No, I am *not*,' he says. Then he says, 'You don't need me. Not for that.'

'I do need you.'

'For *you*? Or for Daniel? I want to know that you see a difference.'

I remember how Andy stood outside the gate of the pre-school with all those wretched parents and promised that Emily and Daniel would one day play together. It was true, for now they do. Even tonight they were playing in the bath, splashing water at one another, giggling. I remember how Andy taught Daniel to call me 'Mummy' because he knew that would delight me, and it did. How to pretend that his trains were having conversations, how to play-act with a puppet.

But these are memories not about Andy, but about Daniel.

'Have you ever been married?' I ask him. It seems an absurd question. In any normal relationship I would have found this out months ago.

'No.'

'A long-term girlfriend of many years?'

'Two,' Andy says. 'Serious girlfriends, I mean. I don't know how many years.'

'OK, then you know that love gets bound up with many other things. With other people, with events, the history of our lives unfolding. It is not isolated, like a seed, but plugged into a world with many branches. It is a sprawling, messy business, or becomes so eventually. I should know.'

He considers this.

I say, 'So, how can you ask me to separate you from everything you've touched and changed? I can't do it.'

He nods. Then he says, 'OK.'

He sleeps for a few hours with me, then rises, goes downstairs, waits for me to join him, for the children who bounce against him as though they think he's rubber, for the day to begin. He has to go to Wandsworth, to a family there with a boy of eight who has just started saying his first words. I will drive the rental car to pick him up and then we are off, together, the four of us. We are heading to Wales.

'Dung,' he said when I suggested this plan to him. 'Who knew I'd get a holiday with you because of dung?'

The rental car is a beautiful Volvo with leather seats and a radio, and also a CD player. It glides as though on air, obedient to the mildest expression of your fingers on the steering wheel, your foot on the brake pedal. So silent, I have tried to start the engine when it is already on. And the seats are like velvet, the way they hug you, the way they smell.

What happened was the rental place gave me the wrong car. But by the time they found out it was too late, I was away. So I get the 'luxury' category for the economy price. It couldn't be better, and the children think it is great fun. Daniel likes all things mechanical. I took him on a test drive last night and he spent the whole ride mesmerised by the purring engine, the movement of the gear shift, the steady clicking of the turn signal. Back home, he ran his hands over the dashboard, eyeing the dials, reading the numbers. He said, 'Mummy has a green car.' It is green, metallic, shiny, like a new American dollar.

For the occasion of our trip I have scrubbed their car seats, which I fix into place now, loading the boot with the luggage, the swimsuits and towels, the sunscreen and plastic buckets, the water wings and beach balls. All of Daniel's special flour and the ingredients for the gluten-free cakes I make, all the vitamin pills and the fresh oranges I will squeeze for their breakfasts.

'I want my talking books,' says Emily. 'The ones Andy gave me.'

The talking books are her newest craze. She has begun to read the highlighted words inside them: us, it, dog, cat, man, child. The code of language reveals itself to her and now she finds, as I once did, that all around her are messages.

'I won't forget them. But please, Emily, you'd be better off in the house with Veena right now.' Emily refuses to leave the car. She will wait as I load it, she says. She will keep me company.

'Darling, it is many hours to Wales. You'll get bored sitting in the car. Why not go play?'

'I'm not bored,' she says.

I explain to her that it will grow very boring there very quickly, but she will not listen. Finally I say, 'Go find all your ponies to bring along! You wouldn't want to leave them, would you?'

She considers this, her finger to her mouth, then traipses back into the house, holding her Mickey Mouse by the neck as usual. I turn to her and say, 'You get chocolate for being cute!' This makes her smile.

I am leaning over the trunk, rearranging the bed quilts

which I've rolled lengthwise, strapping them in shape with a belt. I am considering a thousand details. Do I have enough of Daniel's gluten-free flour? Do I have enough sunscreen? Do I have enough goat's milk? Have I remembered craft paper for Emily, trains and track for Daniel? All these details fly through my mind, so that I don't notice there is someone watching me until he has been there some time.

It is Stephen.

'You don't return my calls any more,' he says. It's a beautiful late summer's morning, the breeze rustling the trees, laden with leaves, opulently green. The sun is low in the sky yet at ten o'clock, so we stand in the shade of buildings. He is wearing his beige suit, a loose tie, brown shoes. He's shaved his face clean, gotten his hair cut. I am wearing Andy's jeans, the ones with no knees, a ripped pocket, the colour of clouds. They are loose on me, but not much. They are long on me, but only by a couple of inches. In them I feel I could hike a mountain, reach the summit and spring cartwheels across the sky.

'I hope you get good weather in Wales,' says Stephen. 'Here the forecast is for rain.'

'Rain is fine,' I say. 'I expect rain.'

'I got a very strange call from an estate agent,' he says.

I nod.

'Hey, it's your house,' he says, opening his hands as though offering me a gift. 'But if you needed help selling it you could have told me so. I'm happy to arrange for the collection of that pile of . . .'

'Shit,' I say.

'To have it removed,' he continues.

I finish sorting the luggage, close the boot of the car, wait for what is next. For surely there is something.

Stephen stands there, looking at me. His hands look empty, his face unsure.

'I'll sign some papers, if that is what you want,' I say now. 'But I need a lawyer. I guess you already have one. Maybe you could do me a favour and not tell Emily anything just yet. I really don't know how much she should be expected to understand.'

He says nothing.

'If we remain reasonable, it might not be so bad,' I tell him. 'So let's try that, OK?'

'I want to be very reasonable,' says Stephen. Then he comes closer to me, folds his arms across his chest, sighs. 'But I don't want a divorce.'

I look at him. His mouth is soft; his eyes search my face. He is being a man more tender than he is used to. It suits him and it moves me. I cannot think too much about it.

'Please,' he says. 'Five minutes. Please talk to me.'

I can remember just after he left to live with Cath, before he went to Penelope, how I hung on the phone begging him to speak to me, to come home. I remember how I made deals with him. 'I won't call you again for three days if you just talk to me now.' And how his silence on the phone felt almost like a weapon. I'd try to make a joke, but he wouldn't laugh. I'd lavish long, verbose arguments for why he needed to stay, why we needed him home, and he'd grow even more curt. If I cried, he stopped talking. If I got cross, he hung up. Now he wants five minutes on a summer's day. And what reason might I have not to give it?

I don't want Daniel and Emily to see their dad – not right now, just as we are leaving – so I tell Stephen to wait a minute. Then I go inside and ask Veena if she will watch them for me. Daniel is on the floor with Play-Doh, making trains and cars. He looks like any other little boy, except that occasionally he swipes the air in front of his eyes with the figures he makes, much in the manner of swiping a credit card through a machine.

'I'll be right back,' I promise.

'Can I bring *all* my ponies?' asks Emily.

Stephen and I walk down the street, passing the Italian pastry shop, which features cheesecakes and loaves of bread studded with herbs, pizza in thin dials, coffee that fills the air with a scent that makes me think of dark wood and ochre, the accents of strange men.

'You look great,' he says, seated with me on a bench in a public park, not far from lovers and drunks, kids on Rollerblades, old ladies with bread for the pigeons.

I cannot believe he has picked this time, this day, this hour. I want to shout at him, Why *now*?

'I've thought about some of the things you've said,' he tells me. 'Maybe you are right that I belong home.'

He says this as though 'the things' I said were said last week. That he's had a good night's sleep and now, in the clear light of day, it seems that I might have been right after all.

I look at him, astonished, amazed. He carries on affably, says the whole thing just seemed to get away from him, that he thought there might be something wrong with Daniel – perhaps his hearing, or maybe he had a problem with speech – but he also thought there was a lot more wrong with me. He didn't make the connection between the two. And once the diagnosis came, he just ran scared.

'I was a coward,' he says, shrugging his shoulders. 'That's what I feel I've been.'

I cannot disagree. But neither can I condemn him for it. Watching him now, I wonder how much he's acting, and why he's doing it. There's a shadow of deceit here, like the dark spot on an ocean's surface that tells you below are sharks.

I say, 'I didn't make it easy. And I didn't really know. I just felt upset all the time, like something terrible was going to happen.' As I say these words, I realise all at once that this is exactly the feeling that has been missing since I let Andy into my life, the dread and dismay, the heaviness that accompanied me everywhere. I am light again, free and young. I am happy once more. I think of Daniel and I see progress, not disability. I look at Emily and I see a girl with a brother who plays with her. I try not to look at Stephen.

'You are a lot smarter than I am,' he says now. 'How did you know?'

'Because something terrible always *does* happen.'

Now, all of a sudden, I am crying a little, wiping my nose with the back of my hand, turning my face down and bringing the hem of my T-shirt up to my eyes. I am crying because I feel that Stephen's sudden return will take away that feeling of well-being I have, that lightness that I have worked hard for, that I have won. Now that he is here he has automatically cancelled out the days and weeks, the months I've had around Andy. All of Daniel's progress seems wrapped up in those months. And it seems that, for some reason, I am crying for Daniel.

In front of me, all at once, is Stephen's handkerchief. I take it, willing myself to stop crying, but finding it harder than it ought to be. Wasn't I lying in Andy's arms just hours ago? Didn't I laugh when he held up the 'ingenious' sign? Wasn't he there in the morning, isn't he waiting now for me to pick him up in our fancy rental car? Can't I hold on to what is good in my life now? Must I relinquish it as stolen booty to which I have no right?

I am entitled. I am a good mother. Perhaps one day I will have the chance again to be a good wife. I tell myself these things. But Stephen always gets what he wants. He is shrewd and utterly unstoppable. *If you think you are leaving without me, you're kidding.* He knows how to work things in his favour, and he has a sense of entitlement that is a force of its own. He takes my hand and I feel powerless to resist his touch. I am thinking now of someone else anyway, not of Stephen or Andy, or even of Daniel and Emily. I am thinking of a young man I knew in what feels a lifetime ago, who I realise all at once was very much like Andy in the way he saw the world through glad eyes and very much like Daniel, who loves mechanical things, trains and motorbikes, racing cars and helicopters. And he loved me. When my mother died, he rode his motorcycle from New York to Boston after getting off the phone with me in the middle of the night. 'I'll be there in three hours,' he said, and he was, too, marching into my flat smelling of exhaust fumes and snow. Something terrible always happens. Will it happen now? And why is it terrible? Listen to him speak, my husband, with his lovely voice and that smouldering look, a look that will win your heart if the words do not.

'It is all my fault, Melanie. I didn't want to hear, didn't want to know. I underestimated you, I'd forgotten who you are. You once asked me if I remembered what I loved about you. Can I tell you now? Will you let me?'

I shake my head. Across my skull my protest echoes, *no no no*.

He is going to tell me anyway. I have no choice. He

says, 'I loved that you were never worked over and shaped and made to be a thing, as I have been. That you were never groomed and polished, never stylised. It was different for me. I was readied to be a particular type of man. And I learned to want to be that man. Am I making any sense? While I was being made into this monstrous gargoyle like the sort you might find on a listed building, you sprang up as though in a meadow, like a wondrous, delightful tree. If you want to know what I loved about you, it was that. Who you were. Who you are now.'

Oh fuck, it's over. I feel Andy receding from my life like vapour. I feel a coldness in my heart where once there was a thrill of possibility. I am with my husband again and he's taken it all away.

'What about Penelope?' I say. Perhaps he has forgotten about her? Shall I remind him now? She is so much more suited to him. I have come from nowhere; I am no one. It always bothered him, this. Rita without the sexiness, Eliza Doolittle without the charm.

'Penelope is thirty-five and she wants to have children. There is nothing wrong with that. But when we started to talk about it I realised something,' Stephen says.

'That you don't want any more kids? That you are afraid the next one might be autistic as well?' I want him to say that. I want him to say it because I think it is the truth and I am terrified of believing any lies.

Stephen shakes his head. 'No. What I realised is that when I think about having kids, there is only one woman who I can imagine being their mother. And that isn't Penelope. It's you. It always was.'

I shake my head. I don't believe him and I wish he'd stop. How will I live with myself, pushing away my children's father? I'd do anything for them and – certainly, definitely, unquestionably – if I didn't have Andy in my life I would take Stephen back like a shot, if only for the children's sake. For Daniel, who looks just like him with his sandy hair, his brown eyes. For Emily, who hangs on his neck when he leaves, calling Daddy.

Emily. If I am going to pitch for her, this is the time.

'Do we have to send Emily to that pre-prep?' I ask. 'Can't we find a school with shorter hours?'

'Sure,' he says. 'If that's what you'd like. And I am willing to let go of the idea of special school as well.'

No hesitation, no sigh of disapproval. Just a straight answer.

'Daniel will not need special school,' I tell him.

He says, 'I trust you.' And I wonder what exactly he means. With the children, I suppose. He trusts me with the children.

I say, 'If something had happened to you, Stephen, if something had happened to you instead of Daniel, I want you to know that I would have fought just as hard. And for as long as it took.'

'I know that,' he says.

And then another thought occurs to me. It appears in my mind like a lit candle, illuminating everything. 'But I don't think you'd fight for me,' I say. 'If something happened, I mean.' And something always does, I think to myself. Haven't I learned that much? Haven't I seen this before with my own eyes?

'Oh, but I would, Mel, I would.' He means it; he believes it himself. His voice is sugar, his words line up like soldiers. But somehow I feel like Eve, being whispered to in the garden.

He sits with me here in a park full of crowded trees and borders of colour, saying all the things I once longed to hear. I am sad for him, and for me, remembering how much I missed him. But I feel there are other forces at work here, things that are not being said, circumstances not fully disclosed. He is so shrewd, and so tempting, awesome in his own way. But he is not telling me the truth – it is the only thing of which I am certain. I think of Penelope, who wishes for a family just as I have done. She is older than me by five years. Five years is not much until you are planning pregnancies. Hit your mid-thirties and you'll find five years counts as a lot. She has pinned her hopes on Stephen, who feels she isn't quite right for him. She was all right to look after him when his marriage fell apart, but not all right to bear his children. Oh dear, what a price he has put on his affections. And I am feeling awfully tired, looking at his pretty face.

I cannot trust him. Perhaps if I tried hard enough I could make myself. I think about what Andy once told me. *He'll come back. Then he will go again.* I can see now that this is true. And when he goes next time, what will he take with him?

I put my lips against Stephen's cheek, my hand across his heart. I kiss him tenderly, as though my lips may bruise him. I realise that I am about to hurt him and that never, in all the years we were together, did I ever before deliberately do him harm. I find it impossible to speak. To say what I must say. I am thinking about what Penelope might feel if she were here with us. I'm thinking about Andy, waiting confidently in Wandsworth for a woman who cannot scare him away even with two young children, one autistic. If I consider them for a moment then I feel better about what I want to do, which is to tell Stephen goodbye. I will say this and everything that was us will recede even further, trickle away until eventually it is nothing. It is not nothing now. Not yet. Stephen is looking at me, hoping it isn't too late. But I know what I will do and he knows, too, because he can see it in my face as I stand up, still touching his shoulders. He knows that I will go now. Already, he is looking away.

'Will you do this one thing for me?' he says. His mouth is heavy, his eyes focus far off. In a clipped, curt manner he asks, 'If it doesn't work out with him, will you let me have another chance?'

I find myself troubled by this question. It's his tone of voice, I suppose. Something has happened that he doesn't like. He has made an error of judgment; he is angry with himself and, of course, with me. And it is as though, in a single stroke, he has shifted all blame for our marriage onto me. Onto my whims and desires. At the same time he has cleverly cast his bid. He is smart. Maybe that is what I found so attractive about him. I do not find it so attractive now.

'I'm not sure,' I say truthfully.

Stephen looks at me, raises his eyebrows. None of this conversation has gone the way he thought it would.

'I have to go,' I tell him.

I start to walk away now, expecting he may try to stop me. All I can think, moving deliberately across the park, out the gates, down the road, is that I have walked away from my children's father and that I will have to keep walking. The sidewalk seems to shift; my legs feel as though they have stretched and no longer operate like normal legs. I trip and stumble, my strides uneven. This is hard for me. Hard for him. I have to think about each step and where I am going and that only a few blocks away are my children, waiting for me. When I reach the house I see Emily through the window. Her mouth opens in a smile and then she disappears from sight, returning with Daniel, who points at me, then turns to his sister and says something that makes Emily laugh.

Stephen has not followed me. There's no sign of him when I look over my shoulder. I am grateful to him for this.

I ring Andy on his mobile and tell him I'm running late. 'I'm just putting the kids in the car,' I say. 'Don't worry.' But there's something about how I sound that he picks up on right away.

'Don't hang up yet,' he says slowly.

I hold the phone to my ear. I don't speak or move. All of a sudden I don't know what I'm doing, where I'm going.

'Melanie,' he says softly. 'Take your time. I'm here. I'm just waiting for you. I'm not going anywhere.'

And so I take my time. Because there is no need to hurry; and anyway, I believe him.